The Christmas
Backup Plan

By Lori Wilde

STANDALONE NOVELS
THE MOONGLOW SISTERS

THE STARDUST, TEXAS SERIES
LOVE OF THE GAME
RULES OF THE GAME
BACK IN THE GAME

THE CUPID, TEXAS SERIES
TO TAME A WILD COWBOY
HOW THE COWBOY WAS WON
MILLION DOLLAR COWBOY
LOVE WITH A PERFECT COWBOY
SOMEBODY TO LOVE • ALL OUT OF LOVE
LOVE AT FIRST SIGHT • ONE TRUE LOVE (novella)

THE JUBILEE, TEXAS SERIES
A COWBOY FOR CHRISTMAS
THE COWBOY AND THE PRINCESS
THE COWBOY TAKES A BRIDE

THE TWILIGHT, TEXAS SERIES
THE CHRISTMAS BACKUP PLAN
THE CHRISTMAS DARE • THE CHRISTMAS KEY
COWBOY, IT'S COLD OUTSIDE • A WEDDING FOR CHRISTMAS
I'LL BE HOME FOR CHRISTMAS • CHRISTMAS AT TWILIGHT
THE VALENTINE'S DAY DISASTER (novella)
THE CHRISTMAS COOKIE COLLECTION
THE CHRISTMAS COOKIE CHRONICLES:
CARRIE; RAYLENE; CHRISTINE; GRACE
THE WELCOME HOME GARDEN CLUB
THE FIRST LOVE COOKIE CLUB
THE TRUE LOVE QUILTING CLUB
THE SWEETHEARTS' KNITTING CLUB

AVAILABLE FROM HARLEQUIN
THE STOP THE WEDDING SERIES
CRASH LANDING • SMOOTH SAILING • NIGHT DRIVING
THE UNIFORMLY HOT SERIES
BORN READY
HIGH STAKES SEDUCTION
THE RIGHT STUFF
INTOXICATING
SWEET SURRENDER
HIS FINAL SEDUCTION
ZERO CONTROL

LORI WILDE

The **Christmas** *Backup Plan*

A TWILIGHT, TEXAS NOVEL

AVONBOOKS

An Imprint of HarperCollins*Publishers*

Excerpt from *The Christmas Dare* copyright © 2019 by Laurie Vanzura.

THE CHRISTMAS BACKUP PLAN. Copyright © 2020 by Laurie Vanzura. All rights reserved. Printed in the United States of America. No part of this book may be used or reproduced in any manner whatsoever without written permission except in the case of brief quotations embodied in critical articles and reviews. For information, address HarperCollins Publishers, 195 Broadway, New York, NY 10007.

First Avon Books mass market printing: November 2020
First Avon Books hardcover printing: October 2020

Print Edition ISBN: 978-0-06-295313-1
Digital Edition ISBN: 978-0-06-295316-2

Avon, Avon & logo, and Avon Books & logo are registered trademarks of HarperCollins Publishers in the United States of America and other countries.

HarperCollins is a registered trademark of HarperCollins Publishers in the United States of America and other countries.

FIRST EDITION

20 21 22 23 24   LSC   10 9 8 7 6 5 4 3 2 1

To Christie Conlee: Who showed up right when I needed her most. You are amazing!

The Christmas Backup Plan

CHAPTER 1

Cupid: In skydiving parlance, slang for altitude expressed in hundreds of feet above ground level.

Wednesday, December 16
The Silver Feather Ranch, Cupid, Texas

"You gotta be shi—"

"Remington Dewayne Lockhart! Watch your language!" At thirty-five, his stepmother, Vivi, was just three years older than Remington, but she lectured him as if he were the same age as her twin toddlers.

Vivi clapped her palms over the ears of Remington's half brother, Rory, who was sitting in her lap. "Reed," she called to Rory's twin halfway across the den stacking blocks. "Cover your ears, son."

Reed looked up, wide-eyed.

"Ears." Vivi nodded and gave him a pointed look. "Now."

Like a well-trained puppy, the boy plastered his palms over his ears.

"I swear I think you Lockhart men just enjoy testing the limit of my patience," Vivi muttered.

"Do you think making a big deal over curse words might draw more attention to them?" Remington drawled, leaning one shoulder against the doorjamb that led from the foyer to the den.

"Swear jar." Vivi snapped her fingers at the bookcase where a glass mason jar sat. Dollar sign stickers and the symbols %$#@^ decorated the jar.

"Hey." Remington raised both palms. "I didn't say it. You cut me off at the knees."

"The intent was there." Vivi got to her feet, rested her fisted hands on her hips.

"Wicked stepmother," he said affectionately. "To my way of thinking, my foul mouth is all your fault for springing Aria Alzate on me."

"Your father and the US Army are to blame for your foul mouth, not me." Vivi retrieved the swear jar and shoved it under his nose. "Five dollars."

"Five dollars? Highway robbery," Remington grumbled, but he got out his wallet and opened it up. "I only have twenties."

"I'll take one." Vivi leaned over to pluck the twenty from his wallet. "You'll cuss around my boys again. Consider your next three curse words prepaid."

"No doubt I will, especially since you blindsided me with Aria. Low blow, Vivi, low blow."

Vivi fluffed her shoulder-length blond hair and grinned. "I do try my best."

His stepmother ran a cowboy wedding venue on the Silver Feather Ranch, and Aria worked for her as a wedding planner. Because of Aria's connection to Austin, where she'd lived for a time, she'd managed to get a write-up in *Texas Monthly*. Vivi's business had exploded as people sought them out for authentic cowboy weddings, and Aria, rising to the occasion, dazzled. They had so much work they'd upped their prices and started turning away business.

Much as he disliked Aria, the woman was pretty good at her job. Remington valued hard work, and he admired that about her, if nothing else.

"Would you have agreed to drive cargo to a wedding in North Central Texas if you'd known Aria was part of that cargo?" Vivi asked.

"Hells to the no."

"Exactly." Vivi held up two fingers. "You only have two curse words' credit now."

"Hell isn't a curse word, it's a place, and you just put me in a vehicle with it for the next eight hours."

Vivi waggled her index finger. "You have one prepaid swear word left."

Tempted to give her all the money he had in his wallet so he could swear up a blue streak, Remington reached for the cash, but his toddler half brothers watched him with mesmerized eyes.

"I'm no more thrilled to get stuck in that paramilitary black SUV with you than you are to have me there," said a tart female voice from the other entryway into the den, this one from the dining room.

He stared across the room, his gaze clashing with the woman standing there. Their eyes narrowed at each other like gunslingers squaring off on the dusty streets of Tombstone.

Looking at Aria Alzate, knowing what was ahead of him for the next several days, Remington made a brash forecast. Thrown together for several days in forced proximity, they would either learn to get along or tear each other from limb to limb.

Remington's money was on the latter. He groaned and briefly closed his eyes. "You could have warned me that she was in the next room, Vivi."

"Look," Vivi said, "I know you two get along like cats and dogs, but I need you both to play nice and get this done. Got it?"

Remington opened his eyes and studied the stunning woman standing in the doorway.

Aria Alzate was a major pain in the ass, but she was sure pretty to look at. Slim and trim, but curvy in all the right places, she studied him through lowered eyelids thick with long dark lashes. Her father, Armand, was Mescalero Apache, and she'd inherited his straight black hair and high cheekbones, while also inheriting a pale creamy complexion from her Irish mother, Bridget.

She was an interesting contrast of dark and light.

Remington had known her his entire life, although he hadn't seen her much in the twelve years he'd been in the Army, most of those spent as a paratrooper. On the few occasions she'd been home when he'd returned on leave, they'd made a point never to be in the same room alone together. They'd always rubbed each other the wrong way, and they literally had nothing in common.

Aria was impulsive, rebellious, quirky, and something of a busybody. Everything Remington was not. They'd grown up together on the Silver Feather in an arid, isolated stretch of Trans-Pecos nestled in the shadow of the Davis Mountains. Her family had worked for the Lockharts. Her father had been the ranch foreman until he'd retired, and his son Archer took over. Her mother had been their housekeeper.

In those terrible times, after his mother, Lucy, died when Remington was ten, Bridget acted as a surrogate mother to him and his three brothers, Ridge, Ranger, and Rhett.

At the moment, Remington was living on the Silver Feather because his paternal grandfather, Cyril, had left the four oldest Lockhart grandsons—this was before Dad had Rory and Reed with Vivi—two-acre parcels of land on each quadrant of the hundred-thousand-acre spread.

Nice of him, but as with everything involving his father's family, there was a catch. None of the four brothers could sell their places without approval from the entire family. And Remington's father would never grant his permission.

So, knowing he had few options with the land, he had a house built on his property while living in a fifth wheel trailer. His contractors had just finished building the house, giving him something to occupy his mind while he recovered from his injuries and adjusted to civilian life. But things still felt alien. He'd been away for twelve years. Living in a third world country had shown him a whole other way of being. And he wasn't really sure who he was anymore, now that he was no longer an Army Ranger.

Besides, Aria reminded him too much of who he used to be. The wild kid he'd worked so hard to shed.

Yes, he and Aria found themselves forever tied, and not just because of their pasts, but also since his three brothers had all married her three sisters. He might as well get used to having her around. It was a weird family dynamic, especially when everyone seemed to expect him and Aria to get together too, just because the others had all gotten together.

Yeah, over his dead body. The woman was sexy, but she was a bona fide flake. She acted first and thought . . . Well, Aria didn't think, did she? Neither before, during, or after jumping in with both feet.

"Why can't she drive herself?" Remington asked, feeling a bit petulant. He wasn't proud of it, but neither was he ashamed.

Aria drilled down on her glare.

"One," Vivi said, "it's a long drive in the winter with a potential ice storm brewing. Two, she's got a lot of stuff to haul, and three, she needs help to set things up once she gets there—"

"It's okay, Vivi, you don't have to make excuses for me," Aria interrupted.

"Excuses?" Remington lifted an eyebrow. What had the harum-scarum woman done now?

"My doctor says I can't drive, okay?" Aria folded her arms over her chest and jutted out her cute little chin. "If it wasn't for that, you can bet your sweet booty I'd drive myself."

"You think my booty is sweet?" he drawled, intentionally provoking her.

Aria made vomiting noises.

"Stop it, you two." Vivi sounded exasperated. "This wedding is important." She turned to Remington. "Besides being one of Aria's best friends, the bride, Olivia Schebly, is the daughter of Twilight's mayor. If we do a good job, we'll have an 'in' with Texas politicians."

"A lot's on the line then," Remington said.

Vivi nodded and turned back to Aria. "So, follow the checklist. Got it?"

"I've got it right here." Aria tapped her temple with an index finger. "Olivia is my bestie. I won't disappoint either of you."

"Write it down, please." Vivi's expression brooked no argument.

"I don't need—"

Vivi interrupted her. "Write it down. I know you have a good memory, but considering recent events, write it down."

"Yes, ma'am." Aria rolled her eyes.

Without missing a beat, Vivi reached down and took a piece of carpet fuzz out of her son's mouth. "Let Remington rub off on you. He's a great planner."

"*Eww*, I don't want Mr. By-the-Book rubbing off on me." Aria pantomimed dusting herself off.

"Don't worry," Remington said. "I have no intention of getting close enough to you to rub off."

"Good." Aria tossed her head, and her long straight hair swished like a curtain. "I hate being boxed in. I follow my muse."

"You can plan and still find inspiration," Remington said.

"Maybe I can." She put a palm across her heart. "But can you?"

"You're ironic, you know that."

She narrowed her eyes and widened her stance. "How so?"

"A wedding planner who doesn't plan." He snorted. "How does that even work?"

"I plan. Just not in the dead boring, extreme minutiae way that you do."

"Why can't you drive yourself?" Remington changed the subject. He didn't want to get into what his first and last serious girlfriend had called his "intractable" ways.

"Not that it's any of your business," Aria sassed, "but I suffered a concussion two days ago—"

Alarm shot through him. Concussion? That wasn't good.

Remington had suffered one helluva concussion two years ago in Afghanistan, and he'd had lingering health issues for months.

He knew firsthand just how serious a concussion could be. While he disapproved of the scatterbrained woman, he didn't want bad things happening to her.

"Are you okay?" he asked.

"It's a mild concussion, I'm fine. I have a slight headache." Aria kneaded her temple. "But no biggie. Still, to be on the safe side, my doctor forbade me from driving for ten days."

Remington shifted his gaze to Vivi. "Should she even be doing this?"

"Dr. Kemper says she's fine to work, just not to drive and especially not to overdo it. As long as she gets plenty of sleep and keeps hydrated, she'll be fine," Vivi said. "That's why she's adding an extra day to her schedule."

Remington eyed Aria. "How did you get a concussion?"

Aria looked embarrassed. "I . . . um . . ." She dropped her gaze and fiddled with the hem of her sweater. "I fell out of the hayloft."

"What were you doing in the hay—" It hit him then that she might not have been alone in the hayloft. Aria dated a lot. "Oh," he said. "Oh."

She fluttered her eyelashes at him and offered up a knowing smirk. "Sometimes I get a little too adventuresome."

"A little?" He arched his eyebrows. It sounded irresponsible to him. Falling out of a hayloft.

She shrugged and stabbed him with a piercing stare as if daring him to judge her. "What can I say? I like to have fun. Unlike some people in this room."

"There's fun and there's just plain foolishness. What's wrong with having sex in a bed like anyone else?"

Aria hooted. "You thought I was having sex in the hayloft?"

"That's what you implied." He scowled. She loved to poke fun at him.

"No, that's what you inferred."

"What were you doing in the hayloft?"

"Hanging Christmas decorations."

"In a hayloft?"

"It was for ambience."

"In the horse barn?"

"Don't be dopey. It was in the wedding reception barn."

That didn't make it any better. People needed to consider the consequences of their actions and plan ahead. If she climbed up in the hayloft to string lights, she should have had help, and a backup plan in case she fell out and concussed herself.

"No one else can drive her?" Remington shifted his gaze back to Vivi.

"Hello!" Aria waved a hand. "In case you haven't noticed, I'm standing right here."

Oh, he'd noticed plenty. That was part of the problem. Annoying she might be, but he found her hot as a firecracker, and that vexed him to no end.

"Duke's out of town," Vivi said. "Ridge and Kaia's third baby is on the way any day, Rhett is running the Christmas toy drive—"

"How about your brother?" Remington asked. Archer seemed the prime candidate to drive her to Twilight, at least in his book.

"Archer has his hands full with the ranch, and Casey doesn't want him traipsing off for five days just before Christmas."

"Maybe a ranch hand then?"

"We give the ranch hands two weeks off at Christmas in case you've forgotten," Vivi said. "That's why Archer is so busy."

"There's absolutely no one else?"

"Everyone's eyeball deep in work. While you, Mr. Dark and Broody, have been moping around your new house feeling sorry for yourself ever since you got discharged from the Army."

Things were a lot more complicated than that, but Remington wouldn't get into the lingering effects of PTSD with Vivi.

"Don't think you're alone in hating this," Aria said. "I've already gone through all the other possible chauffeurs. I even thought about calling an Uber from El Paso to take me, but the cost is beyond astronomical."

"Dammit," Remington muttered.

"Curse again and you'll need to cough up more money." Vivi rubbed her thumb and forefinger together. "You've maxed your twenty."

Okay, he was dragging his feet and grasping at straws. A knot of dismay settled in his gut. He didn't want to do this, but he was a former Army Ranger. He knew how to suck it up and get the job done whenever he got a rotten assignment.

And Vivi was right about one thing. He'd been in a dark cloud mood ever since he'd received the medical discharge for losing the ring finger and pinky of his left hand in a parachuting mishap.

His hand had healed, but in his head, he was still struggling. For the past twelve years the Army ruled his world. Now he was clueless about his future.

"Well?" Vivi's tone irritated him, and if he didn't like his stepmother as much as he did, Remington would have walked off. But Vivi had corralled his old man, who could be a humdinger, tamed Duke as much as was humanly possible, and brought a softness to the family that hadn't been there since his mother died.

"Fine." He sighed. "I'll drive her."

"You can hang out in Twilight until after the wedding." Vivi nodded. "Then drive her back?"

"Yes, yes." He grunted and rolled his eyes. He would do it. He would drive her, but first, he needed to formulate some kind of plan to keep his sanity around the harum-scarum Miss Alzate.

"Don't worry," Aria said. "I'll make it fun."

"That's what I'm afraid of," he muttered.

"Are you always such a sourpuss?" Aria clicked her tongue.

"Pretty much."

"I know how to cure that."

"I have no desire for a cure," he said. "And I have ground rules."

Aria groaned and dropped dramatically onto the couch, clutching her chest as if he'd just stabbed her through the heart. "I'm not a fan of rules."

He caught a flash of her thigh in thin black leggings as the hem of her red-and-green plaid wool skirt rode up, and he felt an odd heat bolt through his body.

Stop that, Lockhart.

"Do you want me to drive you or not?" He stuffed his hands into his pockets and intensified his glower.

"As if I have a choice."

"Good, I'm glad we agree." He nodded but kept his scowl in place just in case she didn't get how serious he was about this.

Vivi was watching them, a bemused smile on her face. Haha. At least someone found entertainment in this farce.

"I'm going to let you two sort out the details," Vivi said, gathering a twin in each arm and balancing them on her hips. The boys peered at Remington and Aria over their mother's shoulder as she waltzed out the door.

"We need a plan," Remington said after Vivi disappeared.

Aria blew out her breath through pursed lips. "Here's the plan. We get in your SUV and drive northeast."

"Not so fast. First, I've got to check the weather." He pulled his phone from his back pocket. "I want to get ahead of this ice storm."

"Then get on it." Aria snapped her fingers. "Chop-chop, time's a-wastin'. It's almost nine."

"Second rule," he said. "No side trips. We're driving straight to Twilight, no delays, no detours, no jacking around."

"Okay, okay." She held up both palms, the many bracelets at her wrist jangling merrily. "But Vivi built an extra day into the schedule just in case something comes up."

He ignored that. "Third rule, no Christmas music."

"No Christmas music! Who are you, the Marquis de Sade?"

"Who's that?" Remington asked. "If the guy hates Christmas music, then yes, I'm the Marquis de Sade."

"He was a famous sexual sadist."

"Then no! I am not the Marquis de Sade."

"Figures," she mumbled. "So, does that mean I *can* listen to Christmas music?"

"On your own device where I don't have to hear it. That's why they make earbuds."

"You are such a grinch."

"Thank you. I consider that a compliment." He nodded. He'd never been a fan of Christmas. At least not since his mom had died.

"His heart is two sizes too small," Aria muttered.

"What?"

"Forget it. How many rules are there?" Aria scrambled to her feet, landing gracefully on the spiky heels of her ankle boots. "Because I've got a really short attention span—"

"Rule four. No putting your feet on my dashboard. I hate it when people put their feet on my dash," he said.

"Good grief, you're such a fussy old man."

"Five," he went on, laying out his plan. "Keep conversations to a minimum."

"No Christmas music, no talking—what? Am I just supposed to sit there like a silent lump?"

"That would be nice."

"You're impossible."

"Look, I've been through some stuff, okay? I don't like idle chit-chat. Or cheerful music—"

"Or cheerful anything, apparently."

"Right. The less cheer, the better."

"I get that you're a war hero and all that . . ." Her gaze went to his missing fingers.

Self-consciously, he tucked his left hand into his right armpit. No one talked about his injury to his face and that's just the way he wanted it.

"But I don't like when people try to micromanage me," she said.

"I don't think this will work." He shook his head. "At all."

"Me either."

"Vivi!" they called in unison, simultaneously rushing for the door.

They made contact at the threshold, Remington's big shoulder plowing into hers. He was so much bigger than her that the impact of their bodies knocked her off her cute little boots. Her arms windmilled in the air, and she teetered.

Adrenaline shot through Remington, and he grabbed her just before she fell, holding her securely in the crook of his elbow. The last thing she needed was concussion number two. What the hell was wrong with him?

"I'm sorry, I'm sorry," he apologized, alarm tightening his chest. "I didn't mean to do that."

Her long dark silky hair trailed down the back of his arm, and she peered up into his face. Her eyes widened and her lips pursed, and that adrenaline in his veins turned to pure testosterone.

Creamed cow chips, what in the hell was this? He was not having a sexual reaction to Aria Alzate. No way, no how, no, no, no.

NO.

"It's okay," she said, her voice softening. "Not your fault. I charged for the door like a galloping rhino."

"There is nothing rhino-like about you," he murmured, shocked to hear how raspy his voice sounded.

"I think you're right," she said, still in his arms and breathing as hard as he was. It was not his imagination.

"I am?" Remington blinked. "About what?"

"A plan. We do need one."

He gulped, nodded, righted her, and stepped away. "And what's your plan?"

"We stay away from each other as much as possible."

"Agreed," he said, his mouth suddenly dry as the Chihuahuan Desert. "I like that plan very much."

"Once we hit Twilight, you go your way and I'll go mine. We meet back up on Monday after the wedding, drive home together, and we never speak of this experience again."

"I'm on the same page. Absolutely."

"Deal?" She stuck out her palm and the charm bracelet at her wrist jangled. The charm bracelet was as disorganized as she was. It held too many charms, and they were an eclectic mix of metals—copper, gold, silver, bronze, even some glass and plastic. But oddly, the charms were cohesive in their messiness.

A lot like Aria herself.

"Deal." Remington sank his hand into hers.

The instant their skin touched, static electricity snapped through them with a charge so strong the air literally crackled. Simultaneously, they both dropped their hands and jumped back.

"Wow," she said, her eyes growing wider. "Static electricity is a humdinger this time of year."

"For sure."

"Well." She brushed her palms together, as if by doing so she could discharge the feeling and sent her charm bracelets jangling again. "We better get your SUV loaded and get on the road."

He nodded. "The sooner the better."

"Yes." She sounded breathless. "The sooner we get this party started, the sooner we get it over."

"I couldn't agree with you more."

"I'll round up the supplies," she said.

"I'll gas up the SUV."

With a curt nod, she turned in one direction and he turned in the other, his pulse thumping the way it did every time he jumped from an airplane.

His reaction to her was weird.

Too weird.

And unwanted. Remington knew one thing with unshakable certainty. It was going to be a very long trip.

CHAPTER 2

Apparent wind: The wind perceived by an observer.

Aria waited beside the open garage door, ticking off the labeled boxes against the wedding checklist that Vivi had sent to her phone app. She went through the motions on automatic pilot, doing what needed doing because inside her head, she felt dazed . . .

No, not dazed.

Dazzled.

By Remington Lockhart.

No way. How was that even possible? This dizzy, light-headed giddiness must be due to her concussion. Yes, okay, he was a giant chunk of hotness, but beyond that, she had zero reason for dazzlement.

Chemistry, what a deviling thing. But why? They'd never had chemistry before.

The sweat gathering between her breasts, the hot snap of awareness that had crackled between them when he'd touched her was from the knock on the head she'd suffered when she tumbled from the hayloft.

Yep, this wild affliction, that dried her mouth and quickened her pulse, had to be from the concussion. Because, c'mon, how could Remington of all people turn her on? She'd known him her entire life.

Except she'd barely seen him over the past twelve years. And had probably spoken fewer than a dozen words to him in the three months he'd been back home.

He kept to his side of the Silver Feather Ranch, far from the main Lockhart mansion, the cowboy chapel, and wedding reception barn that were her domain.

The third Lockhart brother had absolutely nothing to do with her symptoms, other than being in the right place at the right time.

Or maybe it was the wrong place at the wrong time.

Whatevs.

This wasn't happening for like nine gazillion reasons. Primary among them, the fact that her meddlesome, matchmaking sisters bought into some wack-a-doodle love legend.

According to family mythology, whenever the women in her family kissed their soul mates, they heard a soft but distinct humming at the base of their brain, signaling they'd found The One.

Total hooey, of course. Even if a tiny part of her thrilled to the concept of fated love. She might be a romantic, but she wasn't delusional. She heard the humming in her head when she played Bruno Mars too loudly through her earbuds.

Perhaps the talented Mr. Mars was her soul mate. She told that joke to her sisters every time they brought up The Humming, as the fam had dubbed it.

To Aria, it sounded like a horror movie title . . . *The Conjuring, The Shining, The Humming* . . . run for your lives.

Although, if she were being honest, Aria had to admit things had worked out pretty well for her three sisters marrying the three other Lockhart brothers.

Still, she considered their marital bliss was not because of the goofball love legend but despite it.

For, surely, it did not mean that Remington was Aria's destiny just because Kaia had hooked up with Ridge, the oldest Lockhart brother and Kaia's longtime crush. Or that Ember fell hard for Ranger, the second Lockhart brother and Ember's very best friend.

Or Tara had entered into a marriage of convenience-turned-love-match with the fourth brother, sexy single dad, Rhett.

Seriously, how cuckoo was it to assume she and the final single Lockhart brother should hook up? In fact, the odds against such a matchup were astronomical. Plus, scientifically, there was absolutely no way that kissing could trigger humming in the brain.

None. Zero. Zipola.

If her sisters heard a humming, and they claimed it with the fervor of new religious converts, the sound was one hundred percent psychological. A reaction to the fairy-tale seeds that Granny Blue had planted in their heads from the time they were babies. Although that romantic part of her—the wedding planner part of her that spent her days with couples in love—longed to believe that a simple kiss could rock her world.

Briefly, she toyed with the idea of kissing Remington.

Shuddered.

Nopers, nope, nope, nope.

Not doing that. Not going there. Not even in her wildest fantasies. Good grief. She and Remington could barely say a civil word to each other in the best of circumstances.

Kiss him?

No *way in hell-o, Jell-O.*

But every time her big family got together the topic inevitably came up. As if her pairing with Remington was a foregone conclusion. And lately the teasing had gotten worse, now that he was out of the military and moved into his brand-new house on the far west side of the massive Silver Feather Ranch.

The conspiracy to shove them together had gotten so aggressive, Aria avoided family gatherings like the plague.

Remington pulled his SUV to a stop where Aria stood in the driveway. He'd just come from fueling the vehicle at the farm tank on the far side of the massive horse barn, and the faint odor of gasoline burned her nose.

He got out and adjusted the brim of his Stetson, tugging the cowboy hat down lower over his brow. He wore a shearling sheepskin jacket, faded Wranglers, and dark mirrored sunglasses. Beard scruff ringed his jaw. Was he trying to grow a beard or just too lazy to shave every day . . . or even every week?

The man looked like what he was.

A complete badass.

Without a word—*Lord, was he ever the strong, silent type*—Remington started loading boxes into the back of his Escalade.

Her gaze dropped to his left hand.

To the missing fingers. The injury was healing, but still red and raw-looking. She could see the seams of the scars running across the top of his hand.

Aria's breath caught in her lungs. She didn't know the full story. Some kind of incident when he'd parachuted from a plane in enemy territory.

Besides losing his fingers, he'd broken bones and suffered a concussion—apparently one a lot worse than hers. In the aftermath of his trauma, the phrase "lucky to be alive" echoed throughout the town.

Even now, six months after the incident, Aria felt a hard punch of empathy for him. She had a vivid imagination, and if she let herself dwell on the suffering of others, she absorbed it like a sponge, felt the pain as if it were her own.

That ability—or handicap, depending on how you looked at it—to commiserate deeply with others was why she strove to keep her world light and positive. Happy, happy, joy, joy. Unicorns and rainbows and kittens in baskets.

That was why she loved weddings and Christmas music and babies. Such things kept her from latching on to the dark side of life and sinking into the muck, which she could do so easily if she let herself.

Remington had sunk into that muck. Was still wallowing in it according to the persistent scowl on his face.

"Aria." His voice came out a gravelly growl, and he stuck his left hand in his pocket as if he'd caught her staring at his savaged digits.

"Huh?" She blinked and realized she'd been woolgathering.

"Are you going to stand there all day?"

"What?"

He nodded at the back of his Escalade stuffed with boxes of supplies for a Christmas wedding. "I'm done loading up. Unless there's something else."

"Oh." Her mouth dropped open. "Oh well, yes. No, nothing else."

He grunted and climbed in behind the wheel.

Um, okay, Mr. Blunt and Curt. Let's do this thing.

She hopped into the passenger seat. The vehicle smelled of him. An enticing masculine scent that made her think of untamed horses, powerful engines and long winter nights by a hot crackling fire.

"Buckle up."

"Aye, aye, Captain." She lowered her voice to sound more like a man and saluted him.

He did not look amused. In fact, he looked downright peevish. "Aye, aye is the Navy. I was in the Army."

"Does it matter?"

Remington snorted and looked at her as if she were the dumbest thing to crawl out from under a rock. With a shake of his head, he muttered, "Does it matter?"

"Jeesh, don't get your skivvies in a twist. I was just joking."

"And never salute me."

"I want to ask why not, but I really don't want to get my head bitten off." Aria stretched her face into an expression that said, I-will-just-tiptoe-on-these-eggshells.

"You aren't military." He shook his head. "Only people in the military may salute. And that's only if one of them is an officer."

"What if I do salute you? Will the salute police come to arrest me?"

"You have no respect." He gave her the side-eye as he drove out of the driveway and onto the dirt road that would lead them off the hundred-thousand acre spread that encompassed two counties. Eventually.

"And you, sir, have no sense of humor."

He said nothing, just scowled at the road as if it were the enemy.

Okay, so that's how this was going down. Fine. Good. Great. Let him be a chunk of granite. She didn't care.

Aria took out her phone, went down the checklist again, checking off everything. She might be on the flighty side by nature, but she took her job seriously. Satisfied that she'd gotten all the supplies she needed, she hazarded another glance over at Remington.

He sat ramrod straight, hands clamped on the steering wheel and his eyes trained on the road. His jaw muscle clenched so hard the muscle just below his right ear twitched.

Wow. She'd bet anything he ground his teeth in his sleep. He might look gruff and tough, but it was all a front. She saw past it. He was a bundle of repressed nerves.

Aria scrolled down Vivi's checklist, thumbed in a new heading. Centered and bolded the text in all caps and started her own loosely structured checklist that suited her unstructured style.

THE CHRISTMAS PLAN

1. *Pull this wedding off without a hitch.*
2. *Enjoy the process.*
3. *Remember that trying to fix other people never works. Stay in your own lane.*
4. *It is Christmas. Smile!*
5. *Charm the Grinch right out of Remington Lockhart.*

There.

That was as planny as Aria ever intended to get.

REMINGTON MIGHT AS well carve the words "No good deed goes unpunished" on his tombstone because every blasted time he let himself get coerced into helping someone, he paid a heavy price.

His ruined hand a case in point.

And today wasn't shaping up to be any different.

He'd rather help a rattlesnake cross five lanes of traffic than drive Aria to Twilight, and yet here he was, doing it anyway.

At the moment, she was chattering on—as if he was the least bit interested—about the upcoming wedding she and Vivi had planned.

Okay sure, she was very easy on the eyes, but Aria grated on his nerves. He'd always known she was a flake, but since coming home, he'd seen just how frivolous she was—spoiled, pampered, protected. Living it up while people he knew, men and women he loved, had died in the line of duty, all so she could exist in her cushy little world. Didn't she get that?

And she'd saluted him, for crying out loud!

Be kind, Lockhart. She didn't know it was wrong.

Remington shook his head. His entire family thought she was wonderful and the perfect match for him, but he knew better. Her kooky, crazy, annoyingly positive attitude was one big joke. It had to be. No one could be that upbeat all the time, and it rankled him to listen to her blabber on about foolish things.

"Guess what the opening song is for the first dance between bride and groom?" she blathered.

He shook his head. Who cared?

"C'mon, c'mon guess."

"I have no idea." *And I don't want to know.*

"'Uptown Funk.'"

"Um . . . okay."

"You think that's a romantic choice?"

He shrugged, hunched his shoulder over the steering wheel, locked his gaze on the stripes disappearing down the road.

"Don't get me wrong, I adore 'Uptown Funk,' but is it first-dance-as-husband-and-wife material? It's all wrong, but I'm not sure how to broach picking a better tune with Olivia though."

"Are you close with her?"

"So close! Or at least we were until she hooked up with Ben and got too busy falling in love."

"How do you know Olivia?" he asked.

"We were roommates at Sul Ross."

Another mile marker coming up. Ah, just five hundred more miles . . . If he'd survived three tours in the sandbox, he could surely survive eight hours with the chatterbox. Right?

"What song would you pick if it were you?" she asked.

"Huh?" He grunted.

"For the first dance with your wife at your wedding reception?"

He shook his head, quelled an eye roll. "Moot point. I'm never getting married."

"Not ever?"

"No plans for it."

"You don't have a girlfriend?"

"I've only been back stateside since June and half of that I spent in a hospital. Some of us don't move as fast as you."

Aria threw back her head and laughed, not the least bit offended. "Touché."

She didn't speak for a moment, and he thought, finally, at last, she'd run out of things to say, but then she went and spoiled the silence.

"So, let's say you got a girlfriend and things progressed and you asked her to marry you and for some insane reason, she said yes, and then she asks you what song you want to play for the first dance and—"

"I'm not playing 'what if' games. There's no point to it."

"Why not? What else you got to do for the next eight hours?" She grinned.

"Drive. Vivi asked me to drive you and I'm driving. I did not agree to fantasize about 'what if' scenarios. But since you seem inclined to play, how about this one? What if I never ever got married? What then?"

"That would be very sad," she said, her tone softening. "You're too awesome not to have love in your life."

He heard something akin to pity in her voice, but the undercurrent was less disapproving than that. Say what you would about Aria, she did her best not to judge people. He liked that about her.

Rigidity was one of his personal character flaws. He was working on himself, but change wasn't easy.

"Back to 'Uptown Funk.' Your song would be . . ."

"I don't dance."

"But you'd learn, wouldn't you? To dance with your wife at your wedding."

"I know how to dance. I just don't do it."

"Why not?"

"Not my style."

"Not even if your future wife begged you to dance with her?"

He let out a long loud breath. "Okay, I'll dance with my wife at the wedding reception if she insists."

"You romantic devil, you! I can see why the ladies are beating a path to your door." She kicked off her shoes and started to put her feet on the dash.

He darted a don't-you-dare frown at her.

"Oopsy," she said, and lowered her legs. "I forgot about the dash thingy. Anyhoo, my pick for the first dance with my husband would be . . ." She paused for dramatic effect.

In a flash, Remington saw her wearing a silky, chic wedding gown and dancing with some bozo she'd just married. A fiery pulse of emotion burned from his head to his stomach, and he had no earthly idea why.

"'Grow Old with Me,'" she said. "Mary Chapin Carpenter."

"Really?"

"Why do you say it like that? As if it's a bad choice."

"I don't see you as the sentimental type." Or the type to grow old with any one person.

"What do you see me as?"

Forever young. "The kind who has several husbands and then ends up the queen of the nursing home in your nineties."

"Remington Dewayne Lockhart." Her mouth dropped open, and she gave a little gasp. Then she leaned over to swat his shoulder. "What do you take me for?"

At her touch, he tensed instantly.

"Well?"

"A party girl," he said, answering honestly.

"I might be a party girl now," she said. "I'm only twenty-six. But one day, when I meet the right guy, I'll settle down, and we'll live happily ever after and have a dozen kids, and I'll be the fun mom."

He felt it again, that hot kick of emotion, and finally, he identified the feeling. Jealousy. Good grief almighty, why would he be jealous of Aria?

Um, because she knows how to enjoy life and you don't.

"So, back to the wedding song. You never told me which song you would choose for the first dance."

"Cripes, you're like a pit bull with a bone. You won't let this go, will you?"

"We have seven hours and fifty minutes to fill. What do you think?"

"'Crazy Love.'"

"Huh?"

"Van Morrison. 'Crazy Love.' That's what I'd want to dance to."

"I've planned over fifty weddings and I've never heard of that song."

"Yes, you have."

"No, I haven't."

"You have. You probably just never knew the title or the artist. It's on my phone." He picked up his phone from the console and tossed it to her. "Cue it up."

"For someone who says he won't dance at his own wedding, you seem awfully prepared with the music."

"I'm prepared for everything, sweetheart."

Sweetheart.

The word hung in the SUV's cab like a cold side of beef in a freezer locker. Why had he said that? He hadn't meant to say that. He was being sarcastic. Right? That's why he'd said it. He hadn't meant it as a term of endearment. Had she taken it that way? Remington cringed and cast a quick glance her way.

She seemed oblivious. People probably called her sweetheart all the time, and it sailed right over her head. Instead, she was futzing with his phone.

"What's your open code?"

"Here." He stuck out his right hand so that she could scan his fingerprint and unlock the phone.

"You could just give me the number."

"I could stick hot pokers in my eyes, too, but I won't."

"Whew, okey dokey. I get it. You do not trust me."

"Don't take it personally. I don't trust anybody."

"Then how come you haven't upgraded to a facial recognition phone?"

"Money. I don't squander it."

"Duly noted." She grinned. "Which finger is it?"

"Thumb."

She took hold of his wrist with one hand and rolled his thumb over the phone screen. At the feel of her soft fingers closing over him, Remington felt a distinctive tightening below his belt, just as he had in the driveway at home.

"Ta-da. I'm in. I see you have the same music app I do." She poked around on his phone and in a few seconds, Van Morrison was singing "Crazy Love" as they bulleted north toward Twilight.

"You're right, I have heard this song."

"Told you."

"The lyrics are very sweet," she said. "And you called me sentimental." She reached over to tickle his ribs lightly.

"Don't," he snapped. Not because he was mad at her, but rather the way his body reacted alarmed him. He did not want to get an erection.

"Just joking." Wilting like a flower in the desert heat, she retreated, sliding closer to the door and hunching her shoulders.

Instantly, he regretted barking at her, but he wouldn't apologize. If he apologized, she'd drift back over, and he needed no more rib tickles.

He said nothing.

She said nothing.

Van Morrison sang about crazy love.

Aria closed his phone and set it on the console between them. She tucked her legs underneath her—gosh, the woman was limber as a pretzel—reached for her purse, took out her cell phone and earbuds. She peered out the window, head bobbing in time to music he couldn't hear.

Great. This was perfect. No more idle chitchat. No more goofy "what if" scenarios. If the next seven plus hours passed like this, he had it made.

She uttered not a word. Kept staring out the window.

All he could see of her was the back of her head. Sleek, glossy black hair fell in a straight curtain down the middle of her back. His hand itched to run his fingers through the thick, silky strands.

Eyes on the road, Sergeant.

No, not a sergeant, not anymore. Those days were over.

The roads were fairly empty on a Tuesday morning in the Trans-Pecos. A few 18-wheelers, some farmer pulling a tractor on a trailer, and a little red sports car zipping by them with a blonde at the wheel.

Remington monitored that one. She was driving too fast and changing lanes over the yellow line and blasting around those 18-wheelers.

"Put your eyes back in your head, Clark Griswold."

"Huh?"

"National Lampoon's Vacation."

"What?"

"Christie Brinkley in the convertible and Chevy Chase drooling over her."

Remington tossed a frown at Aria. "I was not drooling over her. She's driving like a maniac. I was trying to make sure she didn't hit us."

"It's okay to drool over a pretty woman. Perfectly acceptable. You can't help who turns you on."

"I'm not drooling!"

"And I'm not judging."

He wasn't winning this. "Okay, fine, believe whatever you want."

That put a stopper in the conversation.

They traveled for several more minutes, but it felt like hours and hours. The traffic thickened the farther north they drove. After a while, the silence grated on his nerves, which wasn't like Remington at all. Normally, he loved silence.

Hermit.

That was his calling. To live alone, be alone as much as possible. He really wasn't that good with people unless he was ordering them around. And ordering Aria around was about as successful as herding cats.

CHAPTER 3

Blowout: The abrupt failure of a canopy panel or cell.

Thirty minutes passed without her saying a word. Hot damn! Apparently, she'd gotten the message. Good for her.

Remington peeked over at the passenger seat.

Her eyes were closed, and she had her head thrown back against the seat, and she was mouthing the lyrics to some song. He watched her lips, figured out she was silently singing, "All I Want for Christmas Is You."

Not really sure why, he reached over and touched her shoulder.

She yanked out her earbuds, sat up straight, and batted her eyelashes at him. "Yeah?"

"I've got a question for you."

"Oh! The mighty chunk of granite speaks!"

Remington rolled his eyes. "Never mind."

"No, no, don't retreat. Fire away. All questions accepted."

"Since you're not much for plans, how come you're a wedding planner?" It was a question he'd pondered for some time.

"Aww, but you see," she said, gleefully rubbing her palms together. "Not being much of a planner makes me good at planning weddings."

"How can that be?"

"Spontaneity gives me freedom. If something isn't working, I don't stick with it just because it's part of the plan. I can pivot at the drop of a hat."

"But a plan gives you structure. That's the point of it. You make a plan, plot your course, and if you don't deviate, you achieve your goal."

"In the most boring way possible."

"Meaning?" He lifted one eyebrow, honestly surprised by how much her philosophy fascinated him.

"A plan is just a suggestion. Something you stick up there until something better comes along. And something better always comes along if you give it the time and space to develop. Too much planning keeps you hidebound."

"I don't agree."

"I know." She sounded as if she was speaking to a toddler who insisted he wanted a red Popsicle when there were only orange ones in the freezer.

"You say it as if that's a bad thing."

She shrugged and fingered one of the charms on her bracelet. It was a heart-shaped copper charm. "Not bad. Just mentioning that your approach—make a plan and stick to it come hell or high water—hamstrings creativity."

"In what way?"

She flourished her hand. "Take this drive for instance."

"What about it?"

"You programmed the fastest route into your GPS, and you follow it like the gospel all the way up the boring highway to Twilight."

"It's practical to stick to the highway."

"And boring."

"Side roads take longer."

"And I really don't have to be there until tomorrow afternoon."

"Then why did we leave today?"

"To make time for spontaneity."

"I could have been doing stuff today."

"What stuff? You're unemployed."

"I'm helping Ridge around the ranch," he said.

"That's what he's got my brother, Archer, for and the ranch hands. You have been sitting around brooding ever since they discharged you from the Army. That's how you ended up chauffeuring me around. You have nothing else to do."

Point taken. But he wouldn't tell her that.

"You want me to throw my travel plan out the window?"

She pressed her palms together as if she was saying a heartfelt prayer. "Please."

"Just take off down any road headed northeast?" The idea churned his gut.

"Yeah." She perked up. "Let's do it. Take the next exit."

He tried, he really did, to jump right off the highway, but he clenched his hands on the steering wheel and just kept barreling straight ahead.

"Ha." She folded her arms over her chest. "I knew you couldn't do it."

"Stop pigeonholing me."

"Stop being a cliché."

"There's danger involved in willy-nilly ignoring your plans."

"Granted. That's why it's called an adventure. You're a military man. You should be used to danger."

His gaze dropped to his left hand resting on the steering wheel. Yeah, and deviating from the plan was how he'd lost his fingers. It wasn't his day to jump, but he'd volunteered when another paratrooper got sick. If he'd kept his gloomy ass on the ground, he'd still have an intact hand.

But no, he had to be a hero.

He wouldn't get into all that with Aria. One, it was none of her business, and two, well, he just wasn't ready to talk about it with anyone outside his injured war veterans support group.

"It's okay," she said. "It's too much for you."

That irritated him. "Taking another route is not too much for me."

"I get that stepping outside your comfort zone is a big—"

Remington swerved suddenly, taking the exit ramp with a spur-of-the-moment jerk of the wheel. Son of a carpetbagger, why had he let her goad him into veering off course?

"Whoa!" Aria giggled and clung tightly to the grab bar above her head. "Woo-hoo, adventure here we come!"

Ten miles down the road, Aria regretted hounding Remington into taking the highway bypass.

They'd stopped dead in the middle of the road, a line of cars at a standstill in front of them.

Oopsy, her bad.

"This is what happens," Remington grumbled, and tugged his Stetson lower over his brows as if the cowboy hat had magical powers to make the cars in front of them move. "When you don't stick to your plan."

"There could have been a traffic jam on the freeway just as easily as here," Aria pointed out sensibly.

"But we aren't on the freeway, are we? I can't even check the traffic report because there's no cell reception out here in Bumfu—"

"Please." Aria laid her palms over her ears. "Must you curse?"

"I don't have to, but it's a stress reliever."

"Well, it upsets me. So, if you could skip the cussing, I'd appreciate it greatly."

"And I would have appreciated sticking to the plan—so there, we're even."

"No one made you get off the highway."

"You badgered me into it."

"Seems to me like your ego badgered you into it. You couldn't just stick with your plan. You had to show me that you could be spontaneous, didn't you? It's okay, Remington, everyone isn't cut out for spontaneity."

He cursed again.

"*Hmph.* I should have brought along Vivi's swear jar. I'd be rich as Bill Gates by the end of this trip."

"God bless America, Aria, are you saying I can't be myself?"

"I'm saying, I'm not sticking around if you're going to curse. Be your cussy self all you want on your own time, but you can be it without me." Aria unbuckled her seat belt and opened the door.

"Where are you going?"

"To see what's the holdup."

"Aria, get back in the vehicle."

She ignored that. He wasn't the boss of her.

"You can't go off half-cocked. We need a plan."

"Maybe you do," she said, slamming the door. "But I don't."

She was pretty irritated with him right now, and she needed some air. Which—just as it so happened—was bitter cold.

Dark clouds mounded in the sky, making it seem much earlier than ten o'clock in the morning. She wished she'd put on her coat, but she wasn't going back for it. Not while Remington was sitting behind the wheel glaring at her.

Huddling, she crossed her arms over her chest, bent against the wind, and headed for the front of the traffic jam. She heard the Escalade door slam behind her.

"Aria." Remington's voice rose over the sound of the icy gust. "Get back here. I promise I'll try my best to stop cursing."

Nothing doing, bucko.

She had boundaries and things she wouldn't tolerate. Being cursed at was one of them. She'd had enough of that nonsense in her last relationship.

Be reasonable—he wasn't cursing at you. He was cursing at the situation.

Maybe so, but his cursing triggered her, and he should respect that she didn't want to hear it. She walked past the line of cars, nine in all.

She didn't turn around to see if Remington was following her. She wasn't about to give him the satisfaction.

Up ahead, she spied a herd of goats blocking the road. An older gentleman in a green John Deere cap was trying to shoo them along, but the goats weren't budging.

The goats, however, weren't the only problem.

There was also a minivan half in the ditch, the other half sticking out in the road. No one had gotten out of their cars to help the passengers in the minivan or the John Deere dude herd his goats.

Aria surged ahead. As she approached, she could see the problem. The minivan had blown a tire. Most likely when the driver had slammed on the brakes to avoid hitting the goat parade.

"Aria!"

She turned.

There was Remington running behind her, waving her coat in the air over his head. A woman leaned out of the passenger side of a black Camry and snapped a picture of the scene.

Good gravy, the chick could click content for social media, but she couldn't help a stranded traveler?

Be kind, Aria. It is freaking cold out here. If Remington hadn't ticked her off, she probably wouldn't have gotten out.

Aria reached the driver's side of the minivan, heard Remington's footsteps slapping the pavement behind her.

A young woman, wide-eyed, pale and trembling, sat behind the wheel. In the backseat, Aria spied three little kids, all who looked to be under the age of six, tears tracking down their cheeks. Apparently, the blowout had just happened.

Tapping on the window, Aria smiled and waved at the kids to reassure them that everything would be okay.

The mother put the window down, letting out the sound of the children's sniffles. *Aww, the poor babies.*

"Are you all right?" she asked.

Mutely, the mother nodded. "I think so, but I need to check my kids."

"Let me help."

The mom nodded again.

"Hey, Alzate, put this on," Remington commanded from behind her.

She threw a glance over her shoulder.

He thrust the coat at her.

"Thanks," she said breathlessly. She might be mad at him, but she was grateful for the coat.

As she slipped into her coat, Remington, in that shearling jacket that made him look like a Montana rancher, said, "Help the mother and her kids out of the vehicle if they are okay to move, and we'll try to get it off the road."

"We?" As if they were a team. That one word gave her a warm feeling in the pit of her stomach.

"I'll handle moving the minivan. You just get the passengers out."

"It's cold. Is having them cluster on the side of the road in bad weather really the best idea?"

"I don't know what's wrong with their van. They shouldn't be in it when we move it."

"It's a blown-out tire."

"That might not be all. I don't want it catching fire with them in it." He was overly cautious.

"It won't catch fire."

"I swear, Alzate, you'd argue with a dead possum."

The mom opened her door and struggled to get out of the minivan with it parked half-off at a high angle to the road.

"I'm here." Aria sprang to the woman's side, offering her elbow for the mom to balance herself.

"My kids . . ."

"I'll help you get them out so you can check on them."

The mom opened the back door on the roadside, while Aria went around in the ditch to get a child out on that side.

She cast a glance across the top of the minivan to the road, watched Remington walk up to the next car in line and coax the driver to come help him move the minivan from the road.

Someone from the next car got out to help them, and then a fourth person left their vehicle to assist the goat herder.

Well, look at that, Remington had started a community movement.

Within minutes, Aria had the woman and her children a safe distance away from the minivan as Remington and the two other men guided the minivan all the way into the ditch.

She had to hand it to him. The guy might be a pill with his persnickety overplanning, but when push came to shove, he was rock-solid. It shouldn't have surprised her. He was the kind of guy you could always count on in a pinch.

Rocks can become anchors, whispered a voice at the back of her mind.

Exactly!

Which was absolutely, positively why she would ignore the strange little pop of attraction that burst inside her as she watched him clear the road.

"C'mon," she said to the shivering mom and sniffling children. "Let's go sit in my vehicle where I can crank up the heater and get y'all warm. I have M&M's too."

CHAPTER 4

Airhead: The secure initial position of an airborne assault.

It took twenty minutes, but Remington—with the help of fellow travelers—got the road cleared and the tire on the minivan changed.

When he straightened and looked around, he saw that all the other vehicles had gone on past, save for his SUV that Aria had pulled off on the shoulder of the road with the little family safely inside with her.

She asked him for the key fob to start the car. He'd hesitated at first because she shouldn't drive, but she only had to pull the SUV over, so he'd relinquished it. He couldn't be in two places at once, and it was dangerous to keep the SUV on the road.

Good call all the way.

Remington's ears and cheeks burned from cold. He eyed the sky. Yep. Trouble brewing. Time to get moving. If they didn't, they could end up fighting an ice storm all the way to Twilight.

He stalked to the SUV.

Even before he opened the door, he could hear them singing. Aria was in the driver's seat, the mom in the passenger seat and the three kids in the back. Aria smiled as she led the family in song, keeping the kids occupied and their minds off the wreck. They sang in decidedly off-key notes, "Grandma Got Run Over by a Reindeer."

Remington couldn't stop the grin from spreading across his face if he tried. Aria might be a hot mess, but she was a fun hot mess. And from the looks of things, damn—*watch your language, Lockhart*—er, darn good with kids.

He opened the passenger side door, poked his head inside. "Your car is ready to go now, ma'am."

"Oh, thank you," the young mom enthused. "I had no idea what we would do. Because of the weather and how far we are from any cell towers out here, I couldn't get a signal, and no one was getting out of their cars to help me until you two came along."

"My mama raised me by the golden rule," he said, tipping the brim of his Stetson. "I kept thinking, what if it was her stranded out here with us kids when we were little?"

"I know your mother must be very proud of you," the woman said.

Remington nodded, and his eyes met Aria's across the seat. He hoped she didn't tell the woman that his mother was dead. He hated the pity he saw in people's eyes when they learned he lost his mother at a young age. He didn't like it when people tried to make him feel better about his misfortune.

Aria said nothing, but she gave him a look so tender it yanked at something deep inside his gut.

"Follow me, ma'am, and I'll get you back on the road safe and sound." He took two of the kids on his hips and the mother took the youngest in her arms and he guided them back to the vehicle. Once the family was back on the road, he returned to the SUV.

Aria had resumed her place in the passenger seat, and she was still humming "Grandma Got Run Over by a Reindeer."

Laughing, Remington shook his head and buckled up his seat belt.

"Look at you in a good mood. What caused that?" She canted her head, her hair falling sexily over her shoulder, and grinned big.

"You."

"Me?"

"You," he confirmed.

"What about me?"

"You could make a funeral fun."

She narrowed her eyes. "I can't tell from your dry tone if that's a good thing or a bad thing."

Remington shrugged and pulled back onto the two-lane road, now empty of traffic. "It all depends."

"On what?"

"If you're the kind of person who wants to have fun at funerals."

"You're not that kind of person, are you?"

"I was a soldier. I saw a lot of shi—er, stuff out there. There's nothing fun about funerals."

"Could be, if the person who died was humorous and people tell funny stories about him or her."

"You use humor as a defensive mechanism," he said.

"What's wrong with that?"

"Sometimes humor can derail what's really important."

"Humor is important."

"Not inappropriate humor."

"I'm feeling a little judged here." She crossed her arms. He was ticking her off, and that was not his intention.

"Don't be," he said, trying to smooth things over. "You've got your view of life, and I've got mine. Neither one is right nor wrong. It's what works for you."

"That's as long as you don't hurt other people," she said.

"I would add 'intentionally' to that. As long as you don't *intentionally* hurt other people. We can't help what people take offense to. Especially if we're just being ourselves."

"Like you and cussing?"

"I'm trying here, Aria."

She mulled that over for a moment, bobbed her head. "All I know is that you were a real hero just now."

"Nah. People bandy that word *hero* around too lightly. I moved a minivan out of the road and changed a tire. That is not hero material."

"You were a hero to that woman. No one else stepped up, and there were nine cars behind her."

"Don't put me on a pedestal, Aria. I'll fall right off."

"You?" She hooted. "Mr. Straight and Narrow?"

She had no idea about the dark things in his life, and he wanted to keep it that way. She was as pretty and pristine as shiny new Christmas tinsel. He wasn't about to let his ugliness rub off on her.

"Speaking of heroic," he said. "Don't think I didn't see you slip that mother five twenties."

"*Spptt.*" Aria grimaced. "That wasn't heroic. I just wanted to make sure the woman got that tire fixed."

"See?" he said. "Getting called a hero makes you feel uncomfortable."

"Point taken." She knotted her hands on her knees, the blue veins on the back of her hands flattening out, the tendons at her wrist visibly tightening.

"But while it was nice of you to help the woman," he went on, "she should have thought ahead."

"Excuse me, how could she have planned ahead for goats in the road?"

"Her tires were in bad shape. She should have put new ones on several thousand miles ago."

"Well, Mr. Moneybags, not everyone is Lockhart-rich and can drive around with brand-new tires. She's got three kids. That's where her money goes."

"I'm not judging her."

"Aren't you?"

"I'm just saying it's important to plan thoroughly and then have a backup plan in case things go wrong. I have nothing personal against that woman. Stop making out like I do."

"You're projecting your values onto her." She cleared her throat and climbed up on a soapbox. "Not everyone thinks like you do. And besides, even brand-new tires can blow out. Face it. There are some things in life you simply can't plan for."

"Like falling out of a hayloft?"

She gave him a sassy look, muttered, "Smart aleck."

"If the truth hurts . . ." He shrugged.

"Not everyone can plan ahead, even if they wanted to. Sometimes, life just gets in the way."

Remington hardened his jaw. "That sounds like an excuse to me."

"You wanna know what I think?"

Yes, he did. He was curious to find out how she'd made it through life with such a disorganized approach. "Let's hear it."

"I think adaptability is a much more useful skill than planning."

"Interesting theory," he said, feeling the skin underneath his collar heat.

"People who make the best of the situation they find themselves in and don't get bogged down over the way things were supposed to be or how things didn't go according to plan." She tugged at the hem of her short skirt, trying to pull it down lower.

Had she seen him staring at her legs? God, she had gorgeous legs.

"I'm not saying adaptability isn't a useful skill. What I'm saying is if you planned properly, you wouldn't be in a situation where you had to adapt."

"Did they teach you this philosophy in the Army, or are you just naturally a fuddy-duddy? You gotta cut people some slack."

"Meaning?"

"That woman was moving her three kids to her parents' house after leaving an abusive husband." Aria nodded.

"Really?"

"How could you ever plan for something like that? She'd been squirreling away money for months just to get away from him."

"It's hard when the person you marry turns out to be different than you thought."

She gave him the side-eye. "Do *you* have a marriage checklist?"

"You bet I do."

"Why am I not shocked?" She looked heavenward. "That explains a lot."

"Meaning?"

"Why you're not married."

"I'm not married because I've been fighting in a war for a third of my life. You rarely meet a wife in a militarized zone."

"And why is it that you spent a third of your life at war?"

"It was my job."

"Why?"

"Why what?"

"Why is war your job?"

Her question momentarily stumped him. "T-to protect my country."

"For a third of your life? And you chose it over having a family?"

"You're not married either," he said, realizing he was turning things around on her because he was losing this battle of wills.

"I want to see it," she said.

"What?"

"Your marriage checklist. I know you claim you're not getting married, but you can't fool me. You have a marriage checklist."

"No."

"That bad, is it?"

"Having a checklist for what you want in a mate isn't a bad thing."

"In theory, maybe not, but in practice? Let me guess, your potential wife has to meet certain standards."

"That's the whole point of the checklist."

"I see many lonely nights in your future," she said.

He waited for her to say more, and he could see she was struggling not to give him a piece of her mind.

"Not much different from the mom running from her abusive husband," he pointed out.

"All I'm saying is that a checklist can't save you from making mistakes."

"Maybe not, but it could sure cut down on some of them."

"You really don't understand a thing about love, do you?" She stared at him as if he were some zoo oddity.

"Doubtful," he said, feeling like a bit of an ass for misjudging the mom.

Remington didn't want to keep arguing. They were just going around in circles, each trying to prove to the other that their point of view was right. You couldn't change other people. It always backfired.

He'd learned that with Maggie, his first girlfriend.

As they drove, he'd left the two-lane road and got back on the highway. The detour had cost them forty-five minutes, but he was feeling grungy after changing the tire, and in the activity, he'd also worked up an appetite. He had beef jerky and dried apples in the glove compartment, but he wanted something more substantial, and they'd used half a tank of gas.

Time to fill up.

Remington glanced at the sky. The weather seemed to hold steady. An ice storm was on the way, but a thirty-minute stop for lunch shouldn't put them behind the encroaching storm. He would check the weather report when they got to a truck stop.

"Would you like a quick lunch?" he asked.

She looked surprised and pressed a palm to her stomach. "Sure. I'm starving. I didn't eat breakfast."

"Why not?"

"I'm doing this thing where I don't eat for sixteen hours."

"Huh? Sounds brutal."

"Not really. You get used to it."

"But why?"

"So that I don't have to watch my calories so closely if I keep all my eating in an eight-hour window. I have no willpower around the holidays, and intermittent fasting helps me keep the weight off. Christmas cookies are my downfall."

He eyed her. "Aria, you don't have a spare ounce of fat on you."

"I know. Intermittent fasting works."

"Was that why you fell out of the hayloft? You got dizzy from not eating?" he asked, pulling into the parking lot of a truck stop restaurant.

"No, it was not why I fell out of the hayloft. I had on new boots and they slipped on the straw."

It was all he could do not to lecture her. The concussion was lesson enough. He didn't need to pile on, even though he doubted she'd learned her lesson.

"The same boots you're wearing now?" He eyed her boots.

"Yes."

"Then it's settled, I'm holding your arm when we walk across the parking lot. It's been raining here, and I won't have you slip and hit your head again."

"It's no big deal."

"How is your head?"

"It's fine. A tiny headache, but nothing I can't handle."

"Just sit tight." He jumped out of the SUV and raced around to her side to head her off at the pass.

She already had the door open and was sliding to the ground when he got there. "You need one of those running board things for us shorter people."

"Short people don't normally ride in my vehicle."

"I'm not short," she said, drawing herself up to her five-foot-five-ish frame. "Just shorter than you, gargantuan."

"So now you're calling me names?"

"You called me short."

He smiled, amused. "I'll look into the running boards."

"Thank you. Now was that so hard?"

He extended his elbow to her, gave her a look that said, *latch on.* She hesitated.

"I don't bite."

"You sure?"

"Well, I sharpened my teeth before this trip, so no promises."

Her upper lip twitched as if she was trying not to laugh. "Why, Remington Lockhart, is that a joke?"

"Don't sound so surprised. I have a sense of humor."

"Since when?"

Since he'd started hanging around with her.

The wind gusted, whipping her hair into her face. She tucked the loose strands behind her ear. She had the most beautifully shaped ears he'd ever seen.

Getting turned on by ears, Lockhart? No, not just any ear, Aria's ears.

"It's cold out here." Remington extended his elbow again. "Let's go inside."

Finally, she slipped her arm through his. The second she touched him, he felt it all over again. The snap, crackle, pop of attraction.

"That darn static electricity," she mumbled.

"Yeah," he said, feeling his throat tighten. "That darn static electricity."

Except they both knew it wasn't just static electricity charging between them. It was something way more complicated and way more alarming than that.

CHAPTER 5

Box man: A neutral, face-to-earth body position in which the arms form right angles at the shoulder and elbow, and the legs spread at 45 degrees from the long axis and bend 45 degrees at the knees.

The wind whistled around the 18-wheelers as they walked arm in arm into the restaurant.

People packed the place even at eleven in the morning, and Christmas music played too loudly. A Christmas tree loaded with too many decorations sat near the front entrance, and tinsel fluttered every time the door opened.

The hostess, wearing a heavy sweater, greeted them with menus clutched to her chest. "Table or booth?"

"A corner booth," Remington said. "One that backs up to a wall."

"I'm not sure we have one, but I'll go check." The hostess disappeared.

"Why did you specify a booth in the corner?" Aria asked.

"I like sitting with my back to a wall."

"Is it a military thing? So that the enemy can't flank you?"

"Yes," he said, surprised by her insight. "In case there's trouble, I want to see it coming."

"It's gotta be dark and gloomy."

"What?" he scowled, not following her conversational twist.

"Inside your head. So much distrust."

"Being too trusting can get you killed."

"Not being trusting enough can leave you lonely and isolated."

Touché, Remington thought but did not tell her that.

The hostess popped back into view and motioned for them to follow. Aria's statement rang in his ears.

Yeah, sometimes it was dark and gloomy inside his head. Fact of life. He would always sit with his back to the wall. *Be prepared for anything*, that was his motto. And you couldn't prepare if you didn't see your opponent coming.

Handing them their menus, the hostess disappeared.

"What are you going to get?" he asked Aria when a perky purple-haired waitress showed up.

"Hmm." Aria tapped her chin with her index finger. "I'll have the veggie plate."

"Don't hold back. Get some meat. I'm buying."

"Um . . . I'm a vegetarian."

"Since when? I remember when you were a kid, you ate nothing but corn dogs and bacon sandwiches with mustard. I always thought that was so gross. Mayo goes with bacon, not mustard. Mayo."

"That was twenty years ago, dude. I haven't eaten meat in years. And what's the mad love with mayo?"

"They call it aioli now," the waitress said. "They add things to it like garlic or thyme. I think it's just weird." She shrugged. "But whatever floats your boat."

"So, no meat? Not ever?" Remington asked Aria.

"I try never to say *never*. I mean if it was the zombie apocalypse or something, I'd do whatever I had to do to survive, and if that meant eating Spam, then aloha Spam."

"Because Spam is popular in Hawaii?" the waitress asked. "If I were in a zombie apocalypse, I'd just say screw it and let them eat me. Fighting is too much trouble."

Neither Remington nor Aria commented on that.

Instead, Remington studied Aria. He knew she was flaky and vaguely woo-woo, but he didn't realize she'd gone vegetarian.

Honestly though, he wasn't surprised. Aria had a tendency to jump on whatever bandwagon rolled across social media.

"Well, I'm getting the biggest, juiciest cheeseburger on the menu." Narrowing his eyes, he waited for her reaction. He wasn't being childish . . . was he?

"Okay," Aria said mildly.

"That's it? Okay? You're not lecturing on the virtues of vegetarianism?"

"Is that what you want me to do?" A smug *Mona Lisa* smile curled at her lips, and he realized that without even trying she'd gotten his goat.

"No!" He snorted.

"Are you trying to provoke me?"

"No," he said, a little less forcefully this time.

"Seems like you are."

"Anything to drink?" the waitress asked brightly.

"Water," Remington grunted.

"Herbal tea, thank you, please." Aria passed her menu to the waitress.

"We have nothing herbal. How about decaf?"

"That'll do."

She trotted off.

At the waitress's departure, the conversation stopped dead. Aria took out her phone and started texting.

Remington stared out the big glass window at the parking lot. The sky had darkened considerably since they'd come inside the truck stop restaurant. The weather was coming in faster than he'd expected. He'd rush Aria through lunch and get them back on the road ASAP.

The waitress brought their food, and Aria didn't even glance up from her phone.

Remington stared down at his giant cheeseburger dripping with grease. Such a contrast to the sautéed veggies on Aria's plate. He felt like a total jerk for ordering a greasy burger just to spite her.

"Aria?"

She raised her head, thumbs still posed over the phone screen. "Yes?"

"Could you stop texting for half a second?"

Cocking her head at an inquisitive angle, she said, "What is it?"

"Phone. Down."

"These monosyllables don't really work for me, caveman. I know you're not around people much but—"

"Please."

She chuckled, put her phone down on the table, and gave him her full attention, resting her elbows on the table and her chin in her upturned palms. "I'm listening."

"I apologize."

Her eyes widened, and she plastered a palm to her heart. "Excuse me? Remington Lockhart is apologizing . . . to *me*?"

He held up a palm, shook his head. "Never mind. Forget it."

"No, no. I'll stop making fun. Why are you apologizing?"

"For making a show of ordering a cheeseburger." He sliced the cheeseburger into two pieces with his knife. It was too big to handle, but that seemed to just make things worse because slicing it exposed the thick meat patty cooked medium well.

"You made a show? I didn't notice."

"I lied when I said I wasn't doing it on purpose. I *was* trying to provoke you into giving me a benefit-of-being-vegetarian rant. It was juvenile, and I apologize."

"Not offended, so you don't owe me an apology." She dug into her steamed broccoli. "But I appreciate the sentiment. However, there is a bigger question . . ."

"Yes?" He leaned forward, something about her drawing him, even as he had a strong urge to resist getting any closer.

"Why did you feel the need to poke at me?"

Why indeed? He shrugged, took a bite of his burger, but it didn't taste as good as he thought it would. He chewed, swallowed. "I don't know."

"Sure, you do."

"I do?"

"You were testing me."

"I was?" He scratched his chin.

"You pushed me to see if I'd try to persuade you to change your food choice."

Bingo! She'd nailed it, and he'd been unaware that was what he'd done. "How do you know that?"

"How long have I known you, Remy?"

Remy. It had been so long since anyone had called him that. Coming from Aria it sounded nice and friendly.

Too friendly.

"All your life," he murmured.

"You've always been the type to test people. To see if you can trust them." She gave a rabbit-quick shrug. "I suppose it comes from losing your mother so young and your father being a giant dillhole. You could never trust the ground to be solid beneath your feet."

Her insight blew him away. Years ago, he'd pegged Aria as rather shallow, but there was unexpected depth lurking beneath those dark eyes.

"Remy." She called him by that nickname again, reached across the table, and laid her palm on top of his left hand.

Remington didn't like it when people touched his damaged hand, but with Aria, he didn't pull away.

"I don't expect people to change who they are to suit me. I chose vegetarianism. That's just me. You need not be like me. I see you and accept you for who you are."

Instant goose bumps popped up over his skin.

"Why?"

"Why what?"

"Why do you accept me for who I am?"

"Because I honor and respect you."

"Even if we disagree?"

"Sure. I can't expect other people to think and behave the way I do. What a boring world that would be."

Remington shivered all the way to the bottom of his spine.

"Are you cold?" she asked.

"Yes," he lied.

She accepted him for who he was, unconditionally? Wow. He couldn't say the same. Every time he was around her, he couldn't help thinking how she was too this or too that. Too bubbly. Too chatty. Too kind. Too trusting.

In fact, she was being too nice to him right now. He didn't deserve it.

"People should be able to be themselves," she said. "I know your dad taught you otherwise. Shape up to Duke Lockhart's expectations or ship out. Which you did. Running off to the military as soon as you graduated high school. But that doesn't have to be your reality. You don't have to knuckle under or run away. You can find people who love you for who you are."

Whoa. If she got any deeper, he was going to have to buy a life jacket.

"Let's just agree to be ourselves with each other, okay?" she murmured. "No more pretending."

He nodded.

"Can I have a fry?" She motioned at his French fries.

"Be my guest."

She took a fry and dipped it into the ketchup he'd squeezed onto his plate. He watched her slide the ketchup-smothered potato into her mouth.

"Yum, I should have ordered fries."

"Have another," he invited. It was fun watching her eat. She attacked her food with such gusto.

They ate in silence, finishing up their meal. Just as the waitress dropped off their check, Aria's cell phone dinged, letting her know she'd gotten a new text message.

She picked up the phone, rolled her eyes, and set it back down on the table.

"What is it?" he asked.

"Kaia." Aria blew out her breath on a long sigh.

"Is she in labor?"

"No such luck. My sisters have been driving me bonkers ever since they learned you were the one driving me to Twilight."

"Oh?" Remington took cash out of his wallet and paid the bill.

She waved her hand at the phone. "This is the kind of nonsense I'm talking about. Other people trying to tell you how you should be."

"What's going on?" he asked, getting to his feet.

She stood. "It's goofy."

He helped her on with her coat. "Is it about your Granny Blue's kissing legend? Because Ridge texted me something about that hogwash too."

Leaning over to retrieve her phone, Aria stuffed it into her coat pocket. "Yes! It's *sooo* dumb. Just because our siblings all hooked up doesn't mean it's right for us. I mean c'mon, you and I are night and day. We have nothing in common. Am I right?"

"You are correct."

"Same page! Slap some skin on me." She held up a palm.

Surprised, he surrendered to her enthusiasm and gave her a high five.

The second their palms smacked together he felt a surprising tingle shoot all the way up his arm. He schooled his features, not wanting her to see how much touching her affected him.

Unnerved, Remington guided her toward the front door, but he did not put his hand to her back to guide her. Lord knows he wanted to, and *that* was the problem. This was *Aria*, for heaven's sake.

The cold wind hit them with an icy blast. Aria huddled against the cold, pulling up the collar of her coat. She shivered, violently. Her coat was too thin. Remington put his arm around her shoulders to shield her with his body as they walked to his SUV and tried to ignore the fresh tingles passing through him.

He took her to the passenger side where they were out of the wind.

"Look at this." Aria held up her cell phone.

In the text bubble from her older sister, Kaia, he read: Just kiss the guy already and find out.

"It's so freaking ridiculous," Aria muttered, and shook her head. "Why can't my family mind their own business?"

"Yeah, why?" He looked down into her earnest oval face.

Her eyes were bright, her cheeks reddened from the cold, and she looked as magical as a Christmas elf.

His breath left his body on an extended exhale.

"You know what?" She stuck her phone back into her pocket.

"What?"

"I think we should do it."

"Do what?" he asked, assessing her warily with a sidelong glance.

"Prove it's baloney."

He was so captivated by her lively eyes he wasn't really following her conversation. "Um, what's baloney?"

"The legend." With no further preamble, Aria went up on her tiptoes and planted a quick kiss on Remington's mouth.

The kiss was quick until Remington recovered from his surprise, wrapped his arms around her waist, and pulled her closer. His body wanted a *real* kiss, and damn if he could stop himself from bending her back in his arms and claiming her pert little mouth.

A straight-up, big-screen movie kiss.

Aria gasped, but she didn't pull away. Instead, she melted against his chest and parted her lips, giving him an opening. He took it, running his tongue along her teeth, dipping into her far deeper than he should have.

"Woot, woot," someone catcalled from across the parking lot, breaking the spell. "Get a room!"

Remington raised his head, saw a group of teenage boys gawking at them from the sidewalk. He glared daggers at them, and the teens slunk away.

"You can let me go now," Aria whispered. "I think we've proven our point."

"Yeah." Remington righted her, trying hard to ignore how swiftly his blood was pumping through his veins. "What point was that?"

"That there's zero chemistry between us." She made a little chirping noise and stepped away from him.

Wow, why did he feel let down?

"You heard nothing?" he asked. "No humming."

She shook her head vigorously. "Nope."

"Not even a little buzz?"

"Not a peep. Total radio silence. Quiet. The dead zone."

Hmm, she seemed to be protesting a bit too much, but the whole humming legend was far-fetched as hell. "You felt nothing either?"

She rubbed her lips with two fingers. "Well, you *are* a good kisser . . ."

"So are you," he said, startled to hear how husky his voice came out.

"Thanks. But that means nothing. Right?"

"Oh right. Absolutely."

Except it was one of the best kisses he'd ever had. Right up there in the top ten for sure. Maybe even top five. He tried to remember better kisses and came up empty.

In fact, at this moment, his head was so dizzy, and his nose so filled with Aria's lovely scent, his mouth still watering from the sweet taste of her, he couldn't remember any of the other women he'd ever kissed.

Not even Maggie.

And there was this damned humming sound inside his head. What was that all about? In Aria's family legend it was the women who heard the humming. Not the men they kissed.

It's crackers. You've just got a ringing in your ears because of the icy wind. Get her in the vehicle, man. Get back on the road.

"Remington," she said. "That was . . . you were . . ."

"*Shh.*" He shook his head.

"What?" Aria's eyebrows leaped up her forehead. "Did you just shush me?"

"Dammit, Aria—"

"Language."

Remington grunted, frustrated to the max. Not with Aria, but with himself for agreeing to this outing. Hormones pulsed through his body, hot and sticky. He didn't want to feel this way.

He hated whenever he lost control. He had to tamp down his irritation before he climbed back into the SUV with her.

Clenching his hands as much as he could with missing fingers, he whirled on his heel and marched off across the edge of the parking lot to the vast patch of sandy earth stretching to the horizon.

With his face into the wind, he let loose with a string of curses and immediately felt better, despite the icy chill blasting his exposed skin.

Get it together, Lockhart. Now! You've got four more days alone with her.

What was wrong with him? He was losing his ever-loving mind. Okay, he'd kissed her back. So what? Kissing her had been terrific. Big deal. Move on.

But he heard humming.

That had to be due to the worsening weather. Barometric pressure or something. *Not* her kiss. He had to pull himself together. Look at him. Two hours in Aria's company had him swearing at cactus.

Gulping in big swallows of bracing air, he stalked back to the vehicle feeling somewhat calmer.

She stood shivering where he left her, and he realized he'd forgotten to unlock the SUV before stomping off. *What a jackass.*

"Sorry," he mumbled.

"I get it," she said. "You needed to let off steam."

"Storm's coming." He grunted.

"Yes," she whispered. "Yes, it is." Aria locked eyes with him. She looked like a brave little fawn facing down a mountain lion. It was all he could do not to grin.

He hit the remote control. The SUV chirped. He reached for the door handle, opened it, and put out a hand to help her up. She was right. He needed running boards on his SUV for shorter passengers.

She stared at his hand.

His left hand.

Unnerved, he tucked it behind him and turned to offer her his right hand.

She hesitated.

He couldn't look at her. Didn't want to see pity in her eyes. "Let's get the show on the road."

She took his right hand, let him boost her up. She bounced onto the seat and immediately let go of his hand.

"What *was* that all about?" she asked, gesturing toward the field. "If you don't mind me asking."

Emotional regulation. That's what that was. "I don't want to talk about it."

"But—"

"No talking. My vehicle, my rules."

She bobbed her head. "Okay."

Relieved that for once she wouldn't argue with him, Remington walked around the SUV. He had to remember where his priorities lay. He wanted one thing and one thing only. To get this trip over and done with and get back home to carve out his civilian life. Time to get his act together.

In the three months that he'd been home, he'd been at loose ends. Which was fine, normal even, according to the military therapist he'd seen before his dismissal. He needed to find his bearings.

But he'd moped enough. Time for action. His plans? Help other service members who were going through what he'd gone through. No one could really understand what combat was like except someone who'd been there. A lot of military personnel struggled to adjust once they came home, and he'd like to help them find their way.

But that meant he'd have to heal himself first.

Chapter 6

Vortex: A whirling mass of air, especially one in the form of a visible spiral, and operating with the force of suction, as a tornado.

Aria had not planned for the kiss to turn out the way it did.

It should have been quick and simple and proved a point. That she wasn't meant for Remington Lockhart.

That's what you get for being spontaneous. She heard her mother's voice in her head.

Boy, was she in trouble now.

Big-time.

Her head was humming like a beehive and her knees were rubber and she couldn't help sneaking glances over at Remington, who looked as unmovable as a tank sitting in the driver's seat. His stare focused on the road as the gathering wind whipped against the Escalade.

Not a word had passed between them since he'd gotten back on the road. Well, la-de-da. If he wouldn't speak, neither would she.

But now, she had nothing to do but listen to her incessant thoughts. What was going on here? Why was she hearing that stupid humming noise? And how in the world did she make it stop?

Easy. Don't kiss Remington again.

She thought about texting Kaia, but quickly canned that idea. Her sister would start carrying on about soul mates and happily-ever-after.

With Remington Lockhart?

Not a chance.

She sneaked another glance at him, but Mr. Granite Face hadn't moved a muscle. *It's the concussion.* The logical explanation popped into her head and she grasped at it with both hands. *Yesss!* The concussion. That was it.

Except, she'd suffered the concussion three days ago, and she'd heard no humming until after she kissed him.

Oh crap, why had she kissed him?

What if the legend was true? What if the humming meant she'd found The One? What if he was her soul mate?

No, no, no.

Remington didn't have much of a sense of humor and he was so into rules. He was a black-and-white thinker in a shades-of-gray world. She'd always thought he was a bit of a jerk, but since they'd been on the road together, she'd seen another side of him.

He'd apologized about the cheeseburger thing and when he'd felt the need to curse, he'd honored her wishes and stalked off to cuss at a cactus. He'd been so good to help that woman with her blown-out tire, although he had judged the mom for not having a backup plan.

What was all this pigheaded insistence on planning ahead? As if planning could prevent the unexpected from knocking the pins right out from under you.

Like kissing Remington and hearing the hum.

Dang, she didn't want to admit it, but that had been the best darn kiss of her life. *Shoot, shoot, shoot.*

She tugged on her earlobe as if trying to dislodge water from her ear. Thank heavens the humming was ebbing. She was going with the concussion explanation.

"Um." She licked her lips, and despite her best intentions to the contrary, said, "Should we talk—"

"No."

"You don't even know what I'm going to say."

"Could we just be quiet for a while?" he asked.

"How long is a while?"

"A few hundred miles."

Message received. Shut up for the rest of the trip.

She played a game on her phone. Ignored the occasional texts from her three sisters, asking how the trip with Remington was going. Good grief, didn't any of them have better things to do than stick their noses in her life?

Bored, Aria tugged out her earbuds, tossed them and her phone into her purse, settled back in the seat, and peered through the windshield. Two hours had passed since they'd left the truck stop and it was only one o'clock in the afternoon, but outside, it looked more like four P.M.

She glanced over, studied Remington's face. Admired the firm set of his jaw. Her artist's eye itched to capture the way the shadows fell over the high planes of his cheek. Inspired, she took out the small sketchbook she always kept in her purse and a Blackwing pencil and began to draw.

For a long time, there was nothing but the sound of her pencil quietly scribbling soft circles and sharp lines over the page as she outlined Remington's head.

The sky had darkened. Brooding clouds mounded on the northern horizon, and they headed right toward them. The wind buffeted the Escalade so forcefully, Remington's forearm muscles bunched as he fought to keep it on the road.

And the highway was pretty empty.

The ubiquitous 18-wheelers, but not as many as usual, and two or three passenger vehicles. Remington had the radio on low, tuned to the weather channel. He had a grim set to his chin, and he sat slightly forward in the seat, his spine military stiff.

"What are you drawing?" he asked, and gave a quick peek over at her before returning his attention to the road.

"Nothing." Embarrassed that he caught her drawing him, she stuffed the sketchbook and pencil back into her purse.

From the radio, the weatherman was warning people to get off the roads and take shelter.

"What's up?" she asked.

"Storm's rolling in faster than they predicted."

"Will we make it to Twilight before it hits?"

He shook his head. "Twilight is still four hours away. I seriously doubt it."

"We'll have to drive in an ice storm?" Aria felt her body tense. She wasn't thrilled about driving through bad weather. She'd wrecked on ice once, and the accident had left an impression.

"I'm not driving in ice." His jaw hardened, but he didn't take his eyes off the road. "Too dangerous. I promised Vivi I'd get you there in one piece."

"So, what are we going to do?" She gripped the dashboard with both hands.

"We're going to stop in the next town and get a room until the storm passes. This ice storm is severe, but they don't expect it to last more than a day. The weather will hit the fifties tomorrow so it'll melt. That's Texas winters for you. Burr-ass cold one day, warm the next."

She didn't chide him for saying "ass." She didn't want him stopping the car and marching off into a pasture to curse.

Aria dug her phone out again. Searched the internet. "The next town is Armadillo, and it's twenty miles away."

"Which is why we're stopping there and not trying to make it to Odessa."

She searched for motels in the area. "Armadillo only has one motel. What if it's filled with other people who had the same idea?"

"It'll be fine."

Aria angled him a look. "I thought you didn't like flying by the seat of your pants."

"I don't and I'm not. We'll get a room."

"How do you know they're not already booked up?"

"Because I made a reservation."

She leaned sideways in her seat as far as the belt would let her and squinted at him. "What? When?"

"Yesterday when Vivi asked me to make the drive."

"Wait, what? How did you know the ice storm would roll in early and we'd be far from a bigger town?"

"There's not much but jackrabbits and tumbleweeds between Cupid and Odessa. There are only four towns with overnight accommodations before you reach the Odessa/Midland area. Pecos, Wickett, Monahans, and Armadillo. I made reservations in all of them."

"What?"

He turned his head and grinned. "Backup plan. Do you see how that works? We won't get stuck in the SUV at the side of the road waiting for the storm to pass. You're welcome."

"What if the storm had hit *after* we left Midland?"

"I have reservations in two towns between Midland and Abilene as well."

"You've gotta be kidding me."

"Nope. Stick with me, Aria Alzate, I'm always prepared." The clouds seemed to have landed right on the highway, the Escalade's headlights barely cutting through the encroaching mist.

Storms stirred her anxiety. To keep from fixating on it, she chattered. "But what if all those places charge your credit card?"

"I only picked hotels that had a same day cancellation policy. Well, except the place in Armadillo. Since it was the only motel in the town . . ."

"Gotta hand it to you, Lockhart, I am impressed."

He shot her a smug expression.

"Don't make me regret praising you," she said.

"I did make one mistake." Ice was pelting the windshield now, just as they passed a road sign that said: *Armadillo, five miles.*

"Ooh, the famous planner missteps? How's that?"

"When I agreed to drive Vivi's wedding supplies to Twilight, I didn't know about you. I only reserved one room."

Share a motel room with Remington Lockhart? No way. She'd rather spend the night in the SUV in freezing weather, but she wasn't about to let him know how much the idea panicked her.

She tossed her hair and said breezily, "Maybe they'll have another room available. I have a good feeling about this. It is Armadillo after all. How many people could there be waiting in line for a motel room?"

Then she got on the phone again, texted Vivi and Olivia, telling them about the delay. The wedding wasn't until Saturday. A one-night stopover wouldn't affect things much. It was why Vivi insisted they leave on Wednesday.

Thanks to Remington and his backup plan, everything was going to work out just fine.

Now all she had to do was pray for an extra available room.

HOW MANY PEOPLE could be waiting in line for a motel room in Armadillo?

Quite a few, as it turned out. There wasn't a free parking space, and Remington had to parallel park curbside on the street.

The minute he stopped the vehicle, Aria unbuckled her seat belt and hopped out. But she didn't head up the path to the motel, already icing up from the precipitation, rather she disappeared from his view in the opposite direction.

Where in the hell was she headed?

He got out and walked around the back of the SUV to see her mincing her way across a dried patch of yellowed grass to a small park. There in the middle of the park was a concrete statue of seven armadillos. One big one, one medium-sized one, and five small ones. Papa, Mama, and their babies. Each armadillo wore a jaunty red-and-white Santa cap perched between their ears.

The statues were whimsical, quirky, and kitschy cute.

Right up Aria's alley.

Yes, okay, they were eye-catching if you were into that sort of small-town Americana preciousness, but for crying out loud, the sky was raining ice. If Aria wasn't careful, she was going to slip, fall, and bust her very sexy little ass.

Argh. He readjusted his Stetson. The woman needed a keeper.

She bent over to examine the armadillos close-up, giving him a fantastic view of her rump.

Remington felt his body tighten in the wrong places, and he clenched his teeth. Or maybe he was the one who needed the keeper. "Hey," he hollered at her. "What in the blue blazes are you doing?"

She didn't answer. Instead, she took out her cell phone and started snapping pictures.

Remington rolled his eyes and went after her.

"Remy, look."

Remy. There it was again. The nickname that, when it came from her lips, sounded like a term of endearment.

She sighed breathlessly as he approached. "Aren't they totes adorb?"

"They're concrete armadillos, Aria."

"I know. So, so cute."

"You've got ice in your hair."

"Do I?" She ran a hand through her dark, straight mane, dislodging the crystals that formed there. "I like this town. It reminds me of Cupid."

"Yeah, so far out in the middle of nowhere that the townspeople do dopey things like put Santa hats on armadillo statues."

"Don't be such a grinch, Lockhart. These folks know how to live. They have a *joie de vivre* I can get behind."

"How about you get behind a warm fireplace and a hot toddy?"

"Ooh, that sounds nice."

"Come on." He held out his hand.

She slipped her palm into his.

"Your hand is like ice, woman. You're going to catch frostbite."

"Frostbite isn't something you catch." She giggled. "It's something that—"

"Figure of speech, no need to analyze it to death. Upshot is the same. It's twenty degrees out here and you're taking snapshots of concrete armadillos."

"With Santa caps," she reminded him.

"We can't forget that, can we?" He guided her back toward the motel, careful of where he placed his steps on the treacherous ice quickly slathering the ground.

"Do you think they put bunny ears on them for Easter and Uncle Sam hats for Fourth of July?"

"No doubt."

"Pilgrim hats for Thanksgiving and witch hats for Halloween."

"You should move here," Remington said.

"What?"

"You'd fit right in with their wackiness."

"Why thank you, Remy. That's a sweet thing to say."

"I was being sarcastic."

"I know."

"Just so we're clear."

"Oh, I've got a read on you, mister." She playfully shook a finger under his nose. "You're coming in loud and clear."

What did she mean by that? He would have studied her face, but he was intent on getting them into the motel without the icy sidewalk taking them down.

"You think so?" he mumbled.

"Uh-huh." She hummed.

He was intrigued, but he wouldn't let himself get sucked in. "Here we are."

Travelers and buzzing voices filled the lobby. Suitcases sat stacked on the floor. People milled around the gas fireplace while a long line of others snaked around the front desk.

The desk clerk dinged a bell. "May I have your attention, folks?"

The chatter died down as everyone turned their gazes to the front desk.

"We're completely booked. Unless you have reservations, I'm sorry, you must look for lodging elsewhere."

Immediately, the din started up again, as people protested and complained and worried about what they would do.

"I'm sorry," Aria said, going up on tiptoes next to his ear so that he could hear her over the clamor.

"What for?" He angled his head downward to her.

"Making fun of your planning. Sometimes, your obsessive-compulsive disorder comes in very handy, Remy."

"Wait, what? I'm not OCD."

"Aren't you?"

"No."

"How many people here do you think have reservations at four motels on the off chance they'd get caught in an ice storm?"

"Probably none."

"See? OCD. It's probably why you did so well in the military."

Was he OCD? He liked things a certain way, that was for sure. But did he really have a disorder, or was it that organization and planning were so foreign to Aria, that giving him a label was the only way she could explain his efficiency?

Once they'd heard there were no more rooms, the crowd dispersed and the line in front of them dwindled.

"Look, Remy," Aria said when it was their turn at the desk. On the counter sat sheets of stickers depicting the armadillos in Santa hats. To the clerk, she said, "Adorable. How much are the stickers?"

"Two dollars."

"What are they for?" Remington asked.

"Souvenirs, silly," Aria said, digging money from her purse. "To prove you've stayed in Armadillo."

"Why do we need to prove that?"

"Ignore him," she said to the clerk in a loud whisper behind her hand. "He has no sense of whimsy."

"A fact of which I am quite proud," Remington said.

"Sad." Aria clicked her tongue, and the clerk laughed, checked them in, gave them two keys, and directed them to their room.

For an older motel in a small West Texas town, the room turned out to be surprisingly nice. Nothing fancy, but Remington didn't need fancy. It was clean and had no bedbugs—he checked the mattress—so good to go.

Except Aria was eyeing the queen-sized bed with her bottom lip caught between her teeth.

"We both can't sleep in *that* bed."

"Stop worrying. I have no intention of sleeping in the same bed with you, Aria. I'll bunk on the floor."

"That's not fair. You're paying for the room. You served our country. *I'm* bunking on the floor."

Miss Polished and Pampered offering to take the floor? That amused him. She wouldn't last an hour, but it was nice that she offered and hadn't just assumed she'd get the bed.

"It's not up for debate," he said.

"Maybe they have a rollaway cot."

"Did you not see the lobby? I'm sure the cots are taken."

"But we can ask."

She picked up the phone, called the front desk, and made her request. Wincing, she hung up. "All the cots are taken."

"Look, sleeping on the floor is *nothing* to me. I don't need pillows or fluff. All I need is a place to get horizontal, and this qualifies."

"You're a real badass, huh?"

"I was in the Army Rangers. Badass is what we do."

Aria stepped to the window and gazed out. "Were you ever scared?"

"All the livelong day. But you know what they say about bravery. Feel the fear and do it anyway."

"Gosh, I have no idea what that's like. I get a paper cut and it ruins my day."

"You're not supposed to know what fear is like. You should be cherished and looked after."

Aria rolled her eyes. "Oh, please don't tell me you're one of *those*."

"One of what?"

"Guys who think women are too fragile and helpless to be soldiers."

"I don't think that at all. I've worked with plenty of great female soldiers. I was talking about *you*."

"So now it's personal?" She turned away from the window to face him. "I'm too fragile and helpless?"

"You're twisting this the wrong way."

"Am I?"

"Yes."

"Then what's the right way?"

"You're special, Aria, and you know it."

"Special in a good way or a bad way?" She folded her arms across her chest and stared him down. She looked like a fierce kitten ready to take on a Doberman.

"Why are you trying to pick a fight?"

She shrugged then and dropped her gaze. "I need some space."

"Now?"

"Yes."

"Sooo . . ."

"Could you please find somewhere else to hang out for a while?" she asked.

"There's an ice storm." As if to prove his point, a fast blast of wind rattled the windowpanes and flung a fresh round of sleet against the glass.

"Fine," she said, picking up the purse she'd dropped on the dresser when they'd come in. "*I'll* find somewhere else to hang."

"No, no," he said, putting out a restraining hand. "You stay. I'll go."

"Nope." She barreled for the door. "Already gone."

Then she was out, the door clicking closed behind her.

Swearing under his breath, Remington ran a palm along the top of his head and quelled the urge to go after her. She said she needed her space; well, he needed his space too.

CHAPTER 7

Waffle: The vibratory effect of a canopy or airfoil during an abrupt brake or sustained flare, in which the leading edge trembles or flutters, and the entire surface may ripple or undulate.

Wandering into the motel lobby, Aria wasn't the least bit angry with Remington.

Truth be told, she was the exact opposite of angry. Back there in that small room with one queen-sized bed, funny things had been happening to her stomach. It was as if someone had turned loose a million butterflies inside her.

Big, powerful, sexy, the man took up all the oxygen in the room.

Her reaction to him was strong.

Weirdly, she'd never been one for those macho alpha men types. She preferred creatives—artists, musicians, writers. She'd grown up in the high desert around rugged cowboys, and the softer side of life—beauty, aesthetics, luxury—attracted her.

Generally.

But there was just something about Remington—and this development was brand spanking new—that tickled her. He'd been gone for twelve years, almost half her life, and he was not the same eighteen-year-old who'd shipped off to the Army when Aria was twelve.

Oh sure, she'd seen him from time to time, at family gatherings, the weddings of their siblings, but she had spent a limited length of time in his company. Everything she knew about him was second-hand or steeped in the misty lens of childhood.

A memory came to her then, one she'd completely forgotten about until she'd taken her recent tumble out of the hayloft. She'd been ten to Remington's sixteen.

For some untold reason, she'd ventured out to the barn, a place she normally avoided because it was dusty and stank of poo. In retrospect, she'd probably gone because Kaia, the animal lover, had adopted a new pony. Her parents had gone into town to shop for supplies and left her older brother, Archer, in charge of his younger siblings. Archer had been shooting hoops with Remington's older brother Ridge in the ranch's backyard house, where the Alzates lived, and he hadn't noticed she'd slipped off.

The barn was musty, and the smell made her nose itch. From the hayloft, she heard soft giggles and heavy breathing.

Intrigued, she crept up the ladder to the loft as quietly as possible. She peeked her head over the railing and saw Remington with his girlfriend, Maggie. They were half-clothed and stretched out in the hay kissing up a storm.

Startled, she'd gasped and turned to run away, sort of forgetting in the process that she was standing on a ladder, and she fell a good six feet.

She thrust her hands out in front of her to brace herself and heard a loud crack as she hit the floor, palms extended. Felt pain shoot up her arm and the breath leave her body on impact. She couldn't even cry, it hurt that much.

Through the blinding pain, she felt strong arms go around her and a deep male voice calling to her, "Aria, are you all right?"

She'd been unable to speak.

Remington gathered her in his arms. His shirt was unbuttoned, and he held her pressed against his big strong chest as he carried her to the big house. The girl he'd been with trailed after them, running a hand through her hair and straightening her clothes.

Aria's wrist flopped around with each step he took. The pain was so fierce all she could do was whimper and quiver.

"Hang in there, sweetheart," he coached. "Hang in there."

He'd placed her in the front seat of his old farm pickup truck, heavy with red hair from his cattle dog, Ginger, on the front seat, and sand in the floorboard. Fastidious, even back then, she would have balked at being stuffed inside the dirty pickup, but she got no vote on what vehicle carted her to the hospital.

Maggie came up to the passenger side, where Aria was sitting, but he waved Maggie off. It wasn't an extended cab truck and there was no room for her.

"Call my dad," he told the girl. "Tell him what happened and that I'm taking Aria to the emergency room."

"But then he'll know that I was here."

"So what?"

"I'm scared of your dad," Maggie protested. "He makes fun of me because I'm from poor folk."

Remington glowered her. "Yes, Duke's a jackass, but go tell him anyway."

"He will know why I was here."

"Tell him you came to buy eggs."

"I—"

"Do it," he commanded. "I don't have time to babysit you. Aria's wrist is broken." Then he put the truck in gear and hauled her to Cupid General.

She didn't remember much about the ride, except for the many potholes along the way. Each and every time his truck bottomed out in one, Remington muttered, "Sorry, sorry, I'm doing the best I can."

She wasn't complaining. She felt safe and taken care of, despite the dirty truck, bumpy roads, and throbbing wrist.

Her family showed up not long after they got to the hospital. Everyone kept asking her what she was doing in the hayloft, but she never squealed on Remington being half-naked with a girl. She told her family she couldn't remember, and everyone nodded their heads. Yes, typical Aria, impulsive and unrestrained and not paying any attention to what she was doing.

After her wrist was casted, and the hospital released her, Remington briefly came over, leaned his head down, and whispered, "Thanks for not telling anyone about what me and Maggie were up to."

And just like that, they had a secret.

Not that it was any big thing. Aria pretty well forgot about the incident until she'd tumbled out of a hayloft for the second time in her life. But Remington hadn't mentioned it when he learned about her concussion. Had he forgotten all about the time he'd carried her to the hospital with a broken wrist?

He'd forgotten.

That was over fifteen years ago. He had no reason to remember that little blast from the past. Maggie dumped Remington for his best friend, and in the aftermath, he'd gone into the military.

Parking herself in front of the gas fireplace and propping her feet up on a plush plaid ottoman, Aria settled back to text everyone concerned about them. First, she let Vivi know what was happening and told her there was nothing to worry about. Because of Remington's planning, they were snug as bugs in rugs.

Then she texted her parents. After that, Olivia in Twilight, reassuring her best friend that while they were slightly delayed, they were still planning on being there by the following afternoon. Plenty of time to get prepped for the Saturday noon wedding.

Just as she finished, she was about to text her sisters, but Kaia beat her to the punch and texted her first.

Kaia: Vivi says U R stranded in Armadillo.
Aria: How'd U find out so fast? Just texted Vivi.
Kaia: The kids and I R @ the mansion on playdate with Reed and Rory. Ridge and Duke R helping the hands round up the critters and bring them N from the storm.
Aria: Stay safe.
Kaia: No, no, UR not getting off the hook.

ARIA: What hook?
KAIA: U. Rem. Alone in a motel room.

Darn it. Why had she told Vivi there was only one motel room?
Oh yeah, she'd tried to illustrate that while Remington's preparation
saved them from sleeping in his SUV, his backup plan was far from
perfect.

KAIA: U know this is the perfect opportunity . . .
ARIA: ???
KAIA: To test Granny's legend.
ARIA: No idea what U R talking about.
KAIA: Watch out Pinocchio. UR nose is growing.

She added a Pinocchio gif.

ARIA: I have no intention of kissing Remington. I don't even like him.
KAIA: The lady doth protest too much, methinks.
ARIA: Shakespeare? Really?

She wasn't about to tell her sister that it was already too late.
That freaking kiss had unbalanced her to the point where she was
planning on sleeping right here in front of the fire and leaving the
entire room to Remington.

It was just the concussion. Not the kissing. *Yeah right, grasping
at straws, Alzate.*

KAIA: Remington could be the 1!
ARIA: And what if I kiss him and I hear nothing?
KAIA: At least you'll know.
ARIA: And make things forever awkward between us? No thanks.

Besides, just because she heard humming when she kissed him
didn't mean he was The One. She didn't have to buy into that myth.
That's all it was. A silly myth her sisters believed.

Even if the women from Granny Blue's side of the family had soul mate detectors hardwired into their brains—which sounded totally goofy, but for the sake of argument, she'd roll with it—that didn't mean she should end up with Remington.

They were simply too different, and no amount of humming could change that.

He was way too structured in how he tackled life. But Aria was loosey-goosey and took life as it came. There couldn't always be a backup plan. Sometimes you had to go all in, just leap and trust the net would appear.

KAIA: Kiss him. I dare U.
ARIA: Bye.

Truth. Remington *was* not The One. No matter how loudly her head hummed when she kissed him.

But she could admit he was much nicer than she thought. And he had lost his fingers for his country. She needed to cut him some slack on his rigid approach to life. If she wanted him to accept her for who she was, then she had to let him be who he was.

And she was grateful to him for driving her to Twilight. To show him her gratitude, she'd figure out dinner plans for them.

Plans?

Argh! He was already rubbing off on her.

She wasn't sure whether or not she liked that. She vacated her spot in front of the fire, but the minute she got up an elderly man took her place. So much for spending the night in front of the fire.

Aria asked about room service at the front desk, but they told her they didn't have a restaurant. Usually guests just walked across the street to the fast-food restaurants in the strip mall. But that meant trudging outside in the cold and she'd left her coat upstairs.

She wasn't sure she was ready to see Remington again.

"Better hurry," the desk clerk said. "The restaurants intend on closing soon because of the weather."

Aria spied a heavy parka on the coatrack behind the desk. "Could I borrow that coat?" she asked.

The clerk looked uncertain.

She took a twenty out of her purse and passed it across the counter. He got her the coat.

Bundling up in the parka, she took off across the road. There was a burger joint, a fried chicken place, and a Mexican restaurant. But the lights were off at the burger joint and chicken place.

"Mexican it is," Aria said. Maybe they'd have soup. That sounded delicious. Soup to warm them up on a cold night.

The road was super slick, and she had to proceed slowly to keep from falling. Luckily, there was no traffic. One lone car was in the drive-through, and an employee was outside sprinkling ice cream salt on the sidewalks. The crystals crunched beneath her boots, and she nodded at the employee and went inside.

The inside of the restaurant was awash in Christmas decorations. Every inch of space not devoted to eating or cooking held some kind of ornament, light, garland, or holiday-oriented knick-knack. Christmas music was piped in through a speaker system playing "Santa Claus Is Coming to Town."

She really liked Armadillo. They had the Christmas spirit in spades. She loved the festive feel of the place. In fact, she loved all kinds of parties and decorations. It's why she enjoyed working as a wedding planner, even though her bachelor's degree was in fine arts. She got to use her artistic skills in the course of her job, and when she hankered to do more art, she'd break out her easel and oils, although she'd been doing that less and less as Vivi's wedding business grew.

Outside of holidays and birthdays, weddings were one of the few times people really decorated. She loved the whole process of weddings—the decorations, the dresses, the tuxes, the flowers, the cake.

All of it celebrating love.

And she *loved* love as much as she loved art. So, while she missed the daily practice of creating art, she didn't regret the path her career had taken—at least on most days. When she went to galleries and saw fantastic works of art, she felt a bit as if they had left her behind. But she was lucky and knew it. She preferred to dwell on what she had rather than the things she'd missed out on.

She loved seeing people on the happiest days of their lives. Loved being a part of the hustle and bustle. Remington would probably scoff at love and romance since so many people had trouble holding on to love. Especially as his dad had been married three times.

But Aria couldn't help herself. At heart she was a die-hard romantic.

Look at her parents and her three sisters. They all had rock-solid unions—although, Ember had had a starter marriage that hit the skids. Ultimately, Ember took a chance and married her best friend, Ranger, who worked as an astrobiologist in southern Ontario, Canada, where Ember had a thriving real estate business. They had an adorable two-year-old daughter. Aria didn't get to see them nearly as often as she would like, but they'd be home for Christmas, and she was looking forward to it.

The staff was closing up the kitchen when she walked in, but they took the pinto bean soup from the fridge and reheated it for her. With the smell of cumin, garlic, and onions teasing her nose, she took the containers of soup and a bag of chips with salsa back across the road to the motel.

Bracing herself to deal with Remington again, she put a smile on her face and let herself into the room.

Found him sound asleep, sprawled across the queen-sized bed, spread-eagle.

Ahh, poor baby. He must be exhausted.

She set down the food, searched the closet for an extra blanket, and covered him with it. He didn't stir. Driving in ice was nerve-racking, even for an Army Ranger. The guy was all tuckered out.

Taking one container of soup from the sack, she left him the other one. There was a microwave in the room where he could warm it when he woke. She tiptoed to the door, giving him space to nap.

Aria was not the type to sit quietly. She liked people, conversation, action. She carried her soup to the lobby. A small crowd had gathered by the fire. Other extroverts like her, some armed with small bottles of liquor from the minibars in their rooms.

"May I join you?" she asked.

"Settle in," said an elderly woman who was sitting beside an elderly man dressed exactly like her—blue jeans, crisp white shirts, and plaid mackinaws that had *Glacier National Park* embroidered over the pocket. From their wedding bands and twinsy outfits, Aria assumed they were husband and wife.

The woman scooted closer to the man and patted the space beside her.

"Thanks." Aria sat down, balancing her food on her knees.

"You got the pinto bean soup." The woman nodded her approval. "We just had that, didn't we, Hank?"

"We did." Hank nodded. "Decent soup too."

"I'm Helen, by the way." The woman extended her hand.

Awkwardly, Aria rearranged herself so she could reach out and shake the woman's hand. "Nice to meet you, I'm Aria."

"Like the music?" Hank asked.

"Like the music," Aria confirmed.

"Oh my, what a lovely name." Helen let go of her hand. "Where are you from?"

"Cupid."

"Now *that* is a fun name," Helen said. "Is it in Texas?"

"Yes."

"We're from Idaho by way of Cleveland, where we lived for forty years until Hank retired from the Cleveland Clinic. He was a radiologist."

Hank lifted a hand. "We're on our way to Fort Worth. Our daughter is getting married on Christmas Eve."

"Really?" Aria said. "I'm a wedding planner and I'm on my way to a wedding too."

"Are you traveling alone?" Hank frowned.

"No, I have a driver," Aria said. "But he's napping."

"Your boyfriend?" Helen asked.

"God, no," Aria blurted, then realized she'd said it too harshly. "I mean, we're nothing alike."

"Opposites attract." Helen leaned into Hank's shoulder, tilted her head back, and batted her eyelashes up at him. "Isn't that right, sugar bear?"

Hank dropped a kiss on Helen's forehead. "That's right, love bug."

"Aww," said a middle-aged woman sitting on the couch across from Helen, Hank, and Aria. She had yoga symbols tattooed on her wrist, long auburn hair flowing down her back in lush waves, and she smelled of patchouli. "You two are adorable. How long have you been married?"

Next to Ms. Patchouli sat a younger woman with thick black-framed glasses, a short spiky haircut, and artistic SOCOFY ankle boots. Aria coveted those boots.

Helen and Hank grinned at each other.

"Fifty-two years and counting . . ." Hank said. "Each day I wake up in the paradise of my sweetheart's arms."

"Aww, aww, aww." Ms. Patchouli sighed longingly.

"I totes love your shoes," Aria told the woman in the brightly colored SOCOFYs.

"Thanks." The woman beamed. "My name's Pat, and I design websites."

"And I'm her wife, Audra," Ms. Patchouli blurted as if she thought Aria might try to swoop in and steal Pat from her. "I teach yoga."

"Great to meet you guys." Aria grinned. "How long have you two been married?"

"Just a few years, but we've been together for two decades." Audra slung her arm around Pat. "Haven't we, hon? We met at Lilith Fair in 1999."

"But no pet names for us," Pat said. "I'm not into cornball." Looking chagrined, she held up her palm. "No offense, Hank and Helen."

"None taken," Helen said. "To each his own."

Another older couple were sitting on the other side of the room, watching their group with interest. Aria waved them over, and they pulled up chairs to join the fireside bunch. Their names were Andre and Tanya, and they had been married for thirty-four years. They had four sons and were from Atlanta, where Andre had worked as a Coca-Cola executive until he retired, and Tanya had stayed home to raise their children.

The conversation turned to the staying power of long-term relationships and what it took to keep the romance alive. For Andre and Tanya, it was frequent vacations. For Hank and Helen, it was shared interests. They loved golf, stamp collecting, and fly-fishing. For Pat and Audra, it was shared values.

They talked for hours. At one point, the desk clerk gave them two complimentary bottles of wine. They laughed, joked, and shared memories of their lives as couples, and Aria soaked it all up. She wanted the kind of love these couples had found. A love that not only brought them together in the initial attraction stage but deepened and grew over the years. A love that saw them through the difficulties.

The kind of love that lasted a lifetime.

"So," Aria said to Helen, "if you could boil the secret of a long marriage down to just one thing, what would it be?"

"In a sound bite?" Helen's eyes twinkled.

"If you can."

Helen gave Hank a sidelong glance and caressed his balding pate. He beamed at her as if she was a treasure chest filled with gold coins. "The only secret is in marrying the right person."

"Yes," Hank said. "You've got to marry The One. No halfway measures for a fifty-year romance."

"How do you know if someone is The One?" Aria asked, running the pad of her thumb over her bottom lip.

"I can answer that." Pat reached for Audra's hand. "You know when you're in love because when you're away from that person, you miss them so much it physically hurts."

"If you don't marry the right one," Tanya added, "you can never be truly happy in the relationship, no matter how nice the person might be."

"Tanya was married before me," Andre explained. "She knows what she's talking about."

"That's how I found out the hard way what happens when you don't marry your soul mate." Tanya leaned over to kiss Andre on the cheek.

"Lucky for Tanya, I knew she was The One when she kissed me on the playground when we were six. I waited for her until she came to her senses." Andre cupped his wife's face with his palm and gave her a romantic kiss on her lips.

The desk clerk interrupted to tell them they turned off the fireplace and dimmed the lights at ten, but they were welcome to stay talking in the lobby if they wished.

It was their cue to depart. Hank helped Helen up from the couch, and they bade their companions good-night. Andre and Tanya, Audra and Pat quickly followed, leaving Aria the last one to head upstairs, unsettled by the conversation about The One.

Keyed up, she took the stairs to her third-floor room, her mind churning. How was she supposed to know when she'd found The One? The couples in the lobby had never quite explained that part. They'd claimed they just *knew*. Fat lot of help that was.

Her family would tell her that she was lucky. *She* had a foolproof method in the humming legend. But honestly, wasn't that pure silliness? A fairy tale perpetuated by generations of Blue women.

Just because she might have heard a humming—*might have? You heard a humming when you kissed Remington, that happened—* okay, just because she heard a humming noise in her head when she kissed Remington, did not mean they were fated.

She needed someone who shared her interests and values. Someone who wanted a similar lifestyle. Someone who believed in spontaneity, whimsy, and true everlasting love.

Cautiously, she let herself into the bedroom, being as quiet as she could. Remington was still out, still spread-eagle, taking up most of the bed. It didn't look as if he'd moved a muscle in the hours that she'd been downstairs.

She tiptoed closer to make sure he was breathing.

Yep, his chest was rising and falling. His big, beautiful chest in a black T-shirt so thin she could see the outline of his muscles even in the darkness. Holy smokes, the man was *r-i-p-p-e-d . . . ripped.*

What was she going to do?

Option One: Wake him up and ask him to sleep on the floor, which seemed really tacky since the man fought to defend his country for twelve years. He deserved a cushy bed.

Option Two: Crawl up on the bed bedside him.

At the thought, a million goose bumps carpeted her skin, and her heart trampolined right up into her throat. Okay, that was so *not* happening.

Option Three: Sleep in the chair.

Or Option Four: And this could eventually be combined with option three—finish the sketch of Remington she'd started that afternoon. He was asleep after all. She had a captive model.

Ding, ding, ding. Winner, winner, faux chicken dinner.

Softly, she padded to the bathroom, changed into a sleep shirt, and thick fluffy socks. Brushed her teeth and washed her face.

Once she'd finished, she dug around in the closet, retrieved the last extra blanket and a pillow, took them back to the chair, along with her sketchbook and pencil and snuggled in for a night of drawing before she went to sleep.

CHAPTER 8

Harness: The arrangement of webbing and fabric that holds the main and reserve canopies, together with their attachments, and secures them to the skydiver.

It took a while for Aria to fall asleep in the cramped chair after she finished the drawing of Remington. It was hard to doze when you were twisted up like a pretzel. For another, Remington snored. Not a loud chain saw noise, but rather a series of soft little snorts. Weirdly, the quiet snores were more disruptive than aggressive ones.

She found it funny that the big, strong military dude had a comical snore.

Grinning into the darkness, she turned and spied the digital clock on the bedside. It read: eleven-fifty-two.

Outside, the wind had died down, but it was colder here closer to the window, and she burrowed deeper into the chair cushion and pulled the blanket up to her chin.

She could turn up the heat, but it took too much effort to get out from under the blanket to cross the room. She'd turn the heat up the next time she had to go to the bathroom.

Finally, she must have drifted off because she woke with a start, confused at where she was and what had roused her.

Oh yeah. Road trip. Ice storm. Armadillo.

"Help!" The cry that poured from Remington's lips lifted the hairs on her arms and her nape.

"What is it?"

He bolted upright in bed, eyes so wild and wide all she could see were the whites. "Help! Help! Help me!"

Without even thinking about what she was doing, Aria flew from her chair to the bed and wrapped her arms around him. "Remy, Remy? What's wrong? What's wrong? You're not alone. I'm here, I'm here."

"My hand, my hand!" he howled and clutched his left hand.

Fresh chills chased up her spine. Dear Lord, he was having a nightmare. Or flashback.

Or a nightmarish flashback. She wasn't sure of the difference.

He stared at his left hand, his eyes going even wider. Was he awake? "My fingers, oh God! They're gone! They're gone!"

Aria's heart tore right in two. How horrific to relive the trauma in his dreams. There was no escape for him. Not even in sleep.

Remington groaned and collapsed back onto the bed. Fear was a taste in her mouth, corroded and chalky.

She switched on the bedside light.

He blinked at her, looked confused. "What the devil?"

Snapping her fingers in front of his face, she asked, "Are you awake?"

He sat up again, pressing the heels of his hands against his eyes. "What happened?" he growled, lowering his palms to glower at her.

"You cried out in your sleep," she said. "You were having a nightmare."

"Where are we?" He sounded pissed off. "What's going on?"

While she wasn't into this grumpy bear thing, he was clearly still disoriented from his PTSD nightmare, so she lowered her voice and used a calming tone. "We're in Armadillo. The ice storm forced us off the road. You took a nap. I went to get soup. Do you want some? I could reheat it for you."

"Wait, what?" He shook his head and looked like the world's crankiest grizzly.

"Are you okay?"

"I'm fine. I shouldn't have slept so long. Why didn't you wake me?"

"You seemed exhausted. I didn't want to bother you. Do you want some pinto bean soup? I had a bowl. It's really good."

"I'm not hungry."

"Do you want to talk about the nightmare—"

"No."

"You don't have to bite my head off. I'm just concerned about you."

He gulped, leaned back against the headboard. "I'm sorry you had to witness that. The nightmares are less common since I've been stateside and been in therapy, but occasionally they still get the better of me. I apologize."

"It's not your fault. You've got nothing to apologize for. Feel free to talk to me about it." She reached out and wrapped her hand around his forearm.

Remington jerked his arm away as if she'd touched him with a red-hot pan. "You know, I think I will have that soup." Then he got up and left Aria sitting on the bed, wondering what in the dickens she'd done wrong.

WHY IN BLUE blazes had he admitted to the nightmares?

The second he'd confessed that he was plagued by disturbing dreams, Remington realized he'd made a big mistake. Whenever he told people about his PTSD, especially the women, soft sad looks came over their faces. Pitying looks. Just the way Aria was looking at him right now, sitting cross-legged in the middle of the bed.

"It's okay to have nightmares."

"I don't need your permission," he said, sticking the soup container in the microwave.

She pressed two fingers to her mouth and her eyes turned puppy-dog soft. "I didn't mean it that way."

Lockhart, you're being a jerk. She's just concerned. Don't take it out on her.

"I have two ears, two shoulders, and believe it or not, I do know how to zip my lip when it's important. Please." She patted the spot next to her on the bed. "Talk to me."

It was the kindest invitation he'd had in a long time, and part of Remington wanted nothing more than to curl up beside her and tell her everything. But he'd built high walls around his emotions a long damn time ago. It would take more than a hot woman and an ice storm to break down his defenses.

"Look, I have nothing to tell you."

Her face turned impossibly sad, and slowly, she shook her head as if he'd disappointed her on some bone-deep level. "You were in the Middle East. You were in a war. You lost your fingers. Don't tell me there's no story there."

He shoved his hand through his hair—he was still getting used to having a normal haircut and not the buzz cut he'd worn for twelve years—and paced the length of carpet at the end of the bed. He felt like a caged lion trapped in the zoo.

"Some shi—stuff happened to me over there, but so what? Many people I know have real problems dealing with what happened. Me? I'm *fine*."

"Are you?" She canted her head.

"Yes."

"What about the nightmares?"

"What about them? They're just nightmares."

"Have you talked to someone about them?"

"Yes, that's why I need not talk about them now."

With you.

He realized then, exactly why he didn't want to talk about his experiences with her.

One, he wanted her to see him as a strong protector, and if he told her how scared he was, he'd lose credibility with her. And, two, he didn't want to sully her with his ugly world. She'd grown up in a loving family. She'd never seen the dark side of life. He wouldn't be the one to expose her to it. She deserved to think the world was made of kittens and unicorns and rainbows.

The microwave dinged.

"I'll get that for you," she said, shifting gears and standing up. "You sit down and relax."

For the first time, he noticed the slogan on the red-and-green sleep shirt she wore. *I'm a Good Girl, Santa.* The garment hit her midthigh and showed off long, sexy legs that ended in a pair of Christmas socks. She looked more adorable than a newborn foal.

"Sit, sit." She fussed over him, ushering him toward the chair, then turned and got the soup from the microwave.

He didn't like the fussing, but at least she'd stop pressuring him to talk about the nightmare. He wasn't hungry, at least not for food. His eyes ate her up. That skimpy little sleep shirt was doing him in.

Big-time.

Stop feeling this way. It's Aria.

She brought the soup over to him along with a paper bag filled with tortilla chips.

"Where did you get this?"

"Mexican restaurant across the street."

"You went out alone? In an ice storm?"

"Yep, and I made it back in once piece, so you can relax."

"What if something had happened to you?"

"It didn't."

"What if you'd fallen on your back and broken a bone?"

"I didn't."

"Dammit, Aria—"

"Language."

He gritted his teeth. "I worry about you."

"I'm not your problem. You're not my bodyguard. Your job was to drive me and nothing else."

As he studied her, he had a flash of memory. A moment he'd almost entirely forgotten. Aria spying on him when he was with Maggie in the hayloft at the Silver Feather. She'd fallen off the ladder and broken her wrist.

In a guilt-ridden panic he'd driven her to the hospital. She'd only been ten years old, but already full of spunk and sass. She hadn't tattled on him for being with Maggie in the hayloft, but she'd given him a look that said, *you disappointed me.*

Aria was looking at him now with the same challenging expression in her dark eyes. "Say, thank you, Aria, for bringing me soup."

"Thank you, Aria, for bringing me soup," he parroted and took the bowl and chips she shoved at him. "But you don't have to take care of me."

"Why not?" she said. "You're taking care of me. Why does it have to be a one-way street?"

Why? Because he was unaccustomed to having anyone look after him, and he wasn't sure he liked it. He felt uncomfortable, the same way he had in the hospital when the nurses had tended his wounds.

She sat down on the mattress across from his chair, and peered at him.

"Are you going to stare at me while I eat?"

"You want me to leave again?"

"No."

"What do you want?"

To kiss you silly.

He took two spoonfuls of soup. It was delicious, but he was too wired to eat. He set the bowl down on the end table.

"Is something wrong with it? Is it still cold? I could nuke it a little longer."

"The soup is fine." He locked eyes with her.

"But . . . ?"

"I'm not hungry."

"Why not? Is it the nightmares? You should be hungry." She got up, moved to the soup bowl. "You have eaten nothing since the truck stop—"

"Because," he said, getting up from the chair and coming toward her, "I'd much rather do this than eat."

"Do what?" she asked, tilting her head up.

"This."

He knew he was taking a big risk, but the feelings he was having for her were so bright and shiny and new, he just had to see what would happen if he kissed her again. If she told him to step off, he'd back away, apologize profusely, and sleep in the hallway.

What if she doesn't tell you to step off? What then?

That last thought should have arrested him, because he truly did not have a backup plan for that, but it was already too late. He'd already lowered his head and pressed his lips against hers.

"Oh." She breathed inside his mouth. "Oh."

And then she was kissing him right back.

Ho, ho, ho! Merry Christmas!

Raw, potent emotion gushed from his head to his groin so quickly he almost toppled over. He deepened the kiss, rolling with it. Letting his tongue go where it wanted.

She did not put up any barricades. In fact, she loosened her jaw and let him right on in.

Well, this was one way to shut her up about his nightmares. Maybe not the smartest, but she was no longer talking.

Her little tongue touched the tip of his and he was a goner. Tumbling headlong into the most sizzling, intimate, delicious kiss of his life.

It was a perfect kiss in every way. Just the right amount of heat and moisture and pressure. He closed his eyes and felt the kiss shimmer through his entire body.

Why was it so damn good?

Was it because Aria was such a little firecracker? Yes, but he'd been with fiery women before.

Was it because they had this push-pull thing going on? A bit of the enemies to lovers?

Maybe.

Or was it simply because it had been a damn long time since he'd had sex? Not in six months. Since before he'd lost his fingers.

Probably that one.

Self-consciousness stole over him then as he realized he'd kept his left hand tucked behind his back the whole time.

He stepped back.

They were both panting.

She gazed up at him, doe-eyed, lips glistening.

"Why," she whispered breathlessly, "did you do that?"

"That sleep shirt got to me," he said. "I guess I was trying to prove the slogan wrong."

"What?" She blinked, glanced down at her shirt as if she'd forgotten what it said. Laughed. "Hmm, maybe Santa was planning on giving me a hero for Christmas."

"I'm no hero, Aria," he said, his tone turning dark.

"No?" she whispered.

"Far from it. Don't romanticize me."

For sure, he was no hero. A real hero could resist temptation, but Remington simply could not. Not when she was looking at him with that cat-that-ate-the-canary grin. Not when her hot palms were running up underneath his T-shirt and gliding along his abdominal muscles.

He kissed her again.

She moaned low in her throat.

When he scooped her into his arms, she locked her hands around his neck, and that, friends, was all she wrote.

Remington threw any last shred of hero he might have inside him out the window and carried her to the bed.

CHAPTER 9

Loading hot: The aircraft doesn't stop running after landing from the previous jumpers, and the jumper will practice exits and emplane while the plane is running.

She'd lost her ever-loving mind because her head was filled with nothing but humming. Sweet, beautiful honeybee music.

Aria knew she'd gone down the rabbit hole. Didn't give a good damn.

She surrendered into the rashness of the moment, embraced the wild. Gave herself over to the legend. For this moment, the hum that strummed through her entire being, cried, *This One, This One, This One.*

Chemistry, she told herself. Sexual attraction. *That's* all it was.

He fell back onto the bed, and she straddled him.

Frantically, she helped him wrestle out of his T-shirt, then sat back on her thighs to gaze at the glorious sight of his ripped muscles and quelled the urge to whip out her pencil and draw this too.

Be in the moment, Alzate. What do you want right this minute?

Sweet Jesus, what a loaded question. Right this minute, she wanted to lick him up one side and down the other.

So do it.

Wordlessly, he reached for her and tugged her head down to crush his mouth against hers once more. He wasted no time. His hands were busy, sliding underneath the hem of her sleep shirt, peeling it over her head. Then he froze for a second, his eyes rounding with wonder at the sight of her breasts.

From the look on his face, they had a mutual chest-admiration society going on here.

He cupped her breasts in his palms. She leaned forward over him, sinking her fingers into his rock-hard abs.

They didn't talk. Not a word passed between them. They just kissed and kissed and kissed. Lips and tongues. Heat and moisture. It was exquisite.

Pressure built inside her. The barometric equivalent of an earthquake in a hurricane—shifting, building, churning.

More, she had to have *more*.

Her hands went to his oversized cowboy belt buckle. Those Lockhart men and their oversized everything.

He raised his hips so she could whip the belt from the loops. Once she'd freed the belt, she tossed it over her shoulder and heard the buckle hit the floor with a soft *ping*.

"Hang on," he said, and put her aside.

As fast as he could, he shimmied out of his Wranglers and his underwear with one fell swoop.

Every ounce of air left her body on one forceful exhale as she stared at the man and his magnificent erection.

All that for her?

Her heart beat insanely fast.

He pushed back the duvet and, snagging one hand around her waist, tugged her under the covers with him. The sheets felt cool against her heated back. In contrast, his body against her was hot, hot, hot.

His lips and hands were everywhere—licking, stroking, kneading, molding. He was hard. Everything about him was rock-solid. Not an ounce of extra fat anywhere on this man.

Next to him, she felt like a marshmallow, although she did work out in her home gym four times a week. This man had honed his body through years and years of tough physical labor. First as his father's cowhand, later as Uncle Sam's soldier.

But while his body was granite, his tongue—oh that sweet, hot tongue—was pure softness. Pliable and bendy, his tongue could slip in all kinds of nooks and crannies. The adventuresome tongue explored her, tracing from her collarbones to her nipples to her belly button to oh . . . oh . . . oh . . .

She closed her eyes, awash in daring sensation.

He whisked off her panties, and his tongue found the most sensitive part of her. Wave after wave hit her, growing fast and furious.

The humming was not just in her head, but everywhere. She *felt* the sound. A soul-rocking tidal wave of vibration. She tasted it too.

The humming had the flavor of heated honey, but her lips tingled as if she'd bitten into a jalapeño pepper. It had an aroma as well, the scent of fresh spring clover. She saw it too. The humming. When she closed her eyes and strained to focus on the sounds, she saw rivers of red light flashing on the backs of her eyelids.

It was too much to process.

Remington's tongue.

The humming.

She was out of her mind and let all rational thought fall away. Just let herself enjoy the moment. She would deal with the consequences later.

For now, she and Remington were floating in a vast ocean of each other, and she was overjoyed.

Just when she was on the edge of oblivion, his tongue doing its dastardly fabulous work, he rolled her over onto her stomach.

My! Now what?

She'd only thought her heart was galloping before. Now it was practically jumping out of her chest, pounding against the mattress. She could feel him above her, heard his sharp intake of breath.

"You've a tattoo."

"Silly sorority dares. Drunken college party." Honestly, she'd mostly forgotten she had it. "Shocked?"

"No way," he said. "I'm surprised you don't have more."

"It hurt," she said. "No way was I going through that again."

"Ahh, poor baby."

Then she felt his lips press against the tattoo at her left hip. The warm pressure of his lips stirred up the humming again that had died down when he'd flipped her over.

"Why a feather?" he asked, low and husky. "Is it for the Silver Feather Ranch?"

"While my life has been saturated by Lockharts," she said, "no. The feather stands for me."

"Free spirit," he said.

"Yes."

"Flying away whenever anyone gets too close."

"Oh, don't even," she said, peering over her shoulder at him. "You don't get to analyze me. Not when you won't open up about yourself."

"Are you picking a fight with me, Aria?"

"Oh, heavens no." She turned back over to face him.

He was on his hands and knees above her; the mattress dipping from his weight. Her heart sped up again, jabbing against her rib cage, *boom, boom, boom.*

"That's good," he said. "Because I'm a man who believes in finishing what he starts."

He kissed her again, and she was lost in a sensory avalanche of sweet humming. They kissed until they were both hot and ready.

"Protection," she gasped. "Do you have any?"

"Sweetheart," he said, "who are you talking to?"

"Right." She grinned. "The guy with several backup plans. Let me guess, you have one in your wallet, one in your glove compartment, one—"

"One? You do not know me."

"How many do you have?"

"Check my wallet."

"Oh, so that's why your wallet is so fat, and here I thought you were rich."

"Rich in condoms, baby," he teased.

She leaped off the bed, found his jeans, wrenched out his wallet. Three condoms fell out. She snatched them up, dropped the wallet, bounced back to bed, where he stretched out like an Adonis. One arm slung over the top of his head. The other rested against his thigh. His flag of arousal flying high for her.

Pouncing onto the mattress, she tore the condom wrapper open with her teeth, tossed the foil aside. She placed the condom in her mouth and rolled it over his proud erection.

Her stomach constricted and her throat tightened. Excitement and anticipation got the better of her. She was trembling from head to toe.

"Please," she whispered.

"Please?"

"Now, Remy, now."

"I'm not the type to make a woman beg." He chuckled and positioned her beneath him.

Sighing, she sank into the covers.

He nudged between her thighs, and she opened herself fully to him, letting her knees drop wide. She was heavy and warm and humming in all the right places, waiting not so patiently for him to take his place inside her.

Slowly, he entered her. Inch by careful inch. It was all she could do not to take hold of his ears and use them as handles to pull him in deeper.

When he was finally all the way in, she let loose with a low moan of pure pleasure. "Oooh."

He rocked his hips, filling her up, pushing her to the limits of her endurance. She clenched him with her inner muscles, and he let out a groan of his own.

Ha! She could give as good as she got.

In the throes of heated passion, they moved together. One man, one woman, one unit. Time ceased. They existed only in the sweet bubble of each other's bodies.

Remington stroked her to the threshold of release again and again, but each time she was about to fall into that delicious abyss, he'd stop and edge her back to solid ground. Then work her up all over again.

The tease!

He surely knew what he was doing. Aria was no saint. She enjoyed having a good time, and she knew her way around a bedroom, but this here? With him?

Sex with Remington was beyond her previous experiences.

He started from the beginning, working them both up fresh. A gradually spreading heaviness invaded every cell in her body, broadening and building, until she quivered and throbbed. Sobbed, "Please don't stop this time."

It began in her feet, the magnificent tide. Luminescent threads of sensation shot through her system, electrifying her cells, her flesh, her bones. She stabbed her fingers into his back, holding on for dear life as the rocketing ascent blasted her into another realm.

The force of the orgasm shook her as if she were made of rags, twisting her inside out. She hummed from head to toe. *Buzz, buzz, buzz.* Her entire world trembled with vibration. Caught in the honey of this special moment.

Then she hit the center of it—piercingly hot, furiously alive. Transcendent nirvana. What had he done to her? Where had he learned those tricks?

She lost control, lost everything, but in the crazy process came back around to herself more fully formed and suddenly matured in a way she had not been before. Seconds could have passed as she hung in the treacle of him.

Or it could have been hours. Directionless, timeless, it was as if she were deaf, mute, and blind, while at the same moment, each sense highly attuned to every sight, smell, sound, taste, texture of his body.

Remington cried out and his body stiffened with one final thrust, and they collapsed together as if falling from a great height.

Panting, they drifted, twin capsized boats, overturned and past the point of rescue.

But who wanted to rescue themselves from such a shimmering afterglow?

Not this girl.

THEY DOZED FOR a bit, then Remington roused her, and when she kissed him, he tasted warm and rich and masculine and smelled of their lovemaking.

Lovemaking?

Whoa up there, Aria. This was just sex. Of course. *Lovemaking* was just a figure of speech.

At his touch, her body was covered in goose bumps and her pulse leaped. He skimmed his hand over her, caressing her until her hunger was inflamed and riotous again.

His tongue telegraphed his urgency, quick and thrusting.

"This is . . ." She gasped. "You are . . . I want . . ."

"Yes?"

"This time, *I* want to be on top."

"Your wish is my command, princess."

He positioned her above him, and off they went, pleasuring each other's bodies.

What stamina he had! What control!

Just before dawn, they used the last condom from Remington's wallet. He offered to go to his truck for more, but Aria had to cry "uncle." He'd worn her out. What an unexpected and thrilling night. Like riding a bucket list roller coaster—a blast while it lasted, but you never had to do it again.

Hooking up with Remington had been a lark. The consequences of a road trip, an ice storm, and close proximity.

C'mon, look at the guy. Who wouldn't be tempted? But that's all it was. A good time. Okay, okay, an amazing time, but still. Great sex did not a relationship make.

Um, yeah, but what about the humming?

While they lay together as the first fingers of sunlight pushed through the part in the blackout curtains, bodies joined, staring into each other's eyes, she couldn't help thinking, *what if?*

What if what?

C'mon, even if Remington was The One—and by gum she would not let ringing in her ears control her selection of a proper life mate—they were far too incompatible. Their personalities were night and day. They'd get on each other's nerves in a New York minute. They already had.

"Do you think we bothered the people in the room next door?" She giggled.

"You didn't hear them knocking on the wall around midnight?"

"No."

"Well . . ." His grin was cocky. His arms were wrapped around her waist as he peered into her eyes. She lay with her body across the length of him, her interlaced palms resting on his chest, her chin pressed against the back of her hands. "You *were* in the big middle of screaming out my name."

"Did I?"

"Oh yeah."

"Was I really loud?"

"They knocked on the wall."

Aria felt her cheeks burn and lowered her head. "Oh God."

"I liked the way you let go," he said. "You don't hold back. Inside of bed or out. It's an admirable quality."

"I thought my lack of self-restraint irritated you."

He took her chin and tilted it back up onto her hands so that she had to look at him. He seemed surprised. "Where on earth did you get that idea?"

"Um, the way you frown at me whenever I do something un-expected."

"I'm not frowning at *you*. That's just my face."

"Sour lemon face is your default mode?"

"Do I frown that much?"

"You're not frowning now." She reached out and pressed the pad of her thumb between his eyes.

"I have nothing to frown about right now." He ran the knuckles of his left hand across her cheek.

She took his hand in hers. That poor wounded, damaged hand.

He tensed, that pesky frown cleaving his brow, and tried to pull his hand away, but she clung on. "Aria . . ."

"Shh," she murmured, and pressed her lips against the seam where his last two fingers used to be. Kissed the scars.

"I—"

"Shh."

His face reddened. "It's—"

"Don't be ashamed," she cooed. "I'm not grossed out."

"Maybe *I* am."

"Are you ashamed of being injured?"

"Yeah, maybe." He glanced over her head, a faraway look in his eyes.

"Why?"

"It shouldn't have happened. I shouldn't have let it happen."

Aria sucked in air through clenched teeth.

"I wasn't even supposed to jump, but one of the troops was sick and they tapped me. It was at night, a HALO jump."

She sat up, looked down at him. His eyes turned murky as if he were back in the Middle East on that mission. What should she do? Change the subject or keep him talking? "What's a HALO jump?"

"High Altitude, Low Open jump."

"Um, okay."

"It's a maneuver intended to get troops on the ground rapidly under concealment."

"Is it as dangerous as it sounds?"

He held up his left hand.

"Dangerous, check. Go on."

"Jumpers exit the plane at high altitude and free-fall toward the earth at lightning speed. The troops wait as long as possible to open their chutes to minimize the time the enemy can spot them."

Aria exhaled the breath she'd been holding. Just thinking about Remington making such a jump had her sick to her stomach.

"How *did* it happen?" she asked, caressing his skin where his fingers used to be. "Wait, no. Don't answer that. It's none of my business."

"It was a military SNAFU."

"SNAFU? Could you elaborate?"

"It stands for situation normal: all fuc—er . . . all fudged up."

She giggled.

"What's so funny?"

"You trying not to curse. Cussing is as default as your sour lemon face. But thank you for curtailing the salty language on my behalf."

"You make me sound like an ass—" He paused again. "Asshat. Unless 'ass' is too much of a curse word. Should I say rear end hat?"

"You're hysterical." She laughed again.

"I don't mean to be."

"That's exactly why you are."

"You can turn anything into humor, can't you, Zippy."

"Zippy?" She cocked her head, puzzled.

He smiled at her, a genuine, heartfelt smile that warmed her to the tips of her toes. "Because you're bright and happy and full of sunshine. A regular Miss Zip-a-Dee-Doo-Dah."

Gosh, oh gosh, but she liked that. "Did you just give me a nickname?"

"I did."

"Why Remington Lockhart, look at you, being all whimsical and stuff."

"You like my whimsical side?"

"I adore it. Especially since I didn't know you had one."

"Then watch out, Zippy, you're going to love this." He slid down the mattress, winnowing underneath her.

"Oh, what's this?" She giggled again as he positioned his face between her legs.

"Hold on to the headboard, Zippy," he mumbled, his breath hot against her inner thigh. "We're fully in the amusement park now."

And then he did some very fun things to her that no one had ever done before, and it wasn't until she was quivering in the throes of her fourth orgasm of the night that Aria realized he'd never really told her what had happened to him in Afghanistan.

Chapter 10

Dock: To make controlled physical contact with another skydiver while in free fall.

Remington lay staring at the ceiling, Aria's head resting against his upper arm, her body pressed against his. Her breathing was slow, soft, and sweet.

She'd fallen asleep.

It was well after dawn, the morning sun pushing through the slit in the blackout curtains of their east-facing window.

Normally, he would have insisted on an early start, but even though the weathercasters had said the temperatures would climb into the forties today, that wouldn't happen until noon.

For now, there would still be ice on the ground from last night's storm.

He looked at the top of her head, studying the way her hair parted, and his heart got mushy in all the wrong places. How in the world had he let a simple road trip turn into something so complicated?

From the way she snuggled up against him, Aria was reading far more into their relationship than was there.

Holy drop zone, he was in trouble. How would he get out of this? How could he let her down gently?

Stupid, stupid, stupid. How could he have been so stupid as to let his body run away with his mind? His gut twisted, and his chest tightened.

Remington didn't want to hurt her. She was a good egg, but she was not the right woman for him. He needed someone more even-keeled.

Besides, Aria was way out of his league. She could have any man she wanted, and he was a grumbly old grinch with a wonky hand. Why on earth would she want a rugged road warrior like him?

Feeling how he did before every jump—stomach in his throat, adrenaline slamming through his veins—Remington slowly eased his arm out from underneath her head.

It took him a bit to get free and when his feet hit the floor, he breathed a sigh of relief. Stood up, looked over to watch her sleeping, and . . .

Her eyes were open.

Wide-open.

And she was grinning at him as if he was the candy treat that spilled out of a piñata she'd just whacked open.

Oh, shit . . . er . . . oh, stuff.

For crying out loud, Lockhart. She's even got you monitoring the cusswords in your mind. Who could live like that?

"Good morning, Remy." She stretched her arms over her head and yawned and had the audacity to wink at him.

"Morning," he mumbled, grabbing his jeans off the floor and shimmying into them. When what he really wanted to do was sing "Zip-a-Dee-Doo-Dah" at the top of his lungs.

"Morning!"

Was she always this enthusiastic in the morning or was it the sex? He found his western shirt. "How are you?"

"I'm starved." She swung her legs over the bed, rubbing her palms together briskly. "You should be too. You haven't eaten more than two bites of soup since that truck stop burger yesterday."

He eyed her as he did up the snaps of his shirt. She didn't look needy and clingy. That was good.

"Be right back," she said, and took off for the bathroom, buck naked and not in the least bit inhibited about it.

Remington tried not to stare, but Lord love a duck, she was *naked*. What red-blooded hetero male wouldn't stare? When she shut the bathroom door behind her, he let out a long slow breath and scratched his head.

He didn't know what to make of her or this situation.

Perplexed, he plopped down in the chair near the window, propped his feet on the table near the bowl of soup he hadn't eaten. Dropped his gaze, and there on the floor spied her sketchbook.

It was open.

To a graphite drawing of him sleeping. In slumber, she'd made him look vulnerable as a child with his left arm slung over his face, his damaged hand exposed. His features were relaxed, and beard stubble ringed his chin. The overall impression was one of nostalgic sadness.

At the sight of the picture, he hardened his jaw and thought two things. One, Aria was a mad talented artist. Why was she wasting her skills planning weddings? And, two, was that how she saw him? Soft? Tender? Pitiable?

Before he had time to assess his feelings, she came out of the bathroom.

Not wanting to be caught snooping in her sketchbook, Remington jumped to his feet. She didn't appear to notice his nervousness.

She was *still* naked. Her hair was sexily mussed, and a mischievous grin lit her warm chocolate eyes. Those beautiful breasts stood at attention, perky and just the perfect size. Not too big, not too small. They fit in the palms of his hands as if they'd been tailored for him. Her waist nipped in above those curvy hips and at the sweet juncture of her thighs, black curly hairs had been waxed into the shape of a heart.

Why hadn't he noticed that last night? In the dark, he'd thought it was just the usual V-shape. But no, right there on her body in hair art, she proclaimed to anyone who got intimate with her: she was in love with love.

Sweat beaded his brow. Uncomfortable, Remington shifted his weight from the balls of his feet to his heels and splayed a palm at his nape.

Her grin spread across her entire face, and she said one word. "Pancakes."

"What?"

"I want blueberry pancakes with real maple syrup if we can find it." She pantomimed rubbing her belly.

"Aria, before we go to breakfast, there's something we need to discuss." This conversation felt as serious as packing his own chute before a jump. That took time and care.

"Whoa Nelly, don't look so serious."

"This is important, Aria."

"That frown on your face has me scared. Should I be scared, Remy?" She canted her head and pulled one side of her pert little lip up between her teeth.

Remy.

Dammit, every time she called him that, his heart thawed just a little more. "Nothing to fear, but could you, er . . . please put on some clothes? I would appreciate it."

"Does my nakedness distract you?"

"You know it does," he said through gritted teeth. "It's why you're strutting around buck naked."

"I'm not strutting. I'm standing still."

"You know what I mean."

The impish smile was back. "You wanna watch me strut?"

Hell yes. "I do not. Could you please put your clothes on?"

"Driving you crazy, am I?"

Yes, yes, yes. "Clothes," he commanded, then added in a more reasonable tone, "Please."

"For you?" One eyebrow cocked proudly on her forehead. "Okay."

He blew out a long sigh. Whew!

She knotted her hands at her hips, and glanced around the room, her long dark hair swinging about her shoulders. "What happened to my bra?"

He shrugged.

"Help me look for my bra. Unless you want me to stay like this." She winked and touched the tip of her tongue to her upper lip.

"Lampshade."

"Huh?"

"Your bra is on the lampshade."

"Oh, there it is." She giggled. "How did you get all the way over there, you little rascal?"

Remington couldn't help staring as she jiggled her way across the room.

She snagged the blue satiny bra from the lampshade, and still chuckling, put it on. He noticed Aria was the sort of woman who put it on backward and hooked it in front, then twisted the bra around to her back. As opposed to putting it on the right way and hooking it from behind.

He was going to comment on her bra-hooking method, but then realized that might sound judgy. As if she should put on her bra the way he would if he were a woman.

Glancing up, she met his gaze. "Undies?"

He pointed to where her blue thong panties peeked out from under the corner of the bedcovers.

"My." She patted his cheek as she strolled by him. "Aren't you the observant one?"

His cheek stung pleasantly from her touch. He could tell her that his powers of observation had saved his life more than once, and as a result, he kept honing them, but he didn't want to get into that. If he talked about the war, she'd get that pitying look on her face again, and he didn't want that.

She bent over to step into her panties and he had to close his eyes and breathe deeply to keep from groaning out loud.

"Okay, you can look. I'm all covered up."

He opened his eyes to find her fully dressed, sitting in the chair by the window tugging on her cowgirl boots.

"Fire when ready," she said.

"What?"

"You said we needed to talk." She crossed her legs at the knee, and swung her foot in a casual circle. "Shoot."

He cleared his throat. It felt inequitable, him standing, her sitting, so he sank down on the mattress across from her and reversed their roles from last night. "You know I think the world of you, Aria . . ."

"Since when? Last I heard, you weren't all that fond of me." There was a devilment in her dark eyes. She wasn't making this easy.

"Where did you get the idea that I wasn't fond of you?" Her statement truly puzzled him. Sure, they had nothing in common, but he'd always admired her, even if her impulsiveness drove him up the wall. That was his issue, not hers.

"Um, you've avoided me my whole life."

"I have not."

"Who pitched a fit when he found out that his cargo to Twilight included me?"

"I just don't like being caught unaware. It wasn't you so much as I wasn't prepared. In my head I thought I was going to have a nice, quiet drive and instead got—"

"Me."

"No offense, you're just not quiet."

"So, you like quiet women."

"Not necessarily. I just like knowing what I'm getting into when I agree to something."

"Yes, I bet that was annoying. Finding out your boring trip would turn lively." She was smiling, but she sounded miffed. "Such a shocker."

"I don't dislike you, Aria." He shook his head and softened his voice. "Not at all."

"Well . . ." she said, and then said nothing else, leaving him hanging. She stood up, folded her arms over her chest, and broke out in a wide grin. "Last night convinced me of that."

Um . . . oh, they were back to that. He got to his feet as well, splayed a palm on the nape of his neck. "About last night . . ."

"Yes?"

"We need to talk," he said, trudging past the light in her bright irrepressible eyes. He hated that he was about to hurt her. Bone-deep *hated* it. But couldn't let her be thinking thoughts she shouldn't be thinking about him.

About them as a couple.

"So you keep saying." She took her makeup bag from her luggage, unzipped it and went to the mirror. She took out some flesh-colored cream, squirted a dab onto her finger and started smoothing it over her cheeks. "Go ahead. Talk. I'm listening."

"Could you put the makeup away, sit down, and give me your full attention?"

"Sure." Still blending in the makeup with two fingers moving in circular motions, she plunked down onto the mattress.

He crouched in front of her, captured her gaze.

She stilled and stared right into him as if she could see his soul. It was an unsettling sensation and threw Remington off his game.

His heart jumped right into his throat. "I . . . I . . ."

"Let me guess. You're feeling guilty about last night."

He lifted one shoulder. "I wouldn't say *guilty* exactly."

"What exactly?"

"Um . . ." He raised his eyebrows, twisted up his mouth. "Regretful. I shouldn't have . . . we shouldn't have . . ."

"Dude, no regrets." She shook her head so vigorously her hair bounced. "I don't have any."

"This will change everything."

"Not if we don't let it."

"Are things going to get weird? Things will get weird, won't they? They're already weird." He thought of her sketchbook drawing.

She laughed. "It's funny seeing Mr. Nerves-of-Steel anxious."

"I'm glad my discomfort amuses you."

"Look." Her voice filled with humor, as if them as a couple was a total joke. "No expectations. None at all."

Oddly, Remington felt a little hurt.

"Last night was more fun than an amusement park." She leaned back on her elbows, half stretching out across the mattress. "But that means nothing more than a good time. We had fun. It's over. Move on."

He should have been relieved. He expected to be relieved. Most guys in his shoes would have been over the moon. But Remington did not feel relieved. Instead, he felt . . . well, what did he feel?

A mix of things. He was glad she wasn't reading anything into their encounter, and he was happy that she was happy. But deep inside, he felt a little disappointed. Did he harbor expectations?

Wow, it was a provocative and disturbing thought.

"It's okay, Remy." She reached out with the toe of her cowgirl boot and ran it along the side of his thigh. "I'm not a hothouse flower who will wilt because the guy she slept with only wanted a one-night thing."

"You're not . . . ?"

She cocked her head, gave him a knowing grin. "I'm not what?"

"You're really okay?"

"What are you dancing around, Remington?"

"I don't want to hurt you, Aria."

This time she threw back her head and outright hooted. Yes, she hooted like an owl at him. As if he was the funniest thing she'd ever seen.

"What?"

"Oh, darling," she said. "You must've confused me with one of those clingy girls who thinks sex has to mean something."

"You don't think sex means anything?"

"Do you want me to pine over you, Remy? Is that the thing?"

"No, no. I just wanted to make sure you're okay."

"Fine as wine." She popped up off the bed so suddenly, he toppled backward, landing on his ass. "You're the one who looks off-balance to me."

Quickly, he scrambled to his feet.

"Bottom line, Lockhart. I'm fine. You're fine. Every single thing will be fine. Don't sweat it. Now, let's go get those blueberry pancakes. I'm famished."

CHAPTER 11

Brakes: The lines of the square canopy, used for slowing and turning.

No way in Armadillo was Aria going to let Remington know that last night had meant something to her. Not after the way he reacted this morning. No snuggles and cuddles, just pure raw panic.

He was in damage control mode, and she refused to be the tornado.

So, he wanted meaningless sex? Fine and dandy with her. She could do meaningless sex.

She would not let the best sex of her life wreck her in the ditch. Because it *was* just sex. Remington made sure she understood that. Besides, she *wanted* nothing but sex. Never mind that damn humming in her head.

Yes, siree. She'd keep this smile pasted to her face for the entirety of their trip. He'd never guess her true feelings.

Which bordered on freak-out.

But she'd handle her emotions on her own, thank you very much. It wasn't as if she could text her sisters or Vivi or her mother and ask their advice. They'd all start in on that humming nonsense, and she just couldn't deal.

No matter what he thought, she'd had a wonderful time last night, and she didn't want him ruining what they'd shared by spending the rest of the trip telling her she should forget about what happened. So, she was going to pretend that she didn't care.

And he *was* right. Even though she hadn't given him a chance to tell her that she should forget about what they shared, deep down she knew that she should.

For all kinds of reasons. Head humming aside, there was no way things could work out between them. Never mind that the sex was off the chain. When it came down to it, they were simply too different.

She believed in true love and happily-ever-after, and over the years he clarified that he didn't.

Not that she could really blame him for his belief, especially when she considered his childhood. Remington's mother had died when he was ten, and he simply didn't have a template for what a happy, long-lasting marriage looked like. He wasn't blessed like Aria, with a mother and father who were deeply in love and grew more so every day. His father had been married three times, and his older half brother, Ridge, was from their dad's affair with a stripper.

He simply didn't have the tools to make a marriage work. And Aria wanted to spend her life with someone who shared *her* values and her core belief that life was meant to be lived fully. She needed a man who understood that life wasn't a chore or something to plow through or something that you constantly needed a backup plan for. She needed someone spontaneous and joyful and adventuresome . . .

Hey, girl, jumping out of planes is adventuresome, said a voice in the back of her head.

Maybe, but Remington had jumped out of planes as a job, not for fun. No, Remington was too much a rule follower for her. He didn't color outside the lines. It made him a good soldier, no doubt. But husband material? Father material? No way.

She almost laughed out loud imagining him in charge of rambunctious toddlers, trying to make them follow his backup plans.

Aria did such a good job of cheering herself up that she didn't even quibble when they couldn't find a source of blueberry pancakes within the limited range of the motel.

McDonald's was open, so it won.

During the night, a sanding truck had come along and cleared the road, but the sidewalks and grass were still slick with ice.

Remington insisted on taking her arm, which was a bit like throwing gasoline onto a raging fire. At his touch, Aria's stomach got all fluttery, and her throat contracted, and it was all she could do not to yank her arm away.

"Easy does it," he said as he opened the door into the packed restaurant, slipped his hand to the small of her back, and ushered her inside.

Even through the layers of her coat and clothing, she could feel the heat and pressure of his palm.

The place was crowded, and she shouldn't have been surprised to see the other guests from the motel standing in line to place their orders.

The minute Helen spotted them, she waved them over to join their group in line. "Yoo-hoo, Aria, over here."

"Who is that woman?" Remington asked. He had his Stetson pulled down low, and she had trouble seeing his eyes.

"Someone I met last night while you were sleeping."

He snorted.

"What's that supposed to mean?"

"Do you have to make friends *everywhere* you go?"

"Yes," she said. "Yes, I do."

"Aria! Join us!" Audra was in on it now, waving like a loon along with Helen.

Remington growled. "I'm *not* cutting in line."

Aria shook her head and went up on her tiptoes to wave. "We're good back here, thanks."

"We asked permission for you to cut," Helen shouted. "These folks know you're with us."

The other people in line behind Helen and her posse nodded and waved them up.

"Not cutting." Remington steeled his jaw and shook his head.

"Okay. See ya." Aria moved to join her new friends.

"Aria," he said in a crabby voice. "Get back here."

Gosh, he could be such a stick-in-the-mud. Aria joined Helen and the rest and asked them if they'd mind coming to the back of the line with her since her driver was uncomfortable cutting in line.

"Sure, sure," Helen said. "We get it. C'mon, gang."

Helen led the charge. Hank, Audra, Pat, Andre, and Tanya all followed Helen and Aria back to where Remington stood looking grouchy and gobsmacked.

He tipped back his Stetson and ducked his head so he could mumble in Aria's ear. "What are you doing?"

Remy was so not a people person, which was why it was good for him to get outside his comfort zone and mingle. Ignoring his scowl, she introduced him to the group.

Andre and Hank shook his hand. Pat, Audra, and Tanya nodded. And Helen, bless her heart, went in for a hug.

The shocked look on Remington's face was priceless.

He raised his arms above his head, not hugging Helen back, and glowered at Aria. It didn't seem to bother Helen that he did not return her hug.

"I feel like we're old friends!" She grinned and hugged him even tighter.

Remington's gaze slammed into Aria's, and she read his expression clear as day. *You're gonna pay for this, Zippy.*

She beamed at him. The man spent too much time brooding in his cabin on the backside of the Silver Feather Ranch. It was good to be around people. But if looks could kill, she'd be six feet under with lilies on her casket.

"Were you in the military, son?" Hank asked.

"Army. How d'you know?"

"You got the look." Hank nodded. "I served in 'Nam. Sixty-four to sixty-eight. Army medic."

"Thank you for your service, sir."

And then the two of them were off, talking Army lingo with Remington's face lighting up. Ha! She'd dragged him out of his shell.

Audra and Pat stood talking to Andre and Tanya about the weather.

Helen sidled up next to Aria, and grinning slyly, whispered, "Your young man is delicious. And here you had us believing he was just your driver."

"He is just my driver." Or he had been until last night, but Helen did not need to know any of that.

Helen waggled a knowing finger. "You can't fool me."

"I'm not trying to."

"You two have sizzling chemistry."

Yeah, maybe, but so what? "Remington's just not into me."

"Girl!" Helen lightly swatted Aria's shoulder. "That man wants to eat you up with a long-handled spoon."

Aria quelled the urge to ask her what the length of a spoon had to do with cannibalism. Somehow, she didn't think Helen would get her joke. Or worse, she'd turn it around and make an oral sex joke of her own.

"What makes you say that?" Aria sent a sidelong glance over at Remington, who was hanging raptly on Hank's story of battling the Viet Cong.

"The way he looks at you. As if you're cheesecake and he's on a strict low-carb diet."

"He does not."

"Oh yes, he does." Helen nodded.

Did he? Aria peeked at him again, but he was deeply immersed in his conversation with Hank. He was smiling and his eyes lit up like Christmas. She was glad his mood had brightened, and she wanted him to stay sunny.

"It's not like that with us," she said to Helen. "You're wrong."

"You sure? Because you look a little smitten yourself. When he talks to you, you lean in closer."

Did she? "I'm not saying he's not interesting," Aria said. "But we're not right for each other."

"Why not?"

"We're too different."

"That's what people used to say about me and Hank, but now look at us. We're two little peas in a pod."

"How does that happen?" Aria asked.

"Spend fifty years with someone, honey. You get to know them better than you know yourself. It's a beautiful dance, and if you do it right, it's the most wonderful thing in the world. There's a reason poets write about epic love."

"I can see you and Hank have something special. But not everyone gets so lucky."

"Then again," Helen said, "some people *do* get lucky, but then they let fear talk them out of the best thing that ever happened to them."

"Remington's not The One, and you and everyone else here spent several hours last night convincing me that the only way to a happy, loving, long-lasting relationship is to make sure you marry The One."

Helen reached out to pat Aria's cheek. "Oh, dear one. You are so misguided."

"In what way?"

Helen's eyes were soft and kind. "You've got so very much to learn about love."

Aria was about to protest, but it was their turn at the counter. Helen placed the order for her and Hank. Andre and Tanya and Audra and Pat had been in front of them and they'd already placed their orders and had found a table for eight.

Leaving Aria and Remington alone at the counter.

"Do we have to sit with them?" Remington asked as Aria pretended to study the menu. She knew what she wanted, but Remington's closeness and Helen's conversation had frozen her brain.

"It would be rude not to sit with them, *now*," she told him. To the person taking breakfast orders, she said, "Hotcakes and a large coffee." Turning back to Remington, she continued. "I thought you were enjoying Hank's company."

"I was," Remington said. "Until he started telling me I should marry you."

The center of Aria's chest tightened. She studied him but could read nothing on his face. "Ridiculous, right?"

"Completely."

"Helen and Hank are just romantics because they've been married so long. They want everyone to be as happy as they are," she explained.

"Either that or misery loves company."

Ouch. Aria studied him. Did he really believe that?

Aria glanced around as Remington stepped to the counter to place his order. She really did not want to be alone with him right now.

"Their table is the only empty spot in the place," she said.

"We could eat in the truck or go back to the hotel."

"My hotcakes will get cold by the time we walk across the parking lot."

"Fine." He sighed. "Let's get it over with."

"Yes," she said. "Just one meal and we'll never have to see these meddlesome matchmakers again."

"You're my kind of woman, Aria Alzate." He winked.

That conspiratorial wink just about did her in, and for a fraction of a second, she allowed herself to think, *What if?*

They joined the older couples at their table. Remington ate startlingly fast, and when he finished, he made eye contact with Aria and sent her a look that said, *hurry this up.* Purposefully, she took her time, finished her breakfast, and ignored Remington's pointed glances.

Aria was enjoying her pancakes and the table conversation, which centered on the quaint little town of Armadillo.

"Well, folks." Remington got to his feet the minute Aria put the last bite of hotcake into her mouth. "It was nice to meet y'all, but we've got to get on the road."

After a round of hearty goodbyes, Remington hustled her out the door.

Ten minutes later, they were loaded up and pulling out of the motel parking lot. As Remington headed for the highway, they passed the armadillo statues.

This time, the armadillo family not only wore Santa hats, but were also bundled in scarves and fur-lined parkas. Apparently, someone had shown up during the ice storm and dressed the armadillos for colder weather as if they were real critters.

"Oh my gosh," Aria breathed. "That is so adorable. I *love* this town."

"Good grief, woman, you love everything."

"Better than being a grinch," she said, feeling hurt.

"It's just plain foolhardy. Going out in an ice storm to put parkas and scarves on concrete statues."

"Is it smart? Maybe not. But whimsy lifts people's spirits. I'm grinning just looking at them. It fills my heart with joy."

"It's silliness."

"So?"

"Cheesy."

"What's wrong with cheesy? I like cheese. Just call me Gouda," she said.

"The whole thing is absurd."

"In *your* opinion. The town clearly feels otherwise. Your viewpoint is not the only one on the planet," she muttered and added, "thank God."

He slanted her a sidelong glance. "All right, from a business standpoint, I'll grant you that the armadillos do make a bit of sense."

Confused, she frowned at him. "Business standpoint?"

"The statues are a good backup plan for a town that got bypassed by the interstate."

"Oh no, you're even turning the armadillos into a backup plan?"

"They had to have something to bring people here. And I do see how the armadillos appeal to a certain type of tourist, even though personally, I don't appreciate the sentiment."

"Good thing the entire world doesn't think like you do. What a sad little world it would be if they did." She felt offended. She knew that certain type of tourist too. Tourists just like her. Whimsical, fun-loving, and spontaneous.

Everything Remington was not. The reason he couldn't be The One for her. They had nothing in common.

She was attracted to Remington, yes. The man was hotter than hot. And truthfully, he was the best she'd ever had between the sheets. Not to mention that humming noise that filled her head every time he kissed her, but he was not The One for her.

She would wrap last night up with a Christmas ribbon, mark it "hot memories," and stow it away on the shelf of her mind.

Good times. A sexy encounter during an ice storm. That's all it was. For both their sakes, she simply would not go to bed with him again.

No matter how much she might want to.

CHAPTER 12

Terminal velocity: The speed at which a skydiver falls when the friction of the air on their body is equal to and counteracts the force of gravity so that they no longer accelerate.

The remaining drive to Twilight passed in almost total silence.

Aria had her earbuds in and was listening to an audiobook and drawing in her sketchbook. Birds this time. A flock of migrating cranes in an overcast sky.

Remington kept his eyes trained on the road. The rising temperatures and sand trucks had cleared the highway, but there were still occasional cars ditched on the roadside from the night before.

Every single time he let his gaze drift over to Aria, he saw in his mind's eye how she'd been the night before in his arms. Playful, adventuresome, full of life. Next to her, he felt dull, stodgy, and set in his ways.

"I'm sorry," he said after a bit.

"Huh?" Aria straightened in the seat.

"I apologize."

She pulled out her earbuds. "Hang on, I need to pause the book. It's a good part. The killer has got the detective cornered in a boat-house."

He shook his head. "It's okay. I don't want to interrupt your book."

"No, no," she said. "This is important. You're important. The book is good, but not that good. It can wait. What's on your mind?"

She turned toward him, leaning over the console and giving him a whiff of her spicy, cinnamon-scented cologne.

"I'm not much company to be around, and I'm sorry I'm bringing you down," he said and wondered if she knew how hard it was for him to admit his shortcomings.

"What? You're not bringing me down."

"I'm a crabby guy, Aria. I know that."

"Hey, it's no biggie. We all have bad days."

"Truth is . . ." God, what was he doing? He had no business spilling his guts to her. None at all. She didn't need to carry his burdens. That's what group therapy was for. The place where he got together with other military personnel and they debriefed about their war experiences. A place where no one judged him.

"Yes?" She leaned in even closer until he could feel her warm breath on his neck.

"I'm not a very pleasant person."

"Oh, hogwash." She flapped a hand.

"I have trouble with frivolous things. After you've been in combat, the things most people worry about seem so inconsequential."

"I can't imagine how frustrating that must be for you." Her eyes turned somber. "You came from the place where any minute a bullet or bomb could end your life. Then you return home and people are whining about their cell phone service or that the fast-food joint mixed up their burger order or how two days is way too long to wait for their Amazon shipment."

He smiled. "True."

"I bet you want to holler at them."

"I do."

"But you don't yell at them. An unpleasant person *would* yell at them." She knew just what to say to make him feel better.

"I'm jealous of their ignorance. I wish I didn't know how truly terrible the world can be."

"I can't even imagine what that's like." Her smile was sweet and kind.

"Still," he said, "I owe you an apology for being so cranky about your new friends and the armadillo statues."

"*Pah.*" She waved a hand. "You are entitled to your opinion. Just like everyone else."

"You're a compassionate person, Aria."

"So are you, dude. You just don't seem to realize it. You've buried it under years of hurt, but it's still there."

She hit a nerve. Remington tightened his grip on the steering wheel.

"Have you ever tried art therapy?" she asked.

"What?"

"Did anyone during your rehab suggest art therapy?"

"No." He hazarded a glance over at her. "What is art therapy exactly?"

"A way to explore your emotions through art. It's really therapeutic."

He crinkled his nose. "I'm not very good at art."

"It doesn't matter. That's the magic of it. You are in it for the joy of doing art. It's playing like when you were a kid."

"That's so long ago I can't even remember what it was like to be a kid."

"Even more reason you need art therapy."

"I wouldn't even know what to draw."

"What are you interested in?"

You. The thought hit him like a swat. "I don't know."

"Sure, you do. Landscapes? People? Animals? Still life?"

He shrugged. Art seemed superfluous, but Aria liked it, so he tried. "The Silver Feather, I guess."

"You can do better than that." She twisted herself around so that she was sitting in the seat cross-legged and facing him. He didn't know how she managed it with her seat belt on, but Aria was something else.

She leaned across the console to rest her hand on his belly.

Instantly, his abdominal muscles contracted, and he felt a rush of heat go straight to his groin.

"What is your gut telling you?" she asked.

His gut was telling him to pull over the vehicle, yank her into his arms, and kiss her like the world was ending. Staring out over the hood, he forced himself to concentrate on her question.

"Well?" Thankfully, she took her hand back across the console and tucked it in her lap. Today, she wore blue jeans and a fluffy white sweater with old-fashioned Christmas lightbulbs embroidered along the scoop neck collar.

"Uh . . ." He had nothing. He felt self-conscious and hopelessly inept. His abdomen still burned from the touch of her hand.

"Quick," she said. "What's the first thing that pops into your head?"

But that was the problem. Things didn't just "pop" into his head. He was studied and controlled. He considered things, sorted them, cataloged, and analyzed. He didn't know how to identify an instant thought, seize it, and run with it to an instant conclusion.

As if she sensed his thoughts, she said, "This is how art works." She lightly knocked a small fist against his noggin. "Creativity springs from impulse. You can't be creative when you're wrapped too tightly with rules and regulations. Stop thinking so much, Remy, and just *feel*."

As if it was that easy. She was asking him to go against thirty-two years of being in the world a certain way.

"Look," she said. "A rest stop. Please pull over. I need to pee, and you need to close your eyes."

"Why do I need to close my eyes?"

"To connect with your creative impulse."

"Aria, I don't need to do that. I'm no artist."

She fluttered her eyelashes at him and smiled. "Please? For me?"

Who could resist her? Besides, she needed to go to the bathroom.

He took the exit. Aria clapped and leaned down to put on the boots she'd kicked off during the journey.

He pulled into the rest stop and parked near the bathrooms, killed the engine. "There you go, Zippy."

"No, no, we're doing this first. I'm not giving you the chance to back out." Her palm was back on his belly. "Close your eyes."

From her expression, he knew she wouldn't let this go. Might as well get it over with and make her happy.

He leaned his head back against the headrest and closed his eyes.

"Now," she said, her voice low and coaxing. "What do you see?"

Remington stared at the back of his eyelids, desperate to see something besides the remnants of daylight showing up as white blobs in his field of vision. He had a feeling she would not accept that.

"Look past the shadows and light."

Straining, he peered harder.

"What do you see?" she whispered. "There's no wrong answer."

This creativity stuff was hard.

"I see . . . Geometrical shapes. Squares. Rectangles. Cones."

"Okay, push past the pedestrian answers."

"I see a form," he said, noticing the shapes shifting and changing. He expected her to redirect him again or tell him that he was hopeless.

Instead, she inhaled audibly, and he could feel the warmth of her minty breath against his cheek. Her face was millimeters from his, her distracting palm still flat against his belly. "What kind of form?"

"A person."

"Male or female?"

He couldn't tell. He squinted with his eyes closed, trying to will the shape to come into focus. Nothing. "I'm hopeless at this."

"You're not. You've just never practiced getting in touch with your inner artist."

"Is that what I'm doing?" He opened his right eye and peered at her.

"Eyes closed."

Exhaling loudly to let her know he was tired of this game, he closed his eye again.

"This form . . . is it male or female?"

"Female," he said, just to get her off his back.

"Do you see any colors?"

"No. Just black and white."

"Can you make out her features? Is she old or young or somewhere in between?"

She's you, he thought, but said, "I'm looking at the back of her head."

"Then how do you know it's a woman?"

"Long hair."

"Could it be a guy with long hair?"

Zippy, it could be a unicorn, I am just making this crap up. "No," he said firmly, aching to open his eyes again and get a good look at her face. "Definitely not a guy."

"So, you see the back of a woman's head. Has anything shifted?"

He looked again, and this time, he saw the back of a woman's head. The power of suggestion.

"What do you taste?"

"Huh?"

"What do you taste?"

"I taste nothing." But just then his mouth filled with the taste of Aria.

"What about sounds or textures or scents?"

"You hear sounds and feel textures and smell scents and taste things when you paint?"

"For sure. More than that. I can taste colors and smell sounds and feel the weight of everything. It's called synesthesia."

"And this is without benefit of hallucinogens?"

"I don't do drugs," she scolded. "You know that."

"You're the artist, Aria," he said, still keeping his eyes closed. "I don't hear or smell or taste or feel anything when I close my eyes. I see mostly darkness."

"Ahh," she said, sounding impossibly sad, and he couldn't help feeling he'd let her down in some deeply fundamental way.

"Look, I'm a warrior. That's all I am. I don't have your artist eye or your quicksilver mind."

"You don't give yourself enough credit."

"You give me too much."

"Remy, you are so much more than your job. So much more than the rigid way you've learned to think." She seemed beyond disappointed in him that he couldn't play her game.

God, he wanted to please her, but he couldn't give her what she wanted.

Then she issued a strange little sound, and said, "Oh, I get it."

"Get what?" He was uncomfortable sitting here with his head thrown back and his eyes closed. He felt defenseless.

"You can't allow yourself to let go and explore your creativity because you're terrified that if you do, you'll go where you go in your nightmares."

Ding. She'd hit the nail on the head. He knew it as soon as the words were out of her mouth. Felt the truth of it smack the pit of his stomach.

"Remy." She wrapped a hand around his right wrist. "This is fabulous. This is progress. I am so proud of you."

"You are?"

"Could you try one last time, for me? If your mind takes you back to the war, you can just open your eyes right up. It's not like in a nightmare where you get stuck. I'll be right here with you."

Shows what she knew about PTSD. A person could get caught in the grips of the damn thing with their eyes wide-open. But she had a point. He had been letting his fears of the past hold him back.

Bracing himself for an onslaught of images he did not want to see, Remington gave it one last shot. Drilled a hole through the back of his eyelids, and suddenly something popped, and technicolor images filled his mind.

But thankfully, it was not about his experience in the war.

It was a memory of last night, and he saw it as if it was happening all over again. Aria in his arms. Her taste in his mouth. Her silky hair falling over his skin. Her eyes wide and bright. The sound of his name rolling off her lips.

He laughed then, an unexpected sound that surprised him, and from the way she jumped, he knew it surprised her too. He opened his eyes, unexpectedly full of joy.

"Wow, that smile on your face." She grinned like he'd gifted her with a set of expensive art pencils. "What did you see this time?"

"You." He gave her a wicked smile. "Last night."

"I saw last night too."

"What?"

"I closed my eyes too and when I did, I saw you with me, last night."

"It was a night to remember," he murmured, and locked his gaze onto hers.

She lowered her lashes. "Indeed."

"I had a good time last night."

"So did I."

"It was beautiful." He reached out to tuck a strand of hair behind her ear.

"The best."

"But we're not gonna—"

"Oh no, no, no. Last night was just road trip sex. It doesn't count. You can keep it in your fantasies though."

"Good," he said, but it didn't feel good at all. She seemed to supply that edict pretty fast, no hesitation. He straightened in his seat.

"It's for the best, really." She opened the SUV's door. "I'm just gonna go pee."

While he waited on her to return from the restroom, Remington mulled over the situation. Now, every freaking time he closed his eyes, he saw her. It was like turning a movie on and off every time he lowered his eyelids. Not that he really minded. It was a helluva lot better than war images dancing in his brain.

She got back in, breathless and red-cheeked. "Let's hit the road."

He started the engine, but before he shifted the Escalade into Drive, he said. "I've been thinking. Instead of hanging around for four days, maybe I should just drop you off in Twilight and come back for you on Monday after the wedding."

"The wedding is Saturday. You would just get home and have to turn around and come right back. There's no sense in that. I promise, I can keep my hands to myself if you can."

He looked at her and she beamed at him. Not an easy promise to keep. Not when she was smiling at him with those kissable lips and friendly eyes.

"Sure," he mumbled. "I can do that."

"Great. Now that's settled, let's hit the road." She popped the earbuds back in and returned to her audiobook. "I gotta see how the detective gets away from the killer."

Just like that, she closed herself off to more conversation, leaving Remington feeling shaky and off-balance.

No more physical contact between them was the smart thing, the sane thing, but he didn't know if he could trust himself to hold up his side of the bargain. What he needed was a backup plan. Something that assured him he could keep his word.

Right.

He needed to stay in different accommodations. He'd drop her off at the Merry Cherub, the B and B where Vivi had made their reservations, and find himself another place to stay.

Satisfied with his decision, he drove the final sixty miles to Twilight. An hour later, they arrived.

As Remington navigated the streets, it quickly became clear that Twilight was that special sort of small, lakeside village, a close-knit, yet entrepreneurial bedroom community that capitalized on its proximal separateness from the sprawling Dallas metroplex.

Cowboy heritage was taken quite seriously from Fort Worth westward. Mostly, denizens in these parts didn't drive Teslas or hybrid cars; almost exclusively they owned pickups or dual axle trucks meant for hauling livestock trailers, or SUVs with dark-tinted windows to protect against the relentless Texas sun.

Not much different from home in Cupid. But whereas Cupid was nestled in the isolated high desert terrains of the arid Davis

Mountains, Twilight was blessed with humidity, trees, and abundant tourism.

Ten minutes later, they were standing in the lobby of the old Victorian house converted into a B and B, surrounded by an impossible array of angels, the owners, Jenny and Dean Cantrell, telling them every hotel, motel, and B and B within a thirty-mile radius was booked up. Not only was December the height of Twilight tourist season, but the wedding of the mayor's daughter had filled every space.

He could either drive to Jubilee, the next town over, or stay in the rooms Vivi had booked for them.

It would be okay, he told himself as he followed Aria and their chattering hostess up the stairs past the overdose of heavenly images—angels on the wallpaper, thick and velvety-looking. Angel mobiles flying from the ceiling. Angels carved into the staircase. Angel figurines crowding the curio cabinet in the hallway. Angel umbrella stand. Angel coatracks.

Angels every freaking where.

Jenny Cantrell was in her midforties, had light brown hair mixed with threads of silver pulled back into a bouncy ponytail. She deposited Aria in her room, then she turned and guided Remington to the room right next door.

"Would it be possible for me to swap rooms with another guest? Someone who hasn't arrived yet?" he asked. "On another floor?"

"If you'd arrived last night as planned," Jenny said, "maybe. But everyone is already checked in and settled."

"The ice storm stranded us in Armadillo," he explained.

"I know. Miss Alzate texted me about that. While I do appreciate the heads-up, it's out of my hands." Jenny shrugged. "This will have to do."

"Thanks for trying."

Jenny paused, studying him up one side and down the other. "Could I ask you something?"

He raised his eyebrows.

"Why don't you want to be near Miss Alzate?"

"It's a long story."

"Right." Jenny laughed. "None of my business."

"We were stranded in the same motel room last night. Things didn't go well."

"Ahh." Jenny's eyes glistened with a mischievous light. "Then you've come to the right place."

"Huh?"

"Twilight." She waved her hand as if it was a magic wand. "Has a way of turning everything around."

"How's that?"

"The town is magical," she said. "Especially at Christmas. Especially for lovers." She handed him his key and headed back down the stairs as her husband trudged up with their luggage.

"We're not lovers," Remington mumbled under his breath, which wasn't true. That was the problem.

He let himself into the room—yikes, more freaking angels—heard a door lock click open, turned, and saw Aria standing in the threshold of another door.

"Look." She laughed. "You can't get away from me. Adjoining rooms!"

CHAPTER 13

Dirt dive: To rehearse a skydive on the ground by walking through the positions and stations.

If Armadillo was a slice of cheddar, Twilight was an entire cheese wheel, and Remington was feeling decidedly lactose intolerant.

The angel-imbued B and B was just the start.

Remington walked around the town, shoulders hunched, the hoodie of his heavy sweater pulled up over his head, his face lowered against the cold wind blowing off Lake Twilight. He'd changed from his jeans and cowboy boots into sweatpants and sneakers.

Jogging had saved his sanity in the weeks and months following his accident, and he'd gotten addicted to his daily running routine. The last two days with no exercise left him jonesing for physical activity.

After appearing in the doorway of their connecting rooms—and leaving the door wide-open, dammit—Aria had announced she was going to hang out with Olivia, and he was free to occupy himself for the evening.

Part of him felt relieved she was letting him off the hook and he didn't have to socialize with Aria and her friends. But another part of him couldn't help feeling rejected. Why had she left him out of her plans?

She doesn't want a tagalong, you big galumph.

Galumph.

It was something his father had called him when Remington hit a growth spurt his thirteenth summer and sprouted five inches over three months and ended up clumsy, awkward, and towering over his two older brothers. *Galumph* was as close to a term of endearment as Duke ever got, even though his father had not meant it as a compliment.

So here he was, wandering the streets of this Christmas-addled, touristy lake town with nothing to do except run.

The Merry Cherub was only a few blocks from the town square. In early afternoon on a Thursday, the streets were surprisingly packed. If the town was this crowded on a weekday, he sure as heck didn't want to see it on the weekend.

In the middle of the square sat a stately courthouse built in the late 1800s. It was constructed of limestone in the French Second Empire architectural style popular with many county seats in Texas in its day. The three-story clock tower was a throwback to the wild west. When he'd strolled onto the square, he'd seen a plaque on the side of a building proudly proclaiming that the entire Twilight town square was listed in the National Register of Historic Places.

Decorated Christmas trees graced all four corners of the town square. Carolers strolled the road that was closed off to vehicle traffic by Christmas-themed sawhorses. Vendors had erected kiosks on the courthouse lawn and sold everything from Santa paintings to roasted chestnuts and wassail to henna tattoos. The air was filled with the smell of funnel cakes, kettle corn, and street tacos, and the sounds of Christmas music blasted from outdoor speakers, "Rudolph the Red-Nosed Reindeer."

Too much cheer for this old war vet as a wave of agoraphobia washed over him.

He spied a park and lengthened his stride, eager to get running. A cobblestone walkway continued inside, but even here there was no relief from the whimsy. A metal sign over the stone archway read: *Sweetheart Park*.

Christmas lights were strung from the huge old oak and pecan trees, a far cry from his desert home. Families were everywhere. Moms pushing strollers. Dads carrying kids on their shoulders. Strewn across the grassy areas were various holiday displays, from Santa driving a team of reindeer, to Frosty the Snowman Winter Wonderland, to an elaborate nativity scene.

He jogged over several long wooden footbridges that spanned a small tributary of the Brazos River filtering into the lake.

This was Aria's kind of place. He imagined her face when she saw the park. How her eyes would light up and she'd throw back her head, laugh loud and long as she twirled around in that free-spirited way of hers.

He felt a pang in his gut, a weird kind of longing as if he were missing her. But he wasn't missing her. How could he be? She drove him right up the wall. Besides, he'd just spent two very long days cooped up with her.

But miss her he did.

Remington could smell her on his skin. That sweet spicy scent, and he could feel her soft curves in the palms of his hands. What was going on? Was he losing his mind?

Aria.

What had she done to him? Lord, the woman had burrowed under his skin, and he couldn't stop thinking about her.

Weaving around pedestrians, he picked up speed, pushing himself harder. At the very center of the park, he pounded past a concrete statue of two lovers in old west clothing embracing in a passionate kiss, and damn if he didn't substitute himself and Aria in the statue's places.

More cheese. Slathered with Christmas cheese. The cheesiest of cheeses. He hadn't liked Christmas in a very long time, and now he was really starting to hate cheese too.

To keep his mind off Aria, he mentally ran through every cheese he could think of—mozzarella, Gouda, Swiss, Havarti, provolone, Parmesan, Monterey Jack, Brie, feta . . . Seriously, the town should open a cheese factory. That's how cheesy this place was.

He heard Aria's voice in his head. *What's wrong with cheesy?*

Cheesy was sappy, sentimental, corny, unsophisticated—

Fun? He heard Aria's voice as clearly as if she was standing right next to him. *Playful? Whimsical? Quirky?*

He ran faster, but he could not, no matter how fast he sprinted, stop hearing her in the back of his mind.

Run all you want, Lockhart. You'll never escape yourself.

He was almost through the park, but up ahead, people clustered on the walkway, making it impossible to run around them.

Chuffing, he slowed to a fast walk as he neared the group.

What was going on?

The crowd clotted around an enormous pecan tree with long, thick branches that spanned all the way to the creek. In the summer, it must provide an impressive shaded canopy. As it was now, bare of leaves, the smaller branches were laden with ornaments that had names written on them. A wooden ladder was set up nearby.

People took turns scaling the ladder and plucking off ornaments and reporting the name they'd chosen to a plump fifty-something woman wearing a long blue jean skirt and a crazy-ugly Christmas sweater. She held a tablet computer in her hands and a lanyard badge around her neck that identified her as *Belinda Murphey*.

"I got Nelly Long," someone said, reading off the name on the ornament that they plucked from the tree. "She wants books. I love my cherub!"

Ahh, it was an Angel Tree. Cupid did something similar, except in his Chihuahuan desert hometown, they used a mesquite tree. Remington had already gotten several names off the Cupid Angel Tree at home and bought gifts for the underprivileged children who wouldn't have a Christmas without it.

Erected around the base of the pecan was a white, wooden picket fence along with a stern sign warning: DO NOT DEFACE THE SWEETHEART TREE. Hundreds of names had been carved into the bark of the tree, most of them old and faded with time.

To the left of the tree, in an area separate from the group taking part in the Angel Tree project, was a wooden kiosk with a banner that announced: DON'T CARVE! HANG A CHARM TO SHOW YOUR LOVE INSTEAD.

This cheesy town sure liked its signage.

A few couples were lined up in front of the kiosk where a fit-looking, middle-aged Hispanic woman, whose lanyard identified her as *Terri Longoria,* used a machine to inscribe initials and names into heart-shaped, copper-patinated charms the size of half-dollars.

He'd seen one of those charms before, on Aria's bracelet.

On the front side of the tree, under Belinda Murphey's watchful eye, one group plucked Angel ornaments from the branches. While on the back side of the pecan tree, couples who'd bought the heart-shaped charms from Terri affixed them to a metal framework that had been added around the trunk of the tree.

Curious, Remington stepped closer to watch. Hundreds of the charms had been attached to the metal frame. Clever solution to keep people from carving their names into the stalwart pecan that, from the looks of it, had to be at least two hundred years old. Plus, the charms had to bring in a nice chunk of change to the Chamber of Commerce coffers since, according to the banner, that's who was sponsoring the kiosk.

Cheesy as they might be, Remington had to admire the Chamber of Commerce. They had a solid backup plan to save their Sweetheart Tree. He knew without even asking that there must be a schmaltzy story involved.

He turned to get out of the way of a couple angling for the metal frame, when something caught his eye.

A tiny little Santa hat sticker had been stuck to one of the heart-shaped charms. It was exactly like the Santa sticker Aria had bought in Armadillo. Smiling, he took out his phone to snap a picture of the charm with the Santa armadillo sticker on it, but when he looked at the photograph in his camera roll, he got a little shock.

The cutesy charm was inscribed with: *Aria & Remington were here.*

A shiver went right over him and goose bumps rose on his skin. Aria had stopped, bought a charm with their names on it, and hung it on the frame around the tree for all the world to see?

He couldn't say *why* the charm caused such a visceral reaction in him, but damn if it didn't. Why had she left a mark of their passing through this town? And why had she included him? The charms weren't expensive, but she had to spend money to have it engraved. She'd commemorated their visit here.

Why? What did it mean?

Remington backed up, almost stumbling over a tree root to get away. His chest tightened and his blood pumped loudly through his veins and he felt . . .

Well, hell, what did he feel?

Scared.

Yep, he was scared out of his wits and he had no idea why. He wanted to zoom back to the Merry Cherub, jump into his SUV, and drive away as fast as he could.

Aria *had* done this, but when? She'd headed out to meet up with Olivia only twenty or thirty minutes before he'd gone jogging.

Was she still in the park?

"Excuse me," he said, bumping the couple out of the way who were trying to hang a lovey-dovey charm. He leaned over, snatched up the charm with the Santa hat sticker, and palmed it.

"Hey," said the woman of the couple he'd nudged aside. "You can't take that charm."

"The hell I can't." He growled. "It's got my name on it."

The woman gave him a wide berth, and the man with her said, "You can't talk to my girlfriend like that."

"Sorry," he mumbled, realizing he must seem like a giant ass. "I didn't mean to offend."

You're acting like a lunatic, Lockhart, and over what? A whimsical little charm. Yes, but it was the kind of charm lovers put up.

News flash! They had been lovers. At least for one night.

Taken at face value, the plaque wasn't all that provocative. Just *Aria & Remington were here*. Which was true enough. No *Aria + Remington*. No *Aria & Remington 4 EVR*. No *Aria loves Remington* like the other charms and tree carvings.

He took the charm to the lady named Terri. "Ma'am."

She gave him a bright, cheery smile. "Yes?"

"Do you remember the woman who bought this?"

"Why yes, Aria Alzate? Olivia Schebly's friend. She is so lively. I adore her. She bought the charm earlier this year when she came to town, but just now she asked me to engrave it."

"Did she say why she put this up?" Why was he even asking this woman? What did it matter?

Terri's smile widened. "You must be Remington." She stuck out a hand. "Welcome to Twilight."

Not knowing what else to do, Remington shook the woman's hand.

"Aria couldn't stop praising you and how you'd helped her get here for Olivia's wedding. She told me she wanted to do something nice to commemorate your stay."

"Oh," he said, feeling the tops of his ears burn.

"Did you want to talk to her about it?" Terri asked.

"I . . . er . . ." Did he?

"Because she's right over there." Terri pointed across the park.

Clutching the charm in his palm, Remington turned and immediately recognized Aria's long straight black hair as she stood fifty yards away talking to a group of people.

Remington's heart bounced to his stomach, then trampolined up his chest, and he surged forward, not even knowing what he intended. Still, he was unsure why the goofy little charm was undoing him so completely. It was just like her to do something so off-the-wall and impulsive.

But it made him feel . . . *well dammit* . . . the engraving made him feel wanted and included and part of her life and that was *not* what he wanted to feel.

He was hanging on by a thread here, trying to work up some kind of irritation or indignation, but there was Christmas music playing and the people plucking Angel ornaments off trees to give presents to poor kids and other folks declaring their love for each other on harebrained plaques.

The wall of anger and resentment he'd built up toward Christmas, hanging on to it tight because it was the time of year his mother had died, just imploded right there on the spot.

Leaving his soul shaky and threadbare.

He wanted to be near Aria and her bright shining light. He wanted to hear her happy laughter and smell her special scent. He wanted to kiss her and hold her and tell her that, yes, last night had meant something.

Something really monumental, and he was a coward for not telling her so this morning.

Remington didn't even realize he was rushing across the park toward her. His legs moving of their own accord. His gaze firmly fixed on the sweet curve of her tushy in those tight jeans. His mind both focused and dazed, reeling on a sacred mission and completely without a backup plan.

A big, handsome guy who looked like he could be muscle for a security company, approached Aria's group.

Aria turned toward the man, her face beaming with an angelic light. The fellow rushed toward her, gathered her into his arms, and spun around.

Remington froze to the spot. His jaw unhinged as he watched the tall man put her down and then kiss *his* girl.

It wasn't a passionate kiss. A quick peck on the lips. But to Remington it was a gut punch, and all the unbridled hope that had sent him dashing across the park froze him to the spot.

She had a life he knew nothing about.

He watched as the tall man wrapped an arm around Aria's waist and said something that made her laugh, and then an entire group turned in his direction.

Ugh. He didn't want to meet her friends.

Quick, before she sees you, run!

He should have, but Aria had already spotted him and waved him over. Reluctantly, Remington shoved the charm into the front pocket of his sweatpants and jogged toward her. Mainly because she was grinning like she was happy to see him.

"Remy," she said, reaching out an arm to him when he got closer. "I have some people I want you to meet." Then she slipped her arm around his waist and he felt like the freaking king of the world. "This is Jyl, she's one of Olivia's bridesmaids."

"Hi, Jyl." He nodded at the young woman with too-red lipstick that called attention to her overbite.

"Aria," Jyl said, giving him the once-over. "Why didn't you tell us how delicious he was?"

Ack. Jyl was eyeballing him like he was a juicy steak.

"Nice to meet you, Remy," Jyl purred.

He didn't mind when Aria called him Remy. It felt nice, personal. But from everyone else, he preferred Remington. However, he didn't have to set the record straight. Aria tightened her grip around his waist and told Jyl, "You can call him Remington."

Jyl arched her eyebrows but said nothing.

Aria introduced him to the other bridesmaids. Four in total. He couldn't remember all of their names. He was too dazzled by the feel of Aria's arm around him to pay much attention. But when she let go of him to slip an arm around the tall man, Remington's body went rigid.

"And this is Ryder." Aria playfully rested her head on Ryder's shoulder.

If Remington hadn't noticed the wedding band on the guy's finger, he just might have turned possessive.

"Ryder married Katie Cheek, who is the younger sister of Jenny Cantrell, who runs the Merry Cherub," Aria explained. "Twilight is a lot like Cupid, in that everyone seems to be related to someone in town."

Remington didn't quite follow all that, but he got the most important part of it. Ryder was married. That was a relief, but it didn't stop him from wishing that Aria would stop touching the guy.

"Ryder was in the Army," she said. "Military police. I already told him about your—" She broke off and waved at Remington's left hand.

"Thank you for your service," Ryder said, shaking Remington's right hand. To Aria, he said, "He should come. Why don't you bring him?"

"Bring me where?" Remington asked, sidling closer to Aria.

"Ryder is part of a military support group," Aria said. "And on the third Thursday of the month, they hold art classes in a meeting room at The Horny Toad Tavern from seven to nine P.M. It's great therapy."

Interested, Remington arched an eyebrow. He was always on the lookout for ways to manage stress and mental mind chatter. He'd had tons of physical, occupational, and psychological therapy, but no one had mentioned art therapy for him.

"Our art instructor has the flu," Ryder told Remington. "And we were just going to cancel the class, but when I told Aria, she offered to teach for us. Things get especially stressful this time of year, and doing art really helps us keep centered."

Remington wanted to ask why they needed a teacher to slap some paint on a canvas, but he said nothing.

"You really should come to the class," Ryder encouraged. "Painting is a great way to unwind."

"Plus, veterans get free beer," Aria enticed.

She didn't have to twist his arm. Remington wasn't about to let her go alone to teach an art class to a military support group at a tavern, not even when she knew some of them. No way in hell.

Slipping his arm around Aria's waist and tugging her against his side, Remington met Ryder's bemused stare and said, "Count on it. I'll be there."

CHAPTER 14

Manifest: The hub or center of a drop zone activity.

Nervous, but not about to show it, Aria surveyed the group clustered in the back room of The Horney Toad Tavern turned art studio. It had been ages since she'd taught an art class, and that had been to four-year-olds at her church.

If Remington hadn't been among the students, it might not have been such a big deal, but with him standing there, looking at her expectantly, Aria felt as if a lot was riding on this session. Honestly, she'd been quite surprised he'd agreed to come and a little suspicious too. She'd expected Mr. Grinch to veto the idea.

Why hadn't he? What was he up to?

Canting her head, she studied him. The way he held himself a bit apart from the others, as if he didn't belong. There was a guarded air to him. A rigidity to his shoulders. A tightness around his mouth.

Remington's eyes met hers.

She smiled.

He didn't flinch. Didn't smile back.

Thrown, Aria shifted her gaze back to the other participants. The class was composed of only men, and that surprised her too. In her experience, these kinds of classes that mixed adult beverages and art usually comprised far more women than men, but this audience was geared to military personnel with different needs than the public.

That added to her nervousness.

What if she made a mistake and somehow triggered one of them? She'd taken a couple of classes in art therapy in college, but she hadn't specialized in it. Then again, maybe triggering them was a good thing. It could help them face whatever they'd tamped down or iced over or built an emotional wall around.

"Hi, guys," she said. "I'm just a sub, so we're doing regular art since you have to have a degree to teach art therapy. But I hope you'll still get something out of it. I know art helps me relieve stress. Just a disclaimer, since I'm not a therapist."

"Fine with us," one of the guys said, and everyone else nodded.

She really didn't have a clue what she was doing on that score, but she believed in the power of art to relieve stress and manage symptoms of anxiety, in much the same way as music or exercise. And she loved art and loved sharing art with others. She was in the right place.

The guys trooped in, orderly as kids lining up for the school bus. Mostly, they looked relaxed and in good moods. There were eight students not counting Remington. Three of them wore ugly Christmas sweatshirts and seemed quite proud of their outlandish attire.

Remington stood at the back of the group, hands jammed in his pockets, weight centered on the balls of his feet, shoulders cocked forward, as if he were winged Mercury, ready to blast right out of there given half a chance.

She'd arrived early to set up the space, finding art materials in the supply cabinet in the corner. At first, she planned on having the group do paintings, but then an idea had seized her and instead of getting out canvases, easels, brushes, and paints, she'd hauled out sketching paper and graphite pencils of varying darkness and hardness.

Aria busily sharpened pencils with the Derwent Super Point manual sharpener that honed the pencils to a needle-fine point.

Making sure she had a soft, medium, and hard pencil for every student so they would have a range of values in their artwork, Aria counted up the pencils.

"We're not painting?" Ryder asked.

"I thought tonight we'd focus on drawing," she said. "The quickest way to improve your painting skills is to improve your drawing skills."

"No kidding?" Ryder lifted an eyebrow. "Our regular teacher just has us paint."

Oh dear, was she stepping on toes? "Then drawing will be a nice change of pace."

"Normally, the instructor has us choose artwork to paint," said one of the other students, an older man in his midforties with a Barbie Band-Aid on his thumb.

She knew without asking that he had a little girl in his life. Ryder had told her the man's name was Nate Deavers, and he was a former Navy SEAL.

"It's in that book." Nate nodded at a fat white binder on the table at the back of the room. They'd filled the binder with copyright-free laminated artwork. Aria had gone through it when she first arrived. "Will we be using something like that to pick our artwork from?"

"We will all be drawing the same thing tonight," Aria said, sticking another pencil in the sharpener. "A basic exercise."

"Need any help with that? I could sharpen pencils while you do something else." Ryder came closer to Aria.

Quickly, Remington appeared at her side and settled his arm around her waist. "I'll handle the pencils."

Oh my. Was Remington jealous of Ryder? Amused, Aria bit back a grin.

Just then a waitress from the tavern brought in a pitcher of beer and icy mugs to rousing cheers from the men.

"Should I sharpen your pencils?" Remington asked, leaning so far over to check out the pencils that his shoulder almost grazed her breasts.

Aria sucked in a lungful of air and said in a voice testier than she'd intended, "I can sharpen my own pencils, thanks."

Remington straightened and jammed his hands in his pockets. He seemed edgy and ill at ease. "What should I do?"

"Grab that sketch pad," she said. "There are perforated pages. Tear them out and give each student one."

He looked reluctant to leave her side, but did as she asked, tearing out sketch pad pages and passing them out while the other men poured up beers from the three pitchers the server had placed in the middle of the long art table.

Aria focused on the pencils, making sure each tip was as sharp as it could be, breathing in the woody aroma that never failed to bring a smile to her face. She loved the smell of art supplies.

When all the men were settled and pencils and paper passed out, Aria tugged an easel from the side of the room to the end of the table and settled a large drawing board onto it. She looked down the long table at the row of men. Four on one side, five on the other.

Remington sat at the opposite end from where she stood, nearest to the door and his back to the wall. It occurred to her that he didn't feel safe even in this room of military servicemen.

"Tonight," she said, "we'll be doing one of the earliest exercises they teach in art school. We'll be drawing our hands. You'll use the hand you're not drawing with as the model. I'll draw along with you and take you through it step-by-step."

Surreptitiously, she cast a glance at Remington to see how he was taking the assignment. His eyes narrowed, his mouth pressed into a flat line as he stared at the three fingers of his left hand curled into a half fist.

Was this a blunder? Or a calculated risk? She'd thrown him a curveball. Would he play along? Or did he have a backup plan?

You know he has a backup plan.

Yes, and most likely it included just walking right out the door. Gulping, Aria pulled up a tall backless barstool, positioned it in front of her drawing board, and tried to ignore the rapid pounding of her heart.

"Let's start with the HB pencil," she directed, picking up her honed HB pencil. "The HB graphite grading scale is used to determine the hardness and darkness of pencils. The HB is a middle grade pencil. You might know it best as a number two. It's your standard, all-purpose pencil."

"So basically, HBs are the pencils you have lying around your house," Nate said.

"That's right. The higher the number next to the H," she went on, "the harder the pencil lead is inside." She shot a quick glance at Remington.

He sat perfectly still, watching her. If the man was a pencil, he'd be a 9H. The hardest standard grade pencil there was.

"Does that mean the harder the pencil the darker it draws?" Ryder asked, examining his pencil.

"Actually, the opposite is true," Aria said. "The hardness of the pencil is determined by the amount of clay that is added to the pencil during production. The more clay, the harder the pencil, and that means lighter, finer strokes that smudge less."

"I never knew there was so much to know about pencils," Nate mused.

"So how do we make darker lines?" Ryder asked.

Down at the end of the table, Remington was toying with his pencil, rapping it over the knuckles of his left hand.

Aria kept a cautious eye on him, braced for whatever backup plan he had up his sleeve.

"That's where the B part comes in. B stands for blackness. The higher the number next to the B, the darker the pencil. A B grade pencil means the core has more graphite and will draw bolder, darker lines. But the more graphite it has, the more the pencil will smudge."

"You gave us three pencils to use," Nate said. "The HB, a 2H, and a 2B."

"Yes, these are the most balanced pencils in terms of hardness and darkness and will get you used to developing the different values in your drawings without a lot of smudginess from a very dark pencil or the scratchiness of a very light pencil. But I'm passing around the full range of drawing pencils and some scratch paper so you can experiment with the differences. But for today's assignment we will just use the three I gave you." She slid off her stool, picked up her pencil carrying case, unzipped it and gave it to Nate first since he was sitting next to her.

Everyone nodded.

Everyone, except Remington.

"Remington," she said, "do you have a question?"

"Yes," he said. "What are values?" He met her gaze with a look so raw and vulnerable she lost her breath. But just as quickly as the look appeared in his eyes, it vanished, and he was back to his familiar stony expression.

"Oh," she said, feeling a strange fluttering near her heart. "Values are how light and dark something is. Shadows versus highlights and every shade in between. We'll get into that more as we draw."

"I see." He moistened his lip with the tip of his tongue, and she was so entranced she couldn't have looked away if someone had suddenly yelled *fire!* "I'm guessing then that harder pencils are great for very light sketching, like drafting an initial outline before going over it with a darker pencil?"

"Yes," she mumbled, fascinated by the depth of the highlights she saw in his chocolate eyes. "The line you get from a hard pencil will be quite precise."

"Hmm." His gaze raked over her body and it was as if they were the only two people in the room. "Does that mean that the bolder B pencils are great for loose, expressive sketching and shading?"

She gulped. "Yes."

"But bold pencils are very soft, right?" His voice lowered and his eyes darkened. It seemed they weren't really talking about pencils anymore. If they ever had been.

She let out a little chuff of air, her gaze still wedded to his. "Uh-huh."

"And they dull quickly?"

"Yes, but they smudge well, which can be great for certain shading techniques."

"Ultimately," he said, "every pencil has pluses and minuses."

"They do. It all depends on your purposes."

"I see."

Aria saw too. She and Remington were on opposite ends of the spectrum. While he was as hard and precise as a 9H pencil, she was soft and bold as a 9B. He was for outlining, planning, and building a fine foundation. She was for adding color, smudging, and blending.

Talk about opposing values.

But you need both in a drawing. One to capture the darkness, the other the light.

She was peering down the table at him, oblivious to the other men in the room, who were busy doodling on scratch paper with the various kinds of pencils. Staring straight into the eyes of the deepest, darkest, baddest-assed man she'd ever known.

Dear Lord, how had she ever dismissed him as nothing more than the broody Lockhart brother? Had she really not seen before the multilayers and hidden depths lurking inside him?

How immature she'd been. How shallow.

His pupils widened, overtaking his irises. A circle of black, spreading as his eyes gobbled her up, sucking her into his vortex and tugging her closer and closer and closer to him. She barely realized that she had left her place at the head of the table and arrived at his side. Standing so close that she had to tilt her head to maintain full eye contact.

She'd felt the dramatic attraction last night and then again this morning before they left Armadillo, but nothing that held the overwhelming chemistry of this moment in which it seemed she could see through his eyes and into his soul.

They were in a room full of people, she realized with a start, but she didn't care. Not in the least. *They* didn't care, for he was as latched to her as she was to him.

They were caught in a whirlwind of desire, the two of them. As inexplicable as it was powerful.

In his eyes she could see the power of chained lightning, feel the rumble of thunder.

It was phenomenal. The rush of emotions surging between them, based on nothing more than a conversation about pencils.

But something important had been established. Lines sketched. Values shaded.

How had she lived so many years without this feeling? She felt as if the connection between them was pure energy—which come to think of it, it *was*—and that energy was infusing her with something strange and exhilarating.

Excitement drove a hard shiver through her body.

Finally, Remington wrenched his gaze away and dropped it to the table, a tight expression pulling his mouth taut.

Breathless, trembling, imbued with a shimmering lightness, she raced back to the head of the table. Smoothed her hair, cleared her throat, and said to the class, "And now we're going to draw our hands."

REMINGTON STARED AT what remained of his left hand.

He'd thought he'd adjusted to missing his last two fingers pretty well, and he wasn't complaining. So many military people had it much worse. No way was he about to complain.

It had been six months since the skydiving accident, and while the wound still looked raw and ragged, he'd adapted. He'd learned he could hold a coffee cup without spilling the contents, but the counterbalancing had taken some getting used to. He no longer fumbled with a zipper, although buttons were still a bit of a challenge. He could give the peace sign and a thumbs-up, but his left hand had no future in "hang loose" or "hook 'em horns."

"Really *see* your hand," Aria instructed from the front of the room. "Squint. Squinting visually simplifies the values. It helps eliminate the perception of reflected light to better see the whole."

Hey, it ain't whole, Zippy.

But he ignored that smart-ass voice in his head and squinted anyway, trying to see what he usually overlooked. His two remaining fingers had strengthened, the base of both digits developing thicker muscles. His middle finger slanted toward his palm now more than it once had. Hmm, he should work on that.

"Don't judge what you see," Aria said as if she could read his mind. "Just draw."

Easy for her to say.

"Look for shapes. Your palm is basically a square with five cylinders coming off of it." She illustrated with the drawing of her own hand she was creating on the drawing board propped against the easel at the end of the table.

Yeah, he got that. Except his cylinders were down to three. Even on paper, his hand looked skewed, freakish.

Flipping palm-side down, he squinted at the back of his hand. Moved his remaining fingers and thumb around, looking for an angle that would hide his disfigurement and thought inanely, *I have no ring finger. I can't ever get married.*

All around him, the other students were busily drawing. The scribbling of their pencils was the only sound in the room. The noises seemed to converge and grow louder, filling his head with *scratch, scratch, scratch.*

He felt like he was in the belly of an airplane as it zoomed toward the drop zone, geared up and waiting for the jump. He hadn't been in a plane, hadn't donned the rigging of his trade, since they'd medevacked him after the accident.

Inadequate. He felt inadequate with that damn pencil in his hand and the paper drawn with the outline of a square and three unbalanced cylinders. No capable medical doctor could come along and put Humpty-Dumpty back together again.

This was his third time being injured in battle. Young, and feeling immortal, each of the other two times he'd bounced back with a vengeance. At twenty, he'd lost half his spleen from hand-to-hand combat. Then two years later, he'd taken a bullet through his right shoulder that narrowly missed his lung, when his platoon was ambushed by insurgents.

He'd gotten a medal for that, and his promotion to the Rangers. He'd been rewarded for his injuries. Putting himself in harm's way for the good of his country became a siren's song. He volunteered for rough assignments. Went where others feared to tread. Got high on the accolades. He could see that now. His addiction to heroics.

That's what had landed him here, mangled and broken, his career lost. The very thing that had formed his identity in shambles *because* of his belief that giving himself away would make him whole.

He'd suffered a lot. So very much in his pursuit of that wholeness.

Startled, his gaze fixed on his hand, he saw the illusion of his fingers as if they were still there. In his mind and squinty visions, remnants of the man he used to be. His right hand moved the pencil across the page. He watched the lines form, the drawing take shape. Felt soothed and salved in unexpected ways.

The shading appeared, and the highlights shimmered as the techniques Aria described sprang to life on the paper. Watching his hand move was like a mystery, a puzzlement of graphite turning nothing into shape and form.

It felt like magic, and for the first time since coming back to Texas, he felt a twinge of hope. Maybe he wasn't a lost cause.

He leaned forward, drawing as fast as he could, consumed by an impulse he couldn't control or contain. He was no longer in the room surrounded by men in the same boat as he. No longer restricted by his thoughts or his fears.

At the moment, Remington felt as free as the kid he'd been in the years before his mother died. He'd been in a mental cage of his own making, and the pencil in his hand was the key.

Agog, he gazed at the sketch as if someone else had done it and then back at the reference model. The drawing looked so true, so realistic, he was stunned and impressed that he'd created a picture of his own damaged hand.

He heard a rushing in his ears, a solid sound as swift and frightening as tornadic winds. Felt a tremor run through his body and a hot flush burn around his collar. He should take off his coat, but he couldn't even do that.

The picture held his entire attention, a near perfect depiction of his hand, missing fingers and all.

He closed his eyes, claustrophobic and overwhelmed.

But when he opened his eyes and looked around, he saw Aria standing beside him, a look of concerned awe on her face so sharp and poignant that he recognized with unshakable certainty, *I think I love you.*

Chapter 15

Base: The core around which a free fall formation of skydivers is built.

They didn't talk on the way back to the Merry Cherub.

There was a distance between them, strange and heavy, and Aria was afraid to ask him what was wrong. Something had shifted during that art class, but she had no idea what it was or how she felt about it.

In her purse, she carried the drawing he'd done of his hand. His talent was remarkable, but so much more than that was his stunned disbelief that he'd drawn so well.

She'd jokingly asked what had happened, and he'd said without meeting her gaze, "Something came over me."

And then he took her hand, and they walked the rest of the way in silence. But his touch lit a happy little fire deep in the pit of her belly. A fire she was too scared to warm herself by.

Once they were at the B and B and it was time to climb the stairs together and head to their bedrooms, he'd mumbled about forgetting something back at the tavern and bolted.

Leaving Aria on the porch feeling both confused and relieved.

She did not wait for his return and went to her room. She texted her family and friends good-night, got ready for bed, and fell asleep without hearing Remington ever come in.

Aria spent the night in dreams of him and woke the next morning, Friday, December 18, feeling hot and edgy, the covers twisted around her legs.

She stared up at the angel mural painted on the ceiling, trying to make sense of her feelings for Remington and getting absolutely nowhere. She liked the man. More than she'd ever expected to, and when she kissed him, no matter how much she wished it wasn't so, she heard that infernal humming.

What did it mean?

Forget it. Move on. No time for that nonsense. She had work to do.

The wedding was tomorrow, and she needed to double-check on everything in person—cake, florist, caterers, DJ, photographer. The rehearsal at four, followed by the rehearsal dinner. It'd be a jam-packed day.

A knock sounded on the hallway door.

Remington?

She leaped out of bed but then realized, nah, he'd just use the connecting door. Grabbing her bathrobe, she put it on and tied the belt as she walked to the door. Going up on tiptoes, she peered through the peephole.

Jenny Cantrell stood holding a room service tray.

Aria opened the door. "I didn't order room service."

"Remington ordered it for you."

Aria peered around Jenny. "Where is he?"

"He went out jogging at dawn and asked me to bring you blueberry pancakes and veggie sausages at seven-thirty."

Oh, that sly devil.

"Thank you." Aria took the tray Jenny offered.

"Don't thank me, thank Remington. It was his idea to add the carnation by the way." Jenny nodded at the little red flower in a small bud vase. "He saw the arrangement on the front desk as he was leaving and commented how you appreciate beautiful things."

Aww. Aria wished he was here right now so she could give him a big hug.

She thanked Jenny, took the tray to the bed, and slid back beneath the covers. Plumped the pillows and propped herself up. It felt decadent eating breakfast in bed, and she loved every second.

How sweet of him to spoil her this way. Just as she was polishing off the food, a short tap sounded on the connecting door.

Remington was back!

"Come in," she said, putting aside the tray and pulling the covers to her collarbones. She was braless.

The door between their rooms swung open, but Remington did not come in. He hovered at the threshold as if hesitant to move closer.

"Thank you for the breakfast," she said.

"You're welcome."

His hair was damp from a shower, and even halfway across the room she could smell the sandalwood scent of his shampoo. He wore a plain black T-shirt and black Wrangler jeans. His feet were bare.

She tried not to stare, but damn, the man sure had sexy toes.

He stood studying her but didn't say another word.

Feeling exposed, she lifted the covers all the way to her chin. "I've got a busy day today."

"I know."

Again, that long stretch of silence. "Was there something else?"

"Do you mind if I tag along?" he asked. "I'm at loose ends here with nothing to do. Lazing around is not my thing. I like to stay busy. Maybe I could help?"

Just the thought of him hanging out with her sent a mad thrill shooting through her body, and that wasn't good. She was getting too attached. So maybe she should say no? Yes, she would definitely say no.

"Sure thing," she said. "That'd be great."

He just kept standing there, watching her as if mesmerized.

Aria cleared her throat. "Um . . . I need to get dressed."

"Oh right, yeah." He shook himself and withdrew, closing the connecting door behind him.

Fifteen minutes later, it was Aria knocking on the connecting door. She'd showered the night before so all she needed to do was get dressed and slap on some makeup. She wore boot cut yoga pants that could pass for stretchy black slacks, a sage green sweater, and black ankle boots. Hair pulled up into a ponytail, she'd slipped in Santa earrings and a matching holiday bracelet, and she was good to go.

"Ready." She beamed at him.

He led the way downstairs, then turned when he reached the landing into the lobby and held his hand out to help her descend the final step.

Her heart got all melty. Aww, her Sir Galahad.

Not quite. If memory served from her college Lit class, Sir Galahad was a celibate, and he was definitely not that. But like the fabled seeker of the Holy Grail, Remy was the most perfect of knightly men.

Okay, maybe not perfect.

He painted a scowl on his face from time to time, but she was learning the frown wasn't really anger; rather, he used it as a shield to keep people from digging deeper. That made her want to grab a shovel and excavate.

Aria was fighting to resist temptation. The man was entitled to his secret. It wasn't up to her to change him.

She noticed on the short walk to the bakery that he took the outside, putting himself between the traffic and her, and when she stumbled over the old cobblestones on the square, he reached out for her arm and tucked her against his body.

He made her feel safe, and protected, and she let him do it. Not pulling away until they reached the Twilight Bakery.

Yummy bakery smells greeted them, and Aria was so happy she was full of blueberry pancakes or she'd have ordered one of everything.

"Aria!" The bakery owner, Christine Noble Borden, came from around the counter to embrace her in a big hug. She'd met Christine in person when she'd come to Twilight last year for Olivia's engagement party, and she adored the older woman and her encouraging smiles. "It's so good to see you again."

"Ditto."

Christine, who walked with a limp after an automobile collision twenty years earlier that had ended her Olympic bid in track and field, stepped back and eyed Remington with an appreciative glance. The accident also left Christine unable to have children, but she'd married a cowboy from Jubilee, Eli Borden, who had four kids of his own. And Christine got a ready-made family.

"Hello." Christine extended her hand. "You must be Remington. Thank you for driving our Aria. We couldn't pull off this wedding without her."

"Oh yes you could." Aria waved away Christine's compliment.

"Well, we don't want to find out, do we." Christine laughed gaily. "I suppose you're here to see the cake in person?"

"Yes!" Aria pressed her palms together. "I'd love to see how it turned out."

"This way." Christine crooked her finger, and they left her assistant waiting on customers at the counter.

She led them to the kitchen and the big commercial refrigerators at the back of the room. She opened the door and took out a magnificent three-tiered cake.

"It's beautiful." Aria breathed. "You've outdone yourself."

A blush rose to Christine's cheeks, and she ducked her head. Letting Aria know that even at forty, Christine hadn't fully conquered her natural shyness. "Thank you."

"Olivia will be over the moon."

"Would you like a sample?" Christine went to another refrigerator and got out an array of tiny cakes on a tray.

Aria rubbed her hands together and grinned wide. "I thought you'd never ask."

Christine put one sample on a plate and handed it to Aria along with a plastic fork. "Would you like one, Mr. Lockhart?"

"Remington," he said, and held up his right hand. "But no thanks."

Aria noticed he tucked his left hand behind his back, keeping it out of sight. He did that quite often. "Aww, c'mon. Have some."

"I'm good."

"The recipe is my best seller for winter weddings," Christine said. "A toasted almond cake brushed with Amaretto and filled with caramel ganache and a thin layer of salted caramel. The buttercream icing is infused with caramel as well."

Aria popped a bite of cake into her mouth. "OMG." She groaned and rolled her eyes. "This is the best cake I've ever put in my mouth! Here . . ." With the edge of her fork, she sliced off a small piece, speared it with the tines, and moved over to where Remington was standing with his back to a wall. "You positively *must* try this."

"I'm good, I'm good." He put up both palms now, blocking her way to his mouth. "I'm not a big cake guy."

"You'll be one after you've had a bite of this cake."

"Aria, I—" He opened his mouth to protest, and she wasn't wasting an opportunity. She would lighten this guy up or die trying. Before he got any further, she went up on tiptoes and stuffed wedding cake into his mouth.

Shocked, his eyes flew wide, and he automatically closed his mouth. Chewed. A surprised smile lit up his face. "Wow, that is good cake."

Pleased, Christine clapped her hands. "I'm so happy you guys like it."

"*Like* isn't the word for it. I'm in love!" Aria took another bite.

"Can I have more?" Remington asked.

"See? There you go. Proof enough. The grinch likes your wedding cake, it's a crowd-pleaser."

Christine got more samples and cups of coffee, and they spent the next ten minutes enjoying cake.

"Still not a cake guy?" Aria asked as they thanked Christine and left the bakery. She was so happy that the cake had turned out so well. This was going to be the best wedding she'd ever planned. Especially with the handicap of long-distance planning.

"I try to avoid desserts," Remington said. "But you were right. It is pretty damn . . . er, darn . . . delicious cake."

"I'm so thrilled you approve. Onward and upward. Next stop, the florist. You'll like the Garzas. Gideon lost his left hand in Iraq." She crinkled her nose and pursed her lips. "I believe he was Green Beret."

Remington scowled, back to the growly bear act. "Knock it off, Aria."

"What?" She stared at him, eyes widening.

"It sounds like you're trying to set us up on a playdate. Just because we've got similar injuries and are Army war vets doesn't mean we gotta bond or even like each other."

"I didn't mean to overstep. It's just that you got along so well with Hank back in Armadillo, and the guys last night at the art class . . ."

He shook his head, but his scowl softened. "I didn't mean to jump down your throat. I'm a lot more guarded than you are with people, and it just astounds me how open and friendly you are with people."

"Is that a compliment or a complaint?"

"It's just who you are." He shrugged. "You trust so easily. Me? I'm hypervigilant. I'm always trying to figure out the other guy's angle."

"Aww." Aria clicked her tongue. "That's too sad."

"Being wary has saved my ass . . . er . . . backside more times than I can count."

"It's also stopped you from having close, loving relationships."

Remington's eyes got big, and he looked as if she'd just shot him straight through the heart. "I—"

"Here we are," she said, wishing she'd kept her mouth shut. The last thing she wanted was to hurt him. Putting on a bright smile, she pushed through the door that said: *Marsh's Flower Shop*.

The smell of flowers rolled over them, a dam-burst of fragrance— roses, stargazer lilies, sweet autumn clematis, jasmine. The air was rich with the scent of damp soil. Colorful blooms were everywhere, arranged in artfully designed displays and coolers throughout the small, crowded shop. A feast for the senses. A symphony of blooms.

Aria felt transported into another world, the same way she did when she got out her oil paintings and dabbled on canvas. She glanced over at Remington.

His nose twitching and jaw clenched, his gaze swept around the place as if on the lookout for IEDs among the foliage. How terrible it must be to live on constant alert. Unable to turn off the battle long after it was behind you. She'd not considered how the world must look through his eyes.

A pang of sympathy pushed through her. Well, he might have demons to wrestle with, but whenever he was with her, Aria was determined to keep things light and fun.

In the middle of the store was a counter, and behind it, a woman in her late thirties worked at arranging chrysanthemums in a wooden Santa's sleigh. Her shoulders were hunched, her eyes hooded. She looked worried and not about flowers.

As the door closed behind Aria and Remington, the woman glanced up.

"Aria!" she said, smiling brightly, but her eyes remained troubled. She was trying her best to put on a positive face.

"Caitlyn." Aria reached out her arms as Caitlyn Marsh Garza came from behind the counter to hug her.

Aria had traveled to Twilight many times to visit Olivia, and she always made it a point to stop into the flower shop and buy flowers for her friend each time she came. Aria and Caitlyn had been exchanging texts almost daily, keeping in touch about the flowers for Olivia and Ben's wedding.

"It's so good to see you." Caitlyn hugged her hard.

"You too."

Remington hung back. Aria noticed he had his left hand in his jacket pocket again.

"Hello." Caitlyn stepped away from Aria and extended her hand to Remington. "I'm Caitlyn."

"Remington Lockhart," he said. "I'm Aria's driver."

"Driver?" Caitlyn arched her eyebrow.

Quickly, Aria filled her in about falling from the hay barn loft and her concussion.

"Oh my, I'm sorry to hear about that." Caitlyn rested a hand on Aria's shoulder, her concern genuine. "How are you feeling now?"

"I have this minor nagging headache, but I'm doing really great otherwise."

"That's reassuring, and at least you got a handsome escort out of the deal." Caitlyn winked. "Will you be at the ceremony, Remington?"

"I'll be around to help with anything Aria needs," he said.

"Gorgeous and handy too," Caitlyn said to Aria. "I like him."

"He'll do," Aria teased. "He's also a pretty good driver."

The back door opened, and a handsome dark-eyed, dark-haired man came into the shop. He held a cell phone in his right hand, and he looked worried.

It was Caitlyn's husband, Gideon Garza. He carried himself with the same razor-straight military bearing as Remington. The two men exchanged wary glances and Aria tensed, watching Remington's gaze track to Gideon's robotic left hand.

Slowly, Remington took his hand from his pocket.

Gideon stared at Remington's damaged hand, raised his gaze back to Remington's face, gave a short nod. "Afghanistan?"

Remington returned the nod.

Gideon held up his mechanical left hand. "Iraq."

They eyed each other with respect, and that was the extent of their exchange.

Alpha men. Sheesh.

Caitlyn turned to her husband. "Any word on Danny?"

"They're running blood work." Gideon pocketed his cell phone and moved closer to his wife, put his arm around her waist, kissed her cheek. "Let's not worry until there's something to worry about."

Danny was the couple's eighteen-year-old son, who was attending his freshman year at Southern Methodist University in Dallas.

Caitlyn and Gideon had two other children as well. An eight-year-old son named Wright and a six-year-old daughter, Lillian.

"Is something wrong with Danny?" Aria asked.

Caitlyn bit her bottom lip. "He's been running a bit of a fever, and feeling tired, but mono is going around on campus. That's probably all it is. We'll go see him on Sunday after the wedding."

Aria didn't want to seem selfish by asking if Caitlyn and Gideon were up to decorating the reception hall for the wedding, but she was the wedding planner. It was her job to make sure everyone she'd hired was up to their tasks. She tried to think of a delicate way to voice her concerns, but Remington beat her to the punch.

"Is your son's illness going to affect flower delivery for the wedding?" he asked.

Aria could have kissed him on the spot for asking the question she didn't know how to broach.

Gideon glowered at Remington.

Remington held the other man's stare and didn't flinch.

More alpha man stuff. *Yipes!*

"No, no." Caitlyn shook her head. "Everything is ready." She led Aria over to the coolers and showed her the order. It was everything Aria had ordered. The flowers were fresh and gorgeous. Just perfect.

"You've outdone yourself." Aria complimented her and meant it. "I know you'll pull this off without a hitch."

"Thank you for your confidence. I'm sure everything will be fine. Danny is at the university's infirmary, and they're keeping him overnight there for observation. His girlfriend, Jazzy, is with him."

"Are you sure?" Aria asked as they walked back from the coolers to join the men at the front of the store. "Maybe you should go check on Danny now just to ease your mind?"

"Have no fear. We'll get the job done," Gideon said, his tone brooking no argument. "You let us worry about our family."

"I'm sorry about your son," Remington said. "But Aria's reputation is riding on the outcome of this wedding."

"And you don't think ours is?" Gideon stepped closer until he was almost in Remington's face. "Olivia's wedding is our biggest moneymaker this year. Bigger even than Mother's Day."

Remington held his ground. Both men were similar in size and build, but if it came down to a fistfight, Aria's money was on Remington. He was younger and faster.

"I'm sorry." Caitlyn chuffed. "Gideon didn't mean to sound so testy." She threw her husband a quelling glance. "We're a bit stressed. We'll get the convention center ballroom decorated tonight after the rehearsal and bring the flowers over first thing in the morning."

"I trust you implicitly," Aria said, laying a restraining hand on Remington's forearm. "I know everything is going to be beautiful. I hope Danny gets well soon."

"We won't let you down," Caitlyn promised, her smile reassuring Aria that Remington was making a mountain out of a molehill.

"See you tomorrow." Aria wriggled her fingers and guided Remington toward the door. "Thanks again."

Once they were on the sidewalk, Remington pulled her aside out of the flow of Christmas shoppers. "Those two have a sick kid in another town. *You* need a backup plan."

"We've been over this. You do backup plans. I keep my options open."

"That's a crazy way to live. Olivia is your best friend, and she's counting on you to make this wedding happen."

"Chill out, dude. Caitlyn and Gideon are super responsible, and they've got everything ready to go. It's simply a matter of trucking everything over to the convention center and decorating the ballroom. No biggie for professionals like the Garzas. Trust me."

"I'm sure they are dependable, but shi—stuff happens. And their son *is* sick."

"It sounds like a minor illness. Most likely just a bad cold or the flu."

"People die of the flu."

"Elderly people or people with compromised immune systems. Not healthy eighteen-year-old boys. You're overreacting."

"You're underreacting, Aria. If this wedding goes south—"

Why was he getting so testy? "Look, I appreciate you taking up for me in there. That was nice of you, but this is my business, and Vivi is the only one I have to answer to. I trust the Garzas to come through."

"You trust too easily." He shook his head vigorously.

"You distrust too much. I've found people live up to your expectation of them. If you expect them to do what they say, then they will."

Remington rolled his eyes hard. "Oh Lord, that is a cockamamie attitude."

"Yes, we've already established you think I'm a frivolous, hare-brained idiot."

He expelled a long sigh. "I don't think that about you. You're just naive. You've had a safe, good life. And you have no clue how dark things can get out there in the world. I'm glad that you don't know, and I want you to keep your faith in people. But you need someone to protect you."

"Oh, and you're that guy?"

"Yes. Get a backup plan for tomorrow, Aria. Trust me on this."

"What irony! The most distrustful man this side of the Mississippi asking me to trust *him*."

"Fine." He dusted his palms together. "Have it your way. But don't come crawling to me when things fall apart."

"I won't."

"Good."

"Terrific."

"Perfect."

"Unlike you, I believe in people."

"We'll see how far that takes you."

They stood staring at each other there on the cobblestone sidewalk, foot traffic flowing around them, and Aria had the most profound urge to kiss him. But she wouldn't. Not ever again. What they'd shared was road trip sex, and that was it. No dreaming or fantasizing about what if?

"Where to now?" he asked, the muscle at his jaw twitching.

"Caterer, photographer, and DJ." She ticked the tasks on her fingers. "Then the convention center ballroom for rehearsal and it's off to dinner after that."

"Do you need me for those things?"

"Yes," she said. "I do. You were just going on about how I need protection. Who'll walk me back to the B and B after dinner?"

"You've got plenty of friends in this town. Ask one of them."

"What's the matter, Remington? Don't you want to be with me?"

"It's not you." He waved a hand at the Christmas overload around them—sights, sounds, smells. "It's this place. Too damn cheery by half."

"That's why you need to tough it out," she said, slipping her arm through his. She was pleased when he didn't pull away. She learned that when he got cranky, it was usually because he was having feelings he didn't want to deal with. "Get you over your Christmas hang-up."

"I don't have a Christmas hang-up."

"But you do, Remy. Oh, but you do."

"What can I say? I'm a hopeless case, Alzate. Accept it."

"Good thing for you that I have enough hope for both of us. I intend on showing you the joy of Christmas."

"Yeah?" He looked amused by that. "How?"

"I don't give away my secrets." She tossed her head and sashayed away, leaving Remington running to catch up with her.

Ha!

She had him right where she wanted him.

Intrigued.

CHAPTER 16

Blast: Slang for a parachute jump.

Backup plan.

The woman needed a backup plan.

Why was she so stubborn about having one? From the way she resisted, you'd think contingency planning was toxic.

From the minute they arrived in the ballroom at the Twilight Convention Center overlooking Lake Twilight, worry bit into Remington hard. The place was large and open with a bunch of round tables and chairs. It looked like the kind of place you held business conferences, not weddings.

"Can you just see it?" Aria swept her hand in a panoramic gesture. "The lake in the background, the altar set up over there. Twinkling curtain lights hung from the ceilings. Flowers everywhere. It will be gorgeous!"

It sounded good, if things went off without a hitch. But if the Garzas didn't fulfill their duties, Aria would be left with a mess on her hands. It would take at least six hours to transform this dull space into a wedding venue, double that if it was just Caitlyn and Gideon doing the work.

He would not voice his concerns to Aria though. She'd made it clear she didn't appreciate his opinion on the subject. Fine. Let her deal with the consequences if things fell apart. That's how she would learn.

Yeah, that sounded nice, but no matter how hard-assed he might claim to be, he couldn't help worrying. He thought about texting Vivi, but that was going over Aria's head and he didn't want to pull rank on her.

She introduced him to the bride and groom, Olivia Schebly and Ben Mallory and, Ben's cousin, Roger, who was the best man. Roger had also gone to Sul Ross with Olivia and Aria. He'd been the one to play matchmaker between his college friend and his cousin, Ben.

Then Roger introduced everyone to his partner, Gary.

Aria got everything going, positioning people where they were supposed to be. Remington stepped over to the side to watch her work, keeping his back to the wall as he surveyed the group rehearsing the wedding.

She had so much energy, bopping from one group to the next, that bright and cheery smile forever on her face. He loved how expressive she was. How she gestured with her hands and used her body to emote. She was so free. So comfortable in her own skin.

He envied her.

She seemed to fit wherever she went, as if she'd never in her life met a stranger. She had a buoyant way of looking at the world that boosted the spirits of everyone around her. They all liked her. But who wouldn't? She was captivating. A real showstopper.

The world seemed to revolve around her, and he'd somehow gotten caught up in her orbit and, to his shock, Remington realized he liked it.

A lot.

Being around her felt like wearing a warm coat during a cold winter storm. Or the deep play of children engrossed in a game of tag. Or driving a red Ferrari on a racetrack as fast as it would go. She was a cold drink of water on a hot summer day and he was thirsty as hell. She was a magical place outside the confines of everyday life.

Aww, shit.

He was obsessed with her.

Knew it. Feared it. But he did not understand how he'd gotten here or how to get away.

"Hey there, soldier," she murmured, coming over to take his arm. "What's on your mind? You were a thousand miles away. I called your name twice."

"What?" He blinked at her, inhaling her feminine fragrance.

"Everyone's leaving."

"Oh." He stared at the people departing out the main door. "You're done?"

"Yes."

Her smile undid him in a dozen different ways. It cut him from his moorings and set him adrift on uncertainty.

"We're all going to the Funny Farm."

"The what?"

"It's a restaurant. You'll love it. C'mon."

Ten minutes later, the wedding party assembled in the roped-off street of the town square in front of a family-style restaurant that did not take reservations, but you could go on the list for cattle call seating.

They were on the list for six P.M.

"They have group seating," Aria explained. "Every two hours. You miss one seating, wait two hours for the next one. You only have two hours to eat as well. Once the bell rings, you're out if you're in or in if you're out until they reach the fire code max."

"Weird dining concept," he said.

"The restaurant is so popular, it's the only way they can control the crowds without resorting to reservations. They want to keep the restaurant democratic."

"So, we all stand out here until—"

"Six o'clock." She bobbed her head.

Just as she said that, a hostess in a yellow gingham dress and old-fashioned bib apron rang a large dinner bell mounted on the streetlamp outside the restaurant as if she were calling in field hands. Everyone lined up in an orderly fashion.

The doors opened and guests strolled out, some patting their full bellies, others shifting toothpicks in their mouths, all of them with satisfied grins on their faces. Once the last guest had left, a waitstaff in uniforms designed to look like straitjackets opened the double doors and waved their group inside.

The crowd flowed in, and as people went by the waitstaff passed out plastic cards color coded with seat assignments.

"How many in your party?" an auburn-haired young woman asked Aria.

Quickly, Aria counted heads. "Sixteen."

She handed Aria sixteen cards with Holstein cattle printed on them. "You're in the dairy."

"Thanks," Aria said, raising her voice and the cards over her head. "Everyone in our group, follow me!"

Inside, Remington saw old farming equipment covered the walls and shelves—a horse-drawn plow, an old milk churn, pitchforks. Aria led them into the back of the restaurant to a room decorated in black-and-white and everything dairy cow—milking machines, milking stools, murals of Holstein cows and calves on the wall.

Once everyone was assembled, she guided them to their seats, the perfect hostess. She positioned herself and Remington at the far end of the table, leaving the middle for the bride and groom and their parents.

The group tittered about how fun the restaurant was and praised Aria for choosing it. She blushed prettily, thanked them, and waved over a waitress to start their order. When she had everyone settled, she sat down next to Remington.

"Fried green tomatoes are on the menu tonight," the waitress said. "It's one of our specialties. Should I order several rounds for the table?"

"Yes." Aria nodded. "And four plates of jalapeño poppers too."

"Are you picking up the tab?" Remington asked.

"I've got a budget," Aria said. "I'll take care of the check from that. My job is to make sure everything is stress-free for Olivia and Ben."

"It's going smoothly so far," he said.

"And look." She held up both palms. "No backup plan."

"You're tempting fate."

"Why, Remington Lockhart, are you superstitious?" She cocked her head and gave him a teasing grin.

He was so aware of her—her graceful body, her cinnamon and vanilla scent, the soft fall of her hair over her shoulders. He thought about that night in Armadillo when they'd made love while an ice storm raged outside their window and he felt a stab of yearning deep in the dead center of his chest. Felt a burning sensation roll all the way down below his belt.

Remington gulped, and fought his body's reaction. Beside him, she crossed her legs and her thigh bumped against his.

Whoa!

Quickly, she uncrossed her legs and glanced away. Reached for her silverware bundle and unrolled it. She leaned toward Gary, who was sitting to her left, and stirred up a conversation with him.

Leaving Remington suddenly aware of the draft blowing against the windowpane behind him.

Aria, the queen of making people feel at ease, posed questions, going around the table asking the couples how they'd met. It seemed everyone had lucked into great relationships, a rarity in Remington's experience.

"So, what's your secret?" Aria asked Olivia's parents, Mayor Schebly and his wife, Tammy. "What makes love last thirty years?"

The mayor and his wife exchanged admiring glances and said in unison, "Finding the right one."

Couple after couple had "meet cute" stories and their secret for long-term success, most with a common theme—you had to find the right person. As they passed the conversation around, Remington realized that he and Aria were the only ones at the table not in a relationship.

She got up and started taking pictures. She motioned for people to lean in together to get everyone in the shot and had them saying "Limburger." The groups laughed and teased, ordered more wine, and made toasts.

Remington watched as if from a great distance. He was an outsider here. The interloper.

A familiar position.

Even though he came from the wealthiest ranching family in Jeff Davis County, he'd always had this underlying feeling that he didn't really belong. Perhaps it was his birth position as the third of the first four Lockhart brothers. Perhaps it was because he lost his mother when he was young, but not so young that he couldn't remember her. Perhaps it was being raised by a narcissistic single dad. Perhaps a combination of all three.

But he'd battled the feeling for so long that no one would even notice if he was gone. It was all he could do not to slip away.

This pervasive feeling of not belonging was why he'd gone into the military. Looking for something, he supposed. Even though he loved ranching, no one really noticed his contributions to the family. Ridge, his headstrong, illegitimate half brother, was the one who got their father's attention, but mainly because Ridge and Duke butted heads constantly.

Ranger, his second half brother from yet another mother, had scarlet fever as a kid and Remington's mother, Lucy, hovered over him as if he was made of fragile glass. Fact: Remington had been jealous of Ranger, who got to spend a good chunk of his childhood in bed, playing video games, reading books, and staring through his telescope at the stars in the darkest night sky in the country. Lucy felt sorry for Ranger, whose mother had taken a big chunk of Duke's money to walk away from her son and not look back, and Lucy, kindhearted as she was, went overboard to make Ranger and Ridge feel wanted.

And then there was Rhett, Remington's younger brother, the charmer who'd winnowed everyone's attention from Remington with his spirited antics, especially after their mother died.

Yep, Remington had had to leave the Trans-Pecos to find himself.

He stared down at his left hand resting in his lap. Thought about last night's art class and the drawing he'd done of it. The identity he'd found in the Army was gone now, and he was back where he started.

The square peg in the round hole.

Restlessness pushed at him. Where did he go from here? What was he going to do with the rest of his life? Would he ever find a place where he belonged as he had as a paratrooper?

People kept toasting, first Olivia and Ben, and the bride's parents, and then the groom's parents, and on and on around the table.

Remington, who wasn't a big drinker, went on automatic pilot, raising his glass with everyone else and pretending to drink. He'd zoned out a little. He didn't know these people, and so when the entire room fell silent, it was only then that he snapped to attention.

Everyone was staring at him.

He forced a smile. Um, what the hell? What had he missed?

"To Remington," they said in unison and raised their glasses. "Thank you for bringing Aria to us safe and sound!"

They clinked their glasses as people echoed, "To Remington."

Ugh, now that the spotlight was on him, he didn't like it. Not one bit.

"To Aria," he blurted, eager to shift the attention back to her. "The most accomplished wedding planner who flies by the seat of her pants without a backup plan."

The second the words were out of his mouth, Remington knew they were inappropriate from the uneasy glances on people's faces.

Olivia's eyes rounded as she shifted her gaze to Aria. "You do have backup plans in place, right? In case something goes wrong."

"Everything will be fine," Aria soothed. "Remington's such a worrywart." She threw him a look that said, *thanks oh so much for throwing me under the bus*, and he felt terrible. "I've double- and triple-checked everything. No need to worry, Olivia. You leave all that to me."

Olivia's bright smile was back. "I trust you, Aria. You're my best friend and I know you'd never let me down."

The conversation swung to other things, and Remington vowed to keep his big mouth shut for the rest of the evening.

See? So you don't fit in. You don't know how to keep your size thirteen boots out of your mouth.

The dinner bell rang, signaling that the meal was officially over.

"Before we go, everyone, I have one last event planned for those who are up for it," Aria announced.

"A surprise event?" Olivia beamed and clapped her hands. "Oh yay! I'm so excited."

"What is it?" Ben asked.

"A moonlight boat cruise. I talked Joel MacGregor into reserving us a spot tonight on the *Brazos Queen*. It's my wedding gift to Olivia and Ben."

There were oohs and aahs and thank-yous, and everyone took Aria up on her offer. Aria took care of the restaurant bill, and when Remington moved to help her on with her coat, she looked surprised, but pleased.

"How are you affording this excursion?" Remington whispered. "A boat cruise for sixteen can't be cheap."

"Olivia is one of my best friends, and . . ." She gave him a sly little grin. "It didn't cost me anything."

"No?"

"Joel owed me a favor."

There it was again, that punch of jealousy, but he would not let her know he cared by asking about her relationship with this Joel character. He kept his expression cool. "Who is Joel?"

"I met him when I came to Twilight last year for Olivia's engagement party. Joel was in charge of planning his twin brother's bachelor party and he'd left it to the last minute."

"Sounds like someone else I know," Remington murmured.

"Joel was beside himself that they'd end up at the local bar with no activities planned. I helped him put together something on the fly and since he's good friends with Olivia and Ben, I didn't charge

him. He said if there was ever anything that he could do for me . . ."
She shrugged. "Voilà."

"You *are* simply amazing," he said.

"So, you see . . ." She slipped her arm through his and guided
him out of the Funny Farm behind the rest of their party. "You
have nothing to worry about. Joel is just a friend."

"I wasn't worried."

"Your face says otherwise."

"What?" He put his hand to his cheek.

"The minute I said Joel's name, you got that frown right
here." She leaned in on tiptoes to press the pad of her thumb
between his eyes. "I just wanted you to know there's no reason
for jealousy."

"I'm not jealous," he mumbled, but he heard it in his voice.

"You're so cute when you're deluding yourself. Now, pick up the
pace, Lockhart. They're waiting on us."

By eight-thirty, their group was on the *Brazos Queen*, an old
restored paddle wheel boat, and churning around the lake in the
moonlight.

More ubiquitous Christmas decorations, Remington noticed.
Several trees, fully dressed in the holiday spirit, were on board
the boat. The music was Christmas-themed. Twinkle lights were
everywhere. Considering the number of twinkle lights strung
throughout the whole town, Twilight must have a hellacious electric
bill come January.

There was a dance floor and a live band playing a lively line
dance. People rushed to join in.

"Do you want to dance?" Remington asked, more to be polite
than anything. Although he knew how to slow dance—his mother
had taught him when he was a kid—he wasn't keen on group
dances. He always seemed to be out of step in line dancing.

"Nah, let's leave the family to their party." Aria waved. "Why
don't we go on the upper deck."

"It's forty degrees outside, and on the water it'll feel colder."

"Are you afraid of the cold, snowflake?" she teased.

"Hey, I'm from the desert, and I spent years in the Middle East. My blood is thin."

"Excuses, excuses. C'mon. We've got coats. Besides, I'll snuggle up against you if you need warming up."

That's what he was afraid of.

But he went anyway, following her bouncy butt up the stairs to the upper deck. Once up there, she immediately headed for the bow of the boat.

The moon was a bare sliver in the sky. Only eighteen percent visible. It wouldn't be full until almost New Year's. Remington knew more about the moon than the average guy because of his brother Ranger's interest in astronomy. He hadn't really wanted to learn about the moon and stars and sky, but even back when they were kids, Ranger had been an astrobiologist at heart and couldn't stop talking about his passion.

Aria broke away from Remington, twirling around the top deck like a ballerina. The breeze coming off the water was bracing, but not miserably so. Mesmerized by her energy and exuberance, he went after her.

She hopped up on the railing at the bow of the boat, spread her arms wide, tossed her head to the wind and hollered at the top of her lungs, Leonardo DiCaprio in *Titanic* style, "I'm the queen of the world."

Yes, yes you are.

"Aria," he scolded gently, "get down from there before you fall overboard."

"Come, join me." She motioned for him to climb on the railing beside her.

Lord, the woman would be the death of him.

"It's dangerous." He folded his arms over his chest.

"Life is dangerous, Remy."

"I know, which is why I'm worried about you."

Her hair blew out behind her, a beautiful rich dark chocolate flag. "You can't always be expecting a fight. Sometimes you have to trust, realize you are in a safe place, and live a little."

"You do enough of that for the both of us."

She looked back over her shoulder at him and just laughed.

He motioned to the deck. "Down, now."

She shook her head and, scrambling like a spider monkey, stepped on the top rail, balancing precariously in the wind.

Holy shit. Fear shot his heart into his throat. Demanding that she get down wasn't working. In fact, the alpha man approach was having the opposite effect.

"Please," he murmured.

"Why, Remy." Another glance tossed over her shoulder at him, another saucy smile. "All you had to do was ask." With that, she pushed herself backward off the railing, and for one terrifying moment, he thought she'd jumped.

"Aria," he cried, and ran toward her, arms extended.

He caught her as she fell against him, and the impact sent them tumbling to the deck together.

CHAPTER 17

Backslide: To move backward in free fall relative to a fixed or neutral reference.

"That," Aria declared, staring into his face as her legs straddled Remington's waist, "was a blast and a half."

"You drive me crazy. You do realize that."

"Yep."

"You could have fallen. You could have drowned."

"I didn't."

"If anything happened to you . . ."

"What?"

"I'd never forgive myself."

"I know you've got this macho protector thing going on, but it's not your job to control or save me, Remy."

"Zippy . . ." He shook his head. "I swear you'll be the death of me."

"Or the life." Aria's heart was beating wildly fast, and she wasn't about to tell him, but it had been pretty scary tottering on that railing in the darkness, the water rushing below her.

She hadn't meant to scare him. Hadn't even intended on jumping onto the railing. It had been pure impulse.

She'd only brought him up here because he'd looked so lonely and out of place at dinner. But why wouldn't he feel like an outsider? He didn't know anyone, and she'd just shoehorned him in with all those strangers.

Thoughtless of you, Aria.

Yes, right, which was why she *had* brought him up here, but once they were on the deck, she'd felt weird and jumped onto the bow to hide her feelings.

She did that a lot, Aria realized with a jolt. Used activities to escape from uncomfortable emotions. Usually it worked.

But right now? Acting impulsively, jumping on the rail and then falling into Remington's arms had backfired.

As she looked down into his eyes, a hundred feelings passed through her, ninety-nine percent of them sexy.

From downstairs they could hear and feel "Cotton-Eyed Joe" vibrate up through the floor of the deck. She was still straddling him, her knees digging into the floor, and she could feel his erection against the back of her thighs.

He was hot for her.

As hot as she was for him.

"Remington," she whispered.

"We need to get up—"

"Oh," she said, fluttering her lashes. "I think you are already there."

He tugged her flush against his chest then and kissed her long and hard. Kissed her until all she heard was deep, abiding humming.

Dizzied, she pulled back.

He was staring up at her, into her. "Do you hear it?"

"The music? Yes, way too loud."

"Not that," he said. "The humming. Do you hear it when we kiss?"

"Pfftt." She waved a hand, trying to deny the fear twisting around her lungs, squeezing her tight. Not outright lying, but not about to admit that it sounded as if there were a million honeybees buzzing inside her head.

"That's a no?" His voice came out low and sultry.

"It's a silly myth," she said.

"I thought you liked silly myths." His hands were around her waist as the paddle wheel glided over the lake, and the cold air cooled their heated skin.

"Not that myth. It's dorkier than dork."

"You know," he murmured, "the trip isn't over, so technically we're still on the road."

Her hopes bounced high. "Are you saying you'd like *more* road sex?"

"Yes, Zippy, I am."

"Now we're talking." She scrambled to her feet and put out a hand to help him up.

He took it and his touch electrified her. Lighting her up from the inside out.

Just then, the boat touched back into its dock a little too quickly, and the motion rocked her into Remington's big hard chest.

"Oh my."

He peered down at her. "Oh yeah."

Remington dipped his head, held her close, and kissed her again, slowly, softly. There was a bittersweet quality to his kiss this time, and she could taste it. A deep, soulful kiss tinged with something she couldn't quite identify.

Regret maybe? Wistfulness?

They both understood their time together was fleeting. Just the length of this trip. Why not make the best of it while they could before they got home, and reality crept in?

As the rest of the guests disembarked, they waited until everyone else was gone before they left the paddle wheel. Aria stopped long enough to thank Joel for the ride and introduce him to Remington.

"Treat her like gold," Joel told Remington. "Because here in Twilight, this lady is platinum."

"Count on it," Remington answered, and took Aria's hand.

Feeling exhilarated, as they walked hand in hand through the town square, Aria inhaled the specialness of the moment. The Christmas music had stopped for the night, and the silence served to make the place look even more special. Storefronts were darkened, but a few food kiosks stayed open as did the winery bar, Fruit of the Vine.

They didn't talk, just strolled along in the muted glow from the streetlamps. They could have been inside a Christmas snow globe, caught in a magical land. Too bad they couldn't be snow globe people forever together.

No one was up at the Merry Cherub, and they let themselves in through the front door and tiptoed up to their rooms. Remington paused outside Aria's door.

"Are you coming inside?" she whispered, trying not to sound anxious. She didn't want to assume, but dreaded that he'd think better of taking her to bed and say no.

Remington shook his head. "You have to get up early. Tomorrow is a big day."

Her heart clenched. He was right. She'd barely see him tomorrow in the wedding rush. Then they'd leave town on Sunday and go back to their separate lives. This was their last real chance for another romantic encounter.

"I know," she whispered. "But after this weekend, we'll go home and go back to normal."

"You make it sound like a fairy tale." He chuckled. "We've got until dawn until your carriage turns into a pumpkin."

"I suppose that makes you Prince Charming?" She arched her eyebrows at him and leaned in close.

He smiled and held up his damaged hand. "More like Beast from *Beauty and the* . . ."

"Hmm. You know your fairy tales, Mr. Lockhart. Color me impressed."

"Hey, you forget, your mom plunked me and Rhett in front of those Disney movies along with you and your sisters."

True. This man had been a part of the fabric of her life for as long as she could remember. She couldn't ever forget that, but it was also part of what made this adventure so special. Away from Cupid and the Silver Feather and their family connections, they could be anything or anyone they wanted to be.

"There's always tomorrow night, Princess." He leaned in, pressed his forearm into the door above her head, and lowered his mouth so close to hers.

A sweet shiver winnowed down her spine. "I'm always exhausted after a wedding. Generally, I fall face forward in the bed and sleep like the dead for ten hours straight."

"So." He moistened his lips. "Tonight's the night?"

She held his stare. "If you want it."

He groaned. "Aria, there is *nothing* I want more."

She couldn't stop a wide grin from overtaking her face. "Then what are we doing standing in the hallway?"

Unlocking her door, she turned back to him, intending on motioning him inside. But Remington had other plans. He bent and scooped her into his arms.

"Ooh," she said, startled and pleased. She wrapped her arms around his neck, savoring the feel of his muscular body against hers.

"If we're going to do this," he growled, low and sexy, "let's go all the way and do it up right."

"You're all in?"

"I will be soon." He winked rakishly and carried her over the threshold, kicking the door closed behind them.

"Are we backsliding?" she asked.

He laid her gently on the bed and stepped back to study her. She liked the lingering way he raked his gaze over her. As if she were the most magnificent thing he'd ever seen and he couldn't believe she was there with him.

"What do you mean?"

"We swore it was just one time . . ."

He paused, canted his head, lowered his eyelids halfway. He looked so sexy it was all she could do not to rip off his clothes and pull him down on her immediately. "Do you want me to go?"

"No." She inhaled a lungful of air. "I'm just wondering if we did this again, will it be that much harder to go back to things as they were?"

"Zippy, we barely even had a relationship before this trip."

"Exactly."

"We cannot have a relationship again."

"Really?" she asked, as if that's what she wanted, but it wasn't, not at all, but she was terrified to tell him that.

"I can if you can. We both know we mix like oil and water."

"Yes." She scooted to the edge of the bed, and reached up to unbutton his shirt. "Except on this trip. We've gotten along pretty well away from our families and our routines."

"That's what so special about road sex." Remington watched her undressing him with an amused expression twitching at his lips. "It's a fantasy."

"Yes, right. Nothing real about it."

"Not a damn—er, darn thing."

"You know what?" she said. "I've decided it's okay for you to cuss."

"Why is that?"

"You are who you are. It's not like we're a couple. I have no right to ask you to change for me. Besides, talk dirty to me. Some guys like that."

"No," he said staunchly. "You have a right to set boundaries and make it clear what behaviors you will and won't accept. If I want to be around you, I need to curb my cursing. It's just a bad habit. Military release valve. Curse words don't define me."

"Still—"

"Aria?"

"Yes?"

"Are we going to waste our precious time chitchatting when we could explore each other's bodies?"

"No, no, you're right. I was just wondering . . ."

Heck, what was she wondering? Images rolled through her mind like a rom-com montage. She and Remington back home and dating—skinny-dipping at midnight in the springs at Balmorhea State Park, hiking the Davis Mountains, attending stargazing parties at the McDonald Observatory, sharing a banana split at the ice cream parlor and feeding each other like giggly teens. Holding hands as they strolled through the Cupid Botanical Garden. Riding horses together across the desert plains.

Silly. Romantic. Completely illogical. Remington, after all, was *not* a whimsical guy.

"Second thoughts?" Remington's voice came out thick and clotted.

"What?" She fluttered her eyelids, feeling like Sleeping Beauty awakened from a long sleep by a prince's kiss.

"You seemed a million miles away. We don't have to do this. I don't want to do this if you're not one hundred percent on board."

"Are you kidding?" She stared at him, surprised at how he'd misread her. "I can't wait to jump your bones."

"Scoot over then, Zippy," he said in a lighthearted tone that brightened her expectations. "There's this thing I wanted to try with you the last time we were together, but we just never got around to it . . ."

She collapsed into helpless giggles and scooted over.

"God," he said, gathering her into his arms, "I love how often you laugh."

"It's fun," she said. "You should try it."

"Have you met me?"

"Yes, and you're in direr need of a good laugh than anyone I know."

"Keep working on me, Zippy. Maybe you'll get me there."

Aria couldn't believe she was here again with him. Couldn't believe how eager she was to hear more of that humming. He might not be The One, but he *was* Mr. Right Now, and that was good enough. She wasn't greedy. She would take what she could get and be grateful for it. She couldn't let that stupid humming sway her.

Might as well roll up her sleeves and dive in. By resisting and acting in opposition to Granny Blue's family story, she'd allowed the legend to control her life just as surely as her sisters had allowed it to control theirs.

Still, the minute his mouth claimed hers and it ignited that sweet buzz at the back of her brain again, her heart skipped and she felt a desperate urge to take off and run. But Remington's warm hands were doing wondrous things to her body, and she simply surrendered.

Myth be damned. This was fun! And Aria was all about fun and that's what this thing was. Great, terrific fun.

Um, then why was her head dizzy and her chest tight and she felt the way she did when she had those dreams where she was naked in a crowd?

Hope.

That was the problem. She was hoping for more. Stupid. Yes. She knew that. But the romantic Blue fable of happily-ever-after was pitching a fit with Aria's free-spirited style. Yes, *eventually* she wanted love and marriage. Believed in that version of happiness to the bottom of her soul, but it had to happen on her terms. Not based on some irrational auditory response to a man's kisses.

It wasn't until Remington was kissing her within an inch of her life, and she lay rubbery and breathless in his arms, that she wanted with all her heart and soul to believe that the legend was true.

What if she'd found her soul mate, and she was just too stubborn to admit it?

"There's nothing to be afraid of, Aria," Remington said, uncannily reading her mind. "You're here with me now, and you're safe. We're together right now, and that's all that matters."

"How did you know I was caught up in my mind?"

"When you worry, which granted isn't often, your nose crinkles like a bunny." He caressed the bridge of her nose.

"Really?"

"Absolutely. It's another one of the things I love about you."

"What? The bunny nose or the not worrying often?"

"Both."

"What else do you love about me?" she asked.

"Fishing for compliments?"

"You better believe it. You don't give them out often. Your compliments mean something, Remy."

His smile curled his lips and his eyes. "I like the way you don't hold on to things. How you can so easily let go."

Yeah, that was her—easy come, easy go. Except right now, that trait felt like more of a liability than an asset.

"You're detached," she pointed out.

"That's because I never attach. You can give with all your heart and not have any expectations of receiving in return. That is a true gift. Me? If I never let down my guard, then I don't have to worry about building it back up again."

"Wait." Aria burrowed her head deeper into the pillow, pressed her palms against his chest and pushed him back. "I get it now."

"Get what?" He frowned.

"You're so afraid of losing love that you never let yourself experience love. You're terrified of getting hurt."

"Isn't everyone?"

"You're more afraid than most. C'mon, you haven't had a serious girlfriend—that I know of anyway—since Maggie."

"That might be true. Maggie did a number on me when she took up with my best friend. We were just teenagers, but nothing ever hurts quite as bad as your first broken heart."

"Said like a man who has only had one broken heart."

"How do you know that?" He sounded amazed.

She smiled. "You are far more transparent than you think. You're so afraid of getting hurt again, you avoid anything with the whiff of commitment. You're thirty-two. Most guys your age are married with a family." Aria was aware she was being a bit of a hypocrite. She, too, kept romantic relationships at arm's length, but not for the same reasons he did. She just wasn't ready. He was hiding from that part of life.

"I'm not most guys."

"Which is my point."

"Are we going to talk or are we going to take advantage of this opportunity?" His slightly irritated tone told her now she'd hit the nail on the head. Remington was terrified to give his heart away.

"You're terrified of falling in love," she said.

"And you're not?"

She shrugged. "I take life as it comes. If love is there, I embrace it. If it's not, I embrace that too."

"Maybe that's what I'm doing. Embracing me not having love in my life."

"It's not. You're hiding. There's a difference."

"How do you know?"

"Because you feel compelled to overplan *everything*. There's no spontaneity to you, Remy."

"You want spontaneity?"

"Why, yes, I do."

"I'll give you spontaneity, missy."

"What are you—"

He didn't give her time to finish her sentence. He took her by the hand and tugged her from the bed.

Ooh, what was this? "Where are we going?"

He did not explain.

Intrigued, she let him lead her out of the room and down the stairs.

They were still dressed mostly. Well, she was anyway. His shirt was open, and she'd unsnapped his jeans. The steps creaked beneath their weight as the grandfather clock in the hallway struck twelve.

"Remy?" she whispered. "What are we doing?"

"Just do what you do well, Zippy, and roll with it," he whispered back.

She was nervous now. It was difficult, letting him take charge of the spontaneity. She liked spur-of-the-moment, yes, but it seemed she liked it only if she was the one in control.

Eye-opener!

They tiptoed into the parlor, where there was a gas fireplace. Remington went over to start it up and soon a pretty flame warmed the room. In front of the fireplace was a fluffy sheepskin rug.

"Lie down," he said, letting go of her hand and sinking his knees into the rug.

"Here?" She held back.

"Why not?"

"Anyone could wake up, come downstairs, and catch us."

"Exactly. That's the thrill."

"Um . . ."

He reached for a lap blanket thrown over the sofa. "We'll cover up with this."

It felt wild and kinky and all kinds of fun. And the danger of getting caught just added to the intrigue. Still, she hesitated.

"What?" he asked. "Not such a fan of spontaneity now?"

She tossed her head. He was calling her bluff. By gum, she would not give an inch. "Huge fan."

Remington was kneeling, sitting back on his heels, his shirt open, exposing his hard, taut abs. She salivated.

He held out his arm to her and Aria melted into his embrace. The smell of Christmas was all around them, from the cinnamon-scented pinecones in a basket beside the fireplace, to the piney aroma of the real Christmas tree in the corner.

Snugging her tight against his chest, he kissed her.

Time stopped at this one perfect moment on a sheepskin rug in front of a warm fire on a cold December night with the man who made her feel safer and more cared for than she'd ever felt with anyone.

She listened to the pounding of her heartbeat in her eardrums, felt the humming beat throb throughout her body. She kissed his lower lip, the curve of his chin, the underside of his neck, then flicked her tongue along the hollow of his throat where his pulse pounded as fast as her own.

His familiar scent entered her nostrils, reached down, and tickled her lungs.

Remington.

He reached out to unbutton her blouse, and she let him, lifting her arms so he could slide it off her shoulders.

Dropping his head, he tenderly kissed her bare skin, and she shivered.

Surreptitiously, he turned his head and cast a glance over his shoulder. He was nervous, Aria recognized.

No backup plan in place to save him if someone came into the room and caught them in flagrante. While discovery might turn her on, it made Remington anxious, and she had to respect that.

"Hey," she whispered.

"Yes?" he whispered even lower.

"While I appreciate your stab at spontaneity, honestly, I was much more comfy upstairs."

Relief washed over his face, and she couldn't help being touched that he'd been willing to push himself outside his comfort zone for her.

"Oh, thank God," he said.

She almost laughed at his earnestness but didn't want him thinking that she was making fun of him.

"C'mon, let's take this party back upstairs." Clutching her shirt to her chest, she reached out with her free hand to take his, and this time she was the one leading the way.

CHAPTER 18

Body posture: One's free fall body position.

Back in her bed, they picked up where they'd left off, fully in sync, sliding into their smooth rhythm once again.

It was kind of amazing how well they fit.

How she enjoyed being with him. He was like warm socks on a cold winter night, but way sexier. Stable, steady, trustworthy, but willing to expand his horizons if need be. She liked that about him. How she could depend on him to be himself without being so hidebound that he couldn't bend in a hurricane.

She was the exact opposite. A tumbleweed who flew whichever way the wind blew.

He kissed her, slowly, sweetly.

Aria felt the electrical jolt from her head to her toes. He amplified her, made her feel utterly alive. He was a thrill ride. More fun than Six Flags.

She was accustomed to riding the wave, surfing through life without digging in too deep, skimming along the surface like a butterfly. But with one strategic maneuver, flipping her onto her back and straddling her waist, he pinned her hands above her head to the mattress, anchoring her to the spot, keeping her from floating away.

He lowered his head, nibbled her earlobe, and tightened his grip on her wrist.

She whimpered.

"Do you like that?"

"Oh yes."

"How about this?" His nibble moved to her chin.

She wriggled. Sighed. "Happiness."

"And this?" His teeth nipped at her jawline.

"Less talking, more nibbling."

"You got it."

He skimmed his hands up her belly to her chest, his palms sliding over skin. His fingers skated around to unhook her bra, and the next thing she knew it was off her, flung over his shoulder.

Remington's kiss stole her breath, and her wandering thoughts, when he ensnared her lips with his hot, wet mouth again, his chest brushing against her bare breasts. Radiant heat mushroomed outward, across her shoulders, headed chaotically for her pelvis.

Her pulse bounced, skittered. Her nipples tense, standing erect. She rejoiced in the shelter of his arms and inhaled to the very bottom of her lungs, breathing in the pure essence of Remington Lockhart's scent.

Slowly, he lowered his eyelids halfway, in a sultry bedroom stare. Desire for her flamed in his eyes, and against her thigh, she felt his erection grow stiffer.

It felt so good here with him. She felt so good. The things he could do with that marvelous tongue of his, those dazzling hands. He was spectacular, and she was so grateful for whatever moments she had with him.

"What's your pleasure, Aria?" he whispered. "Tell me what you like."

"You," she whispered back. "I like you." Except the word *like* wasn't nearly strong enough. Her feelings for him couldn't be quantified by mere words. Actions. That's what it required. She'd show him.

She responded in kind, pressing her teeth along his throbbing pulse points, caressing his pounding veins with her tongue. He groaned and speared his fingers through her hair, holding her still while he kissed her again and again and again.

Aching spikes of need pierced her entire body, and she moaned softly into his mouth.

His expert thumbs lazily stroked her nipples, teasing the stiff peaks, driving her over the edge of all reason. Her breath hung up somewhere between her lungs and her throat. Captured. She couldn't breathe. Didn't want to breathe. Just wanted her nose full of his exquisite scent.

The Christmas lights twinkling from the eaves outside their window winked gaily, as if shining just for them.

And in her head, she heard the most beautiful music, that steady sweet hum that seemed to buzz, *he's The One, The One, The One.*

She imagined generations of Blue women who'd kissed a man that caught their fancy and then, when they heard the humming, believed they'd found their soul mates. A lineage of fable and folly.

Or so she'd thought.

Right here, right now, in this blissful moment, Aria was a true believer. Tomorrow, in the light of day, that might all change. But she wasn't one to overanalyze things. She felt what she felt for now. Why question good feelings?

Tenderly, they finished undressing each other and shared more slow, soft, moist kisses. Creating their own Shangri-La in a room filled with angels. Drunk on his kisses, she let go and embraced the sensory assault of angels, and scents, lights and the taste of his salty skin and his peppermint tongue.

For now, they were in a snow globe world. An adorable town, far from home and their meddlesome family members, enrapt in the sweet paradise of each other's bodies. Their own little world.

And it was beautiful.

Once they were fully naked and pressed skin to skin, chest to breast, a pure, aching twinge bloomed between her thighs. Yearning for him. Desperate to have him inside her once more.

Her hands were hot against his taut belly.

Things got down and dirty quickly from there, spiraling out of control in a reassuring way. The best kind of way, in Aria's estimation. Swift and hot kept you from getting bogged down in doubt and worry. *Live in the moment.* The motto that had served her well for twenty-six years.

"Being with you is so damn much fun," he whispered. "More fun than skydiving."

"As much as you love skydiving, that's one hell of a compliment."

"I never knew how fun you were."

"Ditto."

"I thought you were flighty."

"And here I thought you were a stick-in-the-mud."

They grinned at each other as lights from the twinkling Christmas decorations fell across the bed in alternating patterns of color—red, green, blue, yellow, white.

"Here's to not judging a book by its cover," he murmured and, burrowing underneath the covers, found a hot spot.

"Moly holy, Lockhart," she said, so thrown she transposed her words. "What are you doing down there?"

"Settle back and enjoy the ride," he mumbled against her skin.

No one had to tell her twice. Enjoying the ride was her forte.

His tongue did some wild thing between her thighs, and she just melted right into the pillow, her whole body warm and pliable.

Remington took his work very seriously, she discovered. There was something to be said for a studious man on a mission. Especially when her pleasure was the mission.

He rocked her world until every cell in her body was quivering and vibrating and then it was her turn to rock his. He collapsed on the pillow beside her, breathing hard, and she took her place between his thighs.

Instantly, he tensed.

"Relax, big guy."

"How do you know I'm not relaxed?"

"You're always tense."

"*Always* is a sweeping statement. No one is always anything."

"Okay, you're too tense ninety-five percent of the time. Like now."

"Maybe you're too relaxed—ever thought about that?"

"That's very likely," she said good-humoredly. "But you're no longer on the battlefield. You can let down your guard and it will be okay."

There was no reason to argue. She *was* laid-back. She was not gonna lie and pretend she wasn't. Remington was good at keeping her on-target, and that was one of the things she loved about him . . .

Loved?

Okay, wait, wait. Back up the dump truck.

She didn't mean *loved,* loved. She loved him the way she loved homemade peach ice cream and Granny Blue's fry bread. She loved him like fall sweaters and amusement park roller coasters. Like her seventy-two-piece set of pastel pencils and high school football tailgating parties.

Oh crap, she *was* falling in love with him.

Yipes!

It's just that stupid humming that's got you rattled. She and Remington would never work out. Not long-term anyway, and she knew it. They were the proverbial oil and water. Don't even try to mix them.

But here and now, well, wow. What they had going on was nine kinds of spectacular.

She should be panicking right now, but she wasn't. She felt what she felt. And there was no way in Hello Kitty she was going to tell him about it. He'd start reading things into it and mulling things over and searching for backup plans.

"Hey," he murmured, pulling her up to him and tilting her chin with his hand so she had to look into his eyes. "Are you okay?"

"Sure, fine, great. Why wouldn't I be?"

"You seem"—he paused as if searching for the right word—"pensive. Which isn't you."

"No one is *always* anything, right? Sometimes shallow girls can be pensive."

"You're not shallow, Aria." He rubbed her cheek with his knuckle. "I used to think you were, but that's before I understood you."

"Oh ho, so you understand me now?" she challenged.

"I think I do." His smile was as comforting as cool shade on a hot sunny day.

"Stuck with me a few days and you've already sized me up."

"You're a butterfly," he said. "Flying around looking pretty and brightening everyone's life. But like a butterfly, you're so much more than that."

Aww, he was being poetic. *Be still my heart.*

"Butterflies pollinate flowers and help plants grow. You're like that. Encouraging. Optimistic. Opening hearts and minds wherever you go. People love being around you. *I* love being around you."

Aria caught her breath. She shifted until she was sitting cross-legged on the mattress beside him, staring deeply into his eyes. She traced a finger over his lips, listening to the sweet humming in her head.

The shine in his dark eyes rocked her soul. The kindness of his words, the look of genuine appreciation on his face heated her skin, burnished her heart. He splayed his palm over her heart, the warmth of him seeping down deep below her skin.

Goose bumps spread over her skin, and she giggled nervously, overwhelmed by him.

"God," he said, reaching up to curl a lock of her hair around his index finger. "I love to hear you laugh. It's the best sound in the world."

"Oh no. You have a much better laugh than I do, and it's made even better by the fact you use it sparingly."

"I'm not sure my family would agree."

"Who cares what they think? It's just you and me here, Lockhart."

"So it is, Alzate." He smiled at her in the dim lighting and she smiled back and soon they returned to the fevered pitch they were at before the lull in their lovemaking.

They got busy exploring. They tickled and teased. All kinds of love games. Used tongues and fingers. Lips and teeth. Used firm pressure and featherlight touches.

He kissed her body from the top of her head to the tips of her toes. Sending hot signals of excitement blasting through her. She bit lightly the sensitive skin on the underside of his arm, and he shuddered hard.

He licked the back of her knee. She ran her tongue over his collarbone.

They massaged and fondled, squeezed and tantalized until they had both reached a frenzied apex, sweating and panting and craving bone-deep release.

His thumbs brushed her nipples and she let out a desperate moan. Incredible!

She was staggered, stunned, swept away. "Please," she begged. "Please, Remy."

"Please what?"

"I've gotta have you or I'm gonna lose my ever-loving mind," she rasped.

"You ready for this?"

"I've been ready since Armadillo."

He laughed and pulled her on top of him, her legs tucked around his waist, her torso leaning over his. Their noses touched until they were cross-eyed.

She was revved and ready for him. So ready. Slick and slippery, sliding easily over his rock-hard shaft, merging her body with his.

"Aria." He gasped as she moved over him.

She glanced down. At the gorgeous man under her. She was in control. He was letting her be in charge. A butterfly flitting over the iron warrior, and he stared at her with adoring eyes, as if she was the most incredible thing that had ever existed in the history of the universe.

That was a heady feeling. His rapt attention.

My man, she thought greedily. *Mine.*

At least for tonight.

Being with him was like the high point of a wedding, the best part where the officiant looked into the eyes of the bride and groom and asked if they vowed to honor each other for all the days of their lives.

She always lost her breath at that point. When two people did the most intimate thing that they could do fully clothed, pledge their troth in front of their loved ones.

But this here? This was the most intimate thing people could do naked, and boy were they having fun.

She quickened her pace rocking against him with every bit of energy she possessed. Remington groaned and settled his hands on her waist, thrusting deeper inside her.

Throwing back his head, his dark hair spilling over the blanket shiny as oil, exposing his throat twinkling red in the glow of the Christmas lights. She moved against him, floating and wobbling in a sweet steady rhythm.

Her legs were rubber. Her breath raw and raspy.

Remington lifted his head, took hold of her neck and angled her forward so he could capture her mouth and kiss her so hard she couldn't think.

Then he reached out to brush her beaded nipples with his fingers, driving her around the bend. And when he put his hot mouth there and added more pressure, she thought she just might lose her mind.

The heat kicked on, adding more sweat to the process until it felt like the tropics and they were slippery as eels. The Christmas lights bathed them in a carousel of lights. Somewhere far, from outside the window, she heard the faint notes of "O Holy Night."

He rocked his hips in time to her movements. She stared into his eyes, got lost in those chocolate depths.

His thrusts quickened, taking her higher and faster to a place she'd never been before. A whole new stratosphere. Visiting the International Space Station couldn't be this exotic and exciting.

He filled her up, made her whole, and just before she was about to lose it, he said, "My turn on top." He held her tight around the waist and in one smooth motion, flipped her over, all the while staying fully connected to her.

Remington slowed everything down. It was maddening, but wildly effective, making her want him more than she ever thought possible.

His self-assurance took her breath away. The man knew what he was doing. Their bodies undulating in a writhing rhythm as if dancing to unheard music. As he kissed her, their souls tied, bound, connected just as surely as their bodies.

Every nerve in her body was on fire as he drove her closer and closer to the edge. She thrashed against him, so badly wanting what his body had been promising for an hour.

His movements quickened. From slow to staccato, thrusting into her deeper, higher, faster. He was on a mission. Focused and trained. Primal and guttural. But no more primal than she.

Remington guided her legs over her head, opening her wide, entering her as deeply as possible, driving her relentlessly to oblivion.

"More," she cried. "More, more, more."

"Your wish is my command."

"Harder," she gasped. "Faster, faster. I'm almost there."

Slow and leisurely was over. He was moving at warp speed now, thumping into her with a vigorous intensity that stole every last ounce of control from her.

And all she knew was humming.

She tasted it. Smelled it. Felt it. Heard it. Touched it. It was honey and treacle. Sticky and loud. It felt like the past slamming into the future and centered hard on the here and now.

They spun, twisted, turned, lost in the whirl of magic and passion, ensnared by mythology, lore, and the recklessness of amazing sex.

The orgasm was upon them both at once. His noises were as rough and husky as her own. Their bodies jerked in unison.

And as they fell together, they cried each other's names over and over. And as she lay in Remington's arms, Aria silently gave thanks for the Merry Cherub B and B and the whimsical magic of Christmas in Twilight.

"YOU NEVER TOLD me how you lost your fingers," Aria said sometime later when they could breathe again. "You started when we were in Armadillo but we got sidetracked."

Remington felt his body stiffen. It was a topic he avoided, and he didn't want to take the shine off the moment by talking about his stupid hand.

But Aria had that determined set to her chin, the same one she'd had when she'd jumped out of his SUV to go help that family stranded on the road. The chin set that said he would not dissuade her.

"It was a HALO jump," she said. "That's as far as you got before."

He closed his eyes and he was back in that plane, on the night he shouldn't have been there without a solid backup plan. He fisted the three remaining fingers of his left hand as if he could protect them from the memory.

Aria curled against him, and he could feel her hair tickling his chest. He didn't owe her an explanation, but he wanted her to know, to understand him a little better.

But why? Wasn't that whacked? Shouldn't he be distancing himself from her right now, not digging in deeper? Protecting his heart from getting sucked in by the tender feelings churning inside him. They weren't a long-term match. Not a forever kind of fit. He knew that, and yet and yet . . .

"HALO jump, night run, dangerous as hell," he said. "My day off, but someone got sick and I volunteered to take his place. We had intel on insurgents gathering forces in the mountain range that borders Pakistan. Our mission was simply, get in, neutralize the targets, and get out."

She didn't speak, instead stroked his chest hairs as if petting an agitated animal. Which maybe he was.

"The first chute didn't open," he said through clenched teeth. "And it got tangled up in the lines of the second chute. I reached up to untangle it and the last two fingers of my left hand got caught in the line and then the second chute didn't open."

"Oh no, you don't have to say any more!" She plastered her palms over her ears and her eyes rounded to saucers. "I get the picture. But what kept you from hitting the ground entirely? Why are you even alive?"

"I landed in a pine tree. At the last minute the second chute deployed, but too late for a proper landing." He rubbed the stump where his missing fingers used to be, felt the pain all over again. But the physical pain had been the least of it. Mental wounds were much tougher to heal, but he was working on it.

His dream? To open a retreat on the Silver Feather, where former military members who were struggling with PTSD could come for a place to heal—horses, fresh air, bodywork, yoga, tai chi, meditation. He was a long way off from that goal, but it's what he wanted to do with the rest of his life.

He told Aria about it, mainly because he didn't want to keep talking about his injury. It was over and done with. He'd had therapy, both physical and mental, and while healing was an ongoing process, he felt that sometimes too much talking could keep you trapped in the pain. Action. That's what had helped Remington the most.

"Remy, that's an amazing idea about the retreat." She hugged him around the waist. "You should totally do it."

Her enthusiasm warmed him. He'd broached the idea with his old man, but Duke had scoffed and said something about whiny, candy-ass millennials always needing their hands held. His harsh, controlling father was the reason Remington left Cupid twelve years ago and had stayed away except for those big family events like weddings and funerals and births of babies until the Army booted him on a medical discharge.

But he'd learned a few things since he'd been away. Mainly that life was short, and he would not let a petty tyrant direct his future. Duke was who he was. Remington's mistake had been in telling his father about the retreat idea. His grandfather had left him land and a substantial trust. He didn't need his father's permission.

"You'll be so good at that. You are so patient and empathetic."

"Me?"

"Yes, *you.*" She tickled his chin. "You have such a big heart, although you try to hide it through all that gruffness."

His heart felt dangerously mushy.

The feelings scared him right down to his bones. He'd been in love before and Maggie had crucified him. With her, he'd let himself be vulnerable, and then she'd betrayed him in the most fundamental way, having an affair with his best friend when he was overseas. Yep, he was a cliché.

He'd been attracted to Maggie for her optimistic, bubbly nature. But she was too sunny for him. When she'd called to tell him that she'd had an affair with Joey, she'd told him she couldn't stand being alone, that she needed care and attention that he just couldn't give.

He'd dodged a bullet. Last he'd heard, Maggie was on husband number three. But that didn't mean it hadn't hurt like hell when she'd cheated on him.

Aria reminded him of Maggie in a lot of ways, both of them irrepressible and vivacious. Was that what appealed to him about her? Aria, like Maggie, balanced out his broody nature?

But like Maggie, Aria was also fickle. Jumping from one interest to the next. One guy to the next. Not making backup plans. As far as he knew, Aria had never had a serious relationship and she was in her midtwenties. Was it the capriciousness of youth, or a serious flaw in her character?

It's not fair to paint her with the same brush as your ex.

"Remy," she murmured.

"Yes?"

"I want you to know this time with you has been really special."

"It has for me too." His throat tightened and he felt a heaviness in his chest. Aww hell, what was this?

"I'm going to miss this when things go back to normal."

He stroked her hair with his palm. There were so many things he wanted to say to her. Tell her that he didn't want things to go back to normal. That he wanted their relationship to continue. He opened his mouth to say the words but then she said . . .

"Good thing you're the kind of guy who knows how to compartmentalize."

"Um . . . good thing," he echoed.

"Neither one of us are the kind to get sentimental over sex. It's just fun."

"Fun," he echoed.

"Could you imagine the two of us in a real relationship?" She laughed as she drew circles on his chest.

"Not even."

"Me either."

"But we sure know how to have a great time together."

"We do."

The feelings pushing up from his heart stalled in his throat. He wanted so badly to tell her how much he admired her. How, whenever she was around, the world seemed like a much nicer place. How impressed he was by her spontaneity and flexibility. He respected her idealism and her commitment to making the world a better place. He loved how she didn't let setbacks and disappointments get her down. Loved her free spirit and how much she enjoyed life.

How he loved being with her.

But Remington said none of those things. He knew he wasn't right for her. Knew his pessimism, rigidity, and adherence to the rules would only, over time, dim her bright light. And he wasn't about to do anything that could wipe the shine off this beautiful butterfly.

Knowing he simply wasn't good enough for her, he wrapped his arms around her, kissed her again, and made love to her one last time.

CHAPTER 19

Clutch: Slang for the "cut-away release handle," which disconnects a malfunctioning main canopy by the simultaneous release of the riser connections to the harness.

At dawn, Aria woke with a strange feeling in the pit of her stomach. Wedding days were always stressful, but there was something about today that had her feeling especially uneasy. She was pretty good at blowing off unsettling emotions, but a weird dread clung to her.

What was this all about?

It hit her then, when she realized the spot beside her in the bed was empty, what was causing her gloomy mood. Once the wedding was over, she and Remington would go back to their separate lives. No more road trysts. No more late-night spill sessions. No more fun adventures with him.

The Taylor Swift song "Shake It Off" filled her brain.

"Up and at 'em, woman," Remington called to her from the bedroom floor, where he was doing push-ups. "It's wedding day."

Oh, there he was. He hadn't run out on her.

"What are you doing?" Groggily, she peered over the end of the bed at him.

"Besides a short run in the park, I haven't worked out since we left Cupid. I need to burn off some energy."

"Didn't we do that last night?" She laughed and swung out of bed.

"We did, but I need a structured workout."

"Come with me this morning and I'll give you all the workout you need." She pushed her hair from her eyes. "But first, coffee. I need coffee."

"I already brought up a carafe from the kitchen." He nodded at the dresser. "Pastries too."

"My, aren't you Mr. Efficient?" She made a beeline for the carafe. "You light up my life, Lockhart."

"Stick with me, babe, you'll never have to get your own coffee again." He finished his push-ups, stood, and dusted off his palms.

Their eyes met.

She wore nothing but a T-shirt and panties—his T-shirt, actually. He wore Wranglers and a snap-down blue western shirt that set off his tanned complexion.

Aria felt utterly naked.

Remington licked his lips.

"We have no time," she whispered.

"I know." But he kissed her, and her toes tingled and her mind looped.

He poured her a cup of coffee, with lots of cream and sugar, just the way she liked it and wrapped a paper napkin around a bear claw and handed it to her.

"You are a blessing," she announced, perching at the little table near the window that had a view of the lake. But even the coffee, pastry, and Remington sitting beside her at the table couldn't dispel this nagging feeling that something wasn't right.

She turned on her phone to check her messages and there it was . . . a text from Caitlyn Garza at three-thirty in the morning.

CAITLYN: So sorry to bail on you, but Danny's condition worsened during the night and they transferred him from the university infirmary to Presbyterian Hospital. Gideon and I took off for Dallas to be with him. Of course, I will refund all of Olivia's money.

"Oh no." Aria's hand flew to her throat.

"What is it?" Remington asked, leaning across the table.

She showed him her phone with the text. "Caitlyn and Gideon's son's condition has worsened. They're in Dallas."

"The florist?"

"Yes, but please don't say it."

"Say what?" Remington arched his eyebrows.

Aria's bottom lip trembled. "That I should have had a backup plan."

Remington shrugged, but he had the good grace not to gloat.

Aria punched in Caitlyn's cell phone number.

Caitlyn answered on the second ring. "Oh, Aria, I am so deeply sorry to bail on you."

Aria tried her best to keep her disappointment out of her voice. There were more important things than weddings. "No apologies necessary. Your son comes first. I'm just calling to see how Danny is doing."

"He has meningitis." Caitlyn said it matter-of-factly, as if she had to get the words out quick before fear took hold of her and she couldn't speak at all.

Aria sucked in her breath. "Oh my gosh, that's terrible. I am so sorry, Caitlyn."

"Th-thank you."

Aria could hear the tears in Caitlyn's voice. "You must be so scared."

"Terrified." Caitlyn hauled in a deep breath as if to steady herself. "But luckily, it's viral meningitis and not bacterial like they first feared."

Aria splayed a palm to her chest. "Thank heavens for that. It could have been so much worse."

"Yes," Caitlyn said. "We could have lost him. Viral meningitis is far less serious—it usually clears up on its own in seven to ten days. Bacterial meningitis is much more dangerous and faster moving. It's the one that can be fatal if you don't get antibiotics quickly enough."

"I thought you said yesterday that the doctor suspected mono."

"Initially Danny's symptoms presented as mono, but when his bloodwork for that diagnosis came back clear, they kept testing."

"I'll say a prayer for you guys."

"Thank you. I do hate that we left you high and dry."

"No worries, really," Aria said, and meant it. "You take care of Danny. We'll figure everything out over here."

"Christine at the bakery has a key to the flower shop. She knows what's going on, and she'll let you in so you can get the flowers."

Whew. That was something, even though Gideon and Caitlyn were already supposed to have the wedding hall decorated at six A.M. This meant she had to get the flowers from the shop to the venue and decorate it in five hours.

"And honestly," Caitlyn said. "We'll reimburse Olivia for the cost of the flowers and decorations."

"How about we wait on that?" Aria said. "If I can pull this off, Olivia and Ben never need know we had this little glitch."

"I—"

"Just leave it to me," Aria assured her. She switched off the phone to find Remington watching her.

"Well?" he asked.

Aria blew out her breath. "Danny will be okay. Christine can let us into the flower shop to get the flowers, but we're short on time. We need to roll *now*."

DAMMIT. HE SHOULD have insisted she make a backup plan when he'd gotten those tingly spidey-sense vibes about the Garzas yesterday. But Remington would not tell her, *I told you so.* She was suffering the consequences of not having a backup plan. Let her learn on her own.

Now it was time for him to be a good friend, roll up his sleeves, and get to work. "Don't worry, Zippy. I've got your back."

Hurriedly, she dressed in leggings and a festive red-and-green tunic top and brought along a cocktail dress to change into for the wedding. They raced to his Escalade that he'd already started with a remote starter so it could warm up before they got inside. A toasty blast of warm air greeted them as they climbed inside.

"Trust you to think of everything." She grinned.

"We're headed to the bakery to get the key to the flower shop?" he asked.

"No, go straight to the convention center."

"But what about the flowers?"

"Taken care of."

"What? How?"

A sly smile curled her lips. "*My* version of a backup plan."

Puzzled, he pulled into the convention center parking lot to find several people huddled outside the door, among them some members of the wedding party, including Roger and Gary, plus Joel Mac-Gregor, and a funky chick in biker clothes, hobnail boots, and a plethora of tattoos and piercings, who Aria said was named Jana.

In the parking lot sat the Garzas' delivery van.

"How did the van—"

"Shortcut," Aria explained. "I texted Jana and Joel to go after the flowers the second I got off the phone with Caitlyn."

Okay, she was fast on her feet, Remington would give her that, but rallying the troops last minute was not an adequate substitute for a backup plan. What if none of these people had been available or inclined to help on short notice?

"Let's do this thing," Aria said, holding out her fist for a fist bump.

"What? Oh." Remington bumped her fist and immediately felt that hot wash of chemistry the second their skin touched. *Damn*, but their physical connection was fierce.

Aria greeted everyone with a hug and a quick kiss on the cheek. She introduced him to the biker chick, and Jana eyeballed him as if he were a juicy cut of steak.

Amused, Remington noticed that amid Jana's eyeballing, Aria slipped her arm around his waist, sending the other woman a clear message, *he's mine, back off.*

But he wasn't hers, was he? Not long-term anyway.

Longing dragged through him, deep and slow. Remington shook his head, shook off the sudden image that popped into his head of him and Aria dancing at a wedding of their own. *Not happening, big guy. Don't even go there.*

To shift his thinking, Remington held out his hand for Aria to give him the key. She hesitated, but only for a whisper-second before dropping the key into his palm. He opened the double doors and pushed them wide for the group to enter the convention center.

Without even being told what to do, everyone went to work. Jana and Joel headed for the florist van to bring in flowers; Roger, Gary, and four other people went to pull the upturned chairs from the tabletops and settle them onto the floor. Seeing how much work they had in front of them, even with eight helpers, Remington's gut tripped over itself. If Aria pulled this off, it would be a miracle.

But he shouldn't have worried.

Ten minutes after they'd started, five more people showed up. Aria directed everyone, delegating like the pro she was. Within thirty minutes, her workers had removed the tables from the room and arranged the chairs in structured rows that faced the big picture window overlooking the lake.

While one half of the group went to decorate the reception hall, Aria instructed the helpers in the makeshift chapel to put slipcovers over the chairs and erect a dais that would serve as the altar for Olivia and Ben to take their vows.

She seemed in her element, rising to the challenge with a smile on her face and a kind word for everyone. The stress of the situation seemed to whet her work ethic and light a fire under her. She buzzed around, directing, guiding, and offering suggestions, all in an encouraging manner and upbeat spirit.

And people eagerly jumped to help.

To bolster the mood, she hooked her phone to the speaker system and soon everyone was bopping to up-tempo Christmas music as they worked. Then she called Christine and had her send over pastries and coffee for everyone. Most impressive of all, Christine did Aria's bidding—and for free!

For the first time, Remington understood why Aria didn't bother with backup plans. With her people skills, she didn't need them. People fell all over themselves to help her out of a jam.

Wow, he thought, mesmerized. *Just wow.*

"Yo." Jana, in her noisy boots, marched over to Aria and Remington, who were helping put the covers on the chairs. "Glitch."

Aria straightened. "What's that?"

"The tablecloths Caitlyn was going to use for the reception hall are in the trunk of their car. I could send someone to Dallas after them, but it would take someone at least four hours to get there and back, and that'll be too late."

Aria chewed on that news a minute. "I could send someone to buy some, I suppose."

"Do you have the budget for that?" Remington asked.

"No."

"You know," Jana said, "I work part-time at the Twilight Playhouse."

Remington had seen the local historic theater on the square the previous day when they'd been out walking around. The theater was a short distance from the convention center.

"I got a key to the prop room," Jana added, pulling a key from her pocket and dangling it from her index finger. "And I'm one hundred percent sure Emma won't mind if we raid it." To Remington, she said, "The owner of the playhouse is retired actress Emma Parks, although she's Emma Cheek now."

"Really?" Remington was impressed.

Aria nodded. "Thanks, Jana. Great idea. Text Emma for permission, and let's go see what we can find."

"On it." Jana took out her phone. A few minutes later, she gave Aria a thumbs-up.

Remington, Jana, and Aria walked the two blocks to the Twilight Playhouse. The wind coming off the lake was chilly. Remington pulled up the collar of his coat and positioned himself on the outside of the two women so that he was closest to the water, using his big body to help block the chill from them.

The Twilight Playhouse, like everything on the town square, had been built in the late 1800s out of limestone. The posters outside announced that *How the Grinch Stole Christmas* was the scheduled play for that holiday season with Lauren Cheek playing Cindy Lou Who. Today the show times were at two and eight P.M. At this early hour of the morning, no one was about.

"Lauren is Emma's daughter?" Remington nodded at the poster as Jana let them into the theater.

Jana grinned over her shoulder at Aria. "He's not just a pretty face. Better latch on to this one, girlfriend."

He couldn't decide if she was making fun of him or not. But Aria surprised Remington by slipping her arm though his and burrowing closer.

Laughing, Jana led them through the lobby to a side hallway and backstage. The prop room was jammed with costumes, props, and sets. Luckily, it was well organized.

"What specifically are we looking for?" Remington asked, staring at the rows and rows of shelving, racks, and boxes.

"Something to turn into tablecloths," Aria said, diving in.

Remington rubbed his temple, feeling a headache coming on. Time was of the essence and they were wasting it digging through a prop—

"Oh my, look!" Aria exclaimed, opening up a wardrobe stacked with linens. "Jackpot."

Stunned, Remington stared openmouthed. Unbelievable. The woman had some kind of magic touch that whatever she did just somehow worked out for her. Yeah, now he got why she thought backup plans weren't worth the trouble, but not everyone was magical.

She started pulling linens from the wardrobe. "Hold out your arms," she said, loading him down with blue and white sheets.

He eyed the sheets skeptically. Okay, these were makeshift table-cloths, but honestly, they *looked* makeshift, thin and of poor quality. He couldn't see how these paltry sheets could make an acceptable substitute for nice tablecloths and he said as much.

Jana laughed. "O ye of little faith. Hide, and watch the master at work, dude."

Aria reached up to pat his cheek. "You gotta trust in the miracle of Twilight."

Remington grunted.

"Trusting isn't his long suit," Aria told Jana. "But he's still cute."

"I'll say." Jana eyeballed him and licked her lips.

Remington cleared his throat. "Excuse me. I'm standing right here."

"Yes, you are. Now get a move on. We've got a wedding to decorate for and less than four hours to make magic happen." Aria tossed her head, her long dark ponytail bouncing as she led Remington and Jana, weighted down with sheets, back to the convention center.

Once they were in the reception hall and they put the sheets on the tables, Remington's skepticism ratcheted to the ceiling.

Aria had draped the sheets over the tables, but the tables were round, and the sheets were oblong. Plus, having some sheets white and the others blue looked wonky.

He wrinkled his nose. "I dunno about this."

She laughed at him again. "I'm just getting started. We'll be layering everything to create a winter wonderland." The woman had more optimism than sunshine, but it was going to take a lot more than thin sheets to transform this mess into a wonderland.

Time for him to take charge and come up with a real backup plan.

"I need to borrow Roger and Gary," he told her.

She paused in her work, looked up. "What for?"

"I'm going to help you fix this thing."

"Don't worry. It really is gonna be okay. I promise."

"It'll be even more okay when I get back." He motioned toward the groomsmen. "Roger, Gary, you're with me."

They looked surprised but trotted over.

"Where are you going?" Aria asked.

"Store."

"But I don't have the budg—"

"I'm paying."

"I can't let—"

"No time to argue." He pulled the Escalade's key fob from his pocket. "Fellas," he said to Roger and Gary, "let's roll."

BEFORE SHE'D GONE on this trip with Remington, Aria would have been offended at the high-handed way he'd just taken over, but honest to Pete, was she grateful that he'd intervened? Relentless optimism would only get you so far, and she'd been really sweating the sheet situation. All she felt was relief.

"I'm telling you," Jana said, watching Remington's backside as he walked out the door. "You better lock that down or someone else will."

"Back off," Aria said in an amicable voice. "He's with me."

At least for the time being.

"Lucky dog." Jana shook her head good-naturedly.

"Let's get back to these sheets," Aria said. "If we put the white sheets down first, then layer a blue sheet on top, pinned them like this . . ." She pleated the sheet on the table nearest her into a scallop. "We can make this work."

Jana stepped back, inclined her head. "Yeah, I see what you mean. Let me get the staple gun, and I'll get after it."

Together, Aria and Jana got the twenty tables swathed and draped with sheets.

"Not bad," Jana said when they'd finished. "But it looks more like something for a casual luncheon that a wedding reception. We're missing the *oomph* factor of Caitlyn's satin tablecloths."

"Never fear," Remington said as he walked through the door carrying as many sacks as he could fit on his arms. Roger and Gary, trailing behind him, were similarly overloaded.

"What did you get?" Curious, Aria came over to dig through the treasures.

He'd purchased boxes and boxes of wireless Christmas lights, giant white glass snowflakes, blue tinsel, white garlands, pinecones decorated white and blue, and twenty white poinsettias in pots wrapped with festive blue foil.

"This is too much," she said, taken aback by what he'd done for her. "It all costs too much."

"You forget." He lowered his voice so only she could hear. "I'm rich, and I have no one to spend my fortune on. Let me do this for you, Aria."

"Why are you doing this?"

"Maybe because you loved the grinch out of me last night," he murmured, a teasing glow in his eyes.

"B-but I screwed up. I didn't have a backup plan. Why would you save someone who needs to take her lumps for not having a backup plan?"

"You *did* have a backup plan," he corrected

Confused, she shook her head. "What backup plan was that?"

He gave her a lopsided grin that warmed her all the way to her toes. "Me."

She laughed. Having him on her side was a great backup plan. "Okay, thank you. This is so sweet. No matter how hard you try to deny it, Remington Lockhart, you are a real hero." Then she went up on tiptoes and kissed him right in front of everyone.

"It's nothing," he mumbled, and ducked his head, but not before she saw a telltale blush rush up his neck. Her praise had pleased him. "Now, c'mon, I can't wait to see your winter wonderland."

With everyone pitching in, they got the wedding venue and the reception hall decorated with an hour and a half to spare before the ceremony. Just enough time for the wedding party to go home and change and return for the wedding.

Everyone scattered, leaving Aria and Remington alone as she went through one final once-over. The ballroom where the wedding was to be held was draped in flowers, ribbon and bows, a red carpet rolled out, ready for the flower girl to strew it with white rose petals.

She stood looking at the dais, where Olivia and Ben would take their vows with the lake in the background. Her heart was full of gratitude.

Remington came over to rest a hand on her shoulder.

"Everything looks great," he said. "I just wish I'd had time to carve Olivia and Ben a real wedding arch. It would have really been special."

Aria stepped back and gave him a sidelong glance. "You know how to do woodworking?"

"It's my hobby. You didn't know that about me?"

She shook her head.

"I made that wooden bench in the foyer at Dad and Vivi's house."

"Really? I love that thing. You could have made an awesome wedding arch."

"Yes," he said. "Something simple but strong."

"No, no," she said. "This is a wedding. A wedding arch needs to be as special as the people getting married. They need something whimsical and magical."

"I disagree. A wedding arch isn't much good if it collapses. It needs to be sturdy and functional. *That's* what matters."

"Well, now I'm glad you didn't make a wedding arch. We would have ended up in a big fight over it." Her laugh came out high-pitched and skittish.

"Apparently."

"I killed the moment, didn't I?" she murmured.

Remington shook his head. "Or I did."

She sent him a soft forgiving smile. "Let's forget about the wedding arch."

He smiled back. "Sure."

But how could she forget the arch when it represented the reason that they were not a good match? She ached for magic and whimsy and hope. While he was a stone-cold realist, who valued function over form.

"You did it," he murmured, settling an arm around her waist. "You pulled off a miracle *and* without a backup plan."

She leaned against him. "*We* did it, and *you* were the backup plan, remember? Seriously, I could not have made this happen without you. And you're right. I need to think more about making backup plans in future."

"You keep doing what you do, Aria. You don't have to be like me."

"Hello?" She playfully knocked her fist against his forehead. "Is that really Remington Lockhart inside there?"

"Oh my God!" said a voice from behind them.

In unison they turned to see Olivia standing in the doorway, in her wedding dress, her hands clutched to her mouth and tears in her eyes.

Startled and a little terrified at Olivia's reaction, Aria ran to her friend, trying not to think the worst. Had Ben broken up with her?

"What is it?" Aria asked, clasping Olivia by the shoulders.

"You've made me cry." Olivia flapped her hands in front of her face as if trying to shoo away the tears. "I can't cry in this makeup. I'll get mascara all over."

Anxiety twisted Aria's spine. "Why are you crying?"

"After Jyl heard that Caitlyn and Gideon took off for Dallas in the middle of the night, I just knew the wedding was ruined. I tried not to be a big old selfish bridezilla, but it terrified me. It took everything I had in me to stay away from here and trust you'd figure it all out, but—"

"I told her to trust you," said Olivia's mother who came up behind her daughter. "I said Aria might seem flighty, but that's just because she's a creative visionary. She won't let you down."

Was she flighty? Aria didn't like to think of herself that way. She darted a glance over at Remington, who'd come up beside her. She knew he thought she was too impulsive . . . Maybe he was right, maybe she was.

Olivia walked around the room taking it all in. "It's even better than your original vision! If this is your makeshift attempt, you should abandon all plans and always fly by the seat of your pants."

Aria shook her head. She knew this whole thing had only worked out because of Remington and the others who'd pitched in to make it happen.

"I'm so glad you like it." Aria clasped her hands to her chest.

"I don't like it, silly. I *love* it. This is exactly what I imagined when I hired you to plan my Christmas wedding. It is beyond our expectations," Olivia said. "You thrive on chaos, my friend. You do your best work under pressure. Do you remember in college when you'd wait till the last minute to study, and you'd invariably ace the test? I was so jealous of you."

"You're welcome, but honestly, Remington was a big part of why this turned out so well." She touched his arm and smiled at him.

Olivia thanked Remington and shook his hand. "Don't let her get away. She's something special."

"That she is," Remington said, looking at Aria as if she were his favorite flavor of ice cream and he couldn't wait to eat her up.

A thrill shot through Aria and she was so confused. Last night they'd sworn to each other their relationship was just a fling, but standing here, with Remington watching her like that, she realized she wanted so much more.

"I better be getting back to the bridesmaids and make sure that all is well there and let you go get changed," Olivia said.

"Yes." Aria touched her friend's shoulder. "The next time I see you, you'll be walking down the aisle."

"One last hug before I'm Mrs. Ben Mallory," Olivia said, then enveloped Aria in her sweet-smelling fragrance and hugged her fiercely. Then drifted out the door with her mother.

"Olivia's right," Remington said after they were alone again.

"About what?"

"You *are* something special. You took a boring room, created an amazing optical illusion, turning something ordinary into something magical."

"By the seat of my pants," she said.

"From what I've seen"—Remington shook his head ruefully, as if the realization was something painful—"that's part of *your* magic."

CHAPTER 20

Blue skies: A salutation among parachutists based upon a civilian interpretation of conditions for jumping.

The wedding went off without a hitch.

Olivia was a beautiful bride. Ben looked totally smitten. Everyone was on their best behavior. The food was to die for, and the cakes were beyond gorgeous. Aria got so many compliments, she was thinking Olivia was right. Maybe her creativity thrived on chaos.

When the DJ asked the guests at the wedding reception to welcome Mr. and Mrs. Benjamin Mallory to their first dance as husband and wife and "Uptown Funk" poured from the speakers, she peeked across the table at Remington. He grinned at her, sharing their private joke.

Remington, who looked stunning in a suit, started dancing in his chair to amuse her, and when the DJ invited people to join the bride and groom on the dance floor, Remington held out a hand to Aria.

He was asking her to dance?

She flew out of her chair, slipping her hand into his, shaking her booty in time to the music as he led her to the dance floor.

But they'd only danced a few steps when Joel cut in. Aria protested, but Remington turned her over to him and quickly bowed out.

What the heck? What was that about? Why had Remington let Joel cut in?

"I just had to dance with you," Joel said, leaning in to be heard over the loud music.

Oh no. Was Joel interested in her? She was trying to think of a diplomatic way out of the conversation when he said, "Do you think I have a shot with Jana?"

So much for her ego. Aria had to laugh at herself. Joel's question stoked the matchmaker inside her, and she was off, giving him tips on how to win Jana's heart.

After Joel, Roger cut in as the song changed over.

"Why aren't you dancing with Gary?" Aria asked.

"He hates dancing," Roger said. "No one has as much spunk as you, Aria. Your feet will get exhausted tonight. Get Remington to rub them for you."

She didn't bother telling him that Remington wouldn't be rubbing anything on her. That they weren't a couple, but someone tapped on Aria's shoulder. She turned, praying it was Remington coming back to cut in, but it was Ben who held out his arm to her. As they danced, he thanked her profusely for the beautiful wedding and making his bride so happy.

Olivia, who was dancing with her father, waved at Ben. He blew her a kiss. Aria's heart melted. God, she loved weddings!

And she loved her job creating weddings, but she was letting herself get swept up in the festivities and neglecting her duties. She needed to make sure everyone was having a good time. When the song ended, she gave Ben back to Olivia and went to coax people off the sidelines, encouraging them to find a partner and dance. Several people asked her to dance, but she laughed and smiled and kindly told them she had work to do.

Some folks were deep in conversation along the wall and at the tables, and she left them alone, but those who looked isolated or out of place, she herded them on the dance floor or introduced them to others, and soon everyone had someone they were talking to or dancing with.

She did one last turn around the room and there, in the far corner behind the DJ and the tower speakers, she saw him standing in the shadows watching her intently.

Remington.

She moved toward him shaking her head and waving at the dance floor.

A faint smile tipped his lips, but he didn't move to meet her half-way. Instead, letting her come to him.

Stepping over speaker wires as the DJ played the ubiquitous "YMCA," and almost the entire room was bouncing on the dance floor, she approached him.

"What are you doing way back over here by yourself?" she asked.

"Watching you."

"Oh?" she said lightly, but the feeling in the pit of her stomach was anything but light.

His eyes were shiny, and she wondered if he'd been drinking, but no, he seemed stone-cold sober.

"That dress"—he raked his gaze over her body—"is stunning."

Feeling self-conscious and not sure why, she ran a palm over the silky bodice of her emerald green bridesmaid dress, smoothing out imaginary wrinkles. That man could fry eggs with the heat of his stare.

"*You're* stunning."

"So are you," she said.

"It's fun watching you flit from group to group. As if they were all flowers and you were a butterfly, infusing them with your energy and brightening up the whole room. You're electric."

She felt her cheeks flush. "Just doing my job."

"You're not. You're making people happy. You go straight for the folks who seem awkward, shy, or isolated and you draw them out of their shells. It takes a special talent to do that, Aria. You're special."

"Because I'm the queen of optical illusions?"

"What?" He blinked.

"Earlier today you said I took a boring room and created an optical illusion."

"I meant that as a compliment."

"Did you?"

Remington looked sad. "I know I have a reputation as being a crusty son of a bi—" He paused when she frowned at him and finished with, "Biscuit eater, but Aria, I love what you've done. I love how you can take something ordinary and make it extra-ordinary."

Love?

Her heart beat faster. *Calm down. He said he loved your skills, not you.*

That thought produced so many crazy feelings inside she had to shake them off. "You're giving me way too much credit."

"How so? Look around. You created *this*."

His praise warmed her like a fire, but she couldn't get too used to it or the look in his dark eyes. "It's a wedding. People feel lively and inclined to have fun at weddings. I just give the reluctant ones a little push to get them started."

"That's it?" He raised his eyebrows.

"It doesn't take much. Good music, wine, a celebration, and it's a party."

"Life with you must feel like one giant party," he murmured, but it was as if he was speaking more to himself than to her. "I don't know how—"

The song switched to "Shut Up and Dance with Me."

Aria took his arm and said firmly, "Shut up and dance with me, Lockhart."

Shaking his head and grinning, he didn't resist. Prancing like a pony, she guided him onto the dance floor to join the wriggling couples. Eyes on only each other, they danced with every ounce of daring and flair they had in them.

"Up for a waltz?" she asked as the DJ started the song she'd requested him to add to the playlist. "Crazy Love."

He looked at her with such tenderness in that moment, Aria thought her heart cracked just a little.

Remington held out his arms, and she slid right into them like hot butter. As if she'd always belonged there. He wrapped his arm around her waist and waltzed her around the floor.

Everyone else ceased to exist.

They were all alone, just the two of them, twirling in time to Van Morrison softly crooning, "Crazy Love."

Yes. This was crazy to think the feeling she was having for Remington could turn into long-term love. It was a road trip romance. Nothing more. She knew that and yet, and yet . . .

He gathered her closer, holding her hands in his. She craned her neck to look up at him. He lowered his head. He didn't kiss her, but his mouth hovered so close. A promise of a kiss. Her body ached for him, head to toe.

He was not a man who willingly embraced public displays of affection, and she was the wedding planner who adored PDA. She should be more circumspect, but how she wanted him to kiss her!

Her nerve endings tingled, yearning, longing, buzzing with need . . .

For *him*.

Here in his arms, the reception hall was a magical winter wonderland—the twinkly lights, the couples swaying in each other's arms, the lake glistening coolly in the distance through the window. They could be in some romantic movie where two opposites attracted, and enemies could become lovers.

Yes, all that made great fodder for romantic fantasies, but in reality? It was the people who were alike that made it. Couples who shared values and goals and similar dreams. Couples who were so much like each other that they didn't argue over every little thing, because generally they agreed on what was really important.

It was a sound theory. Made total sense.

Except, she couldn't help thinking about the couples she'd met in Armadillo. Pat and Audra, Hank and Helen, Andre and Tanya.

They'd all claimed they were different as night and day. Their theory had been that you had to find the right person. That everything else could be overcome if you found The One.

As she stared into Remington's eyes, listening to "Crazy Love," they stopped dancing. Just stood in the middle of the dance floor absorbed with each other. Without even kissing him, she heard the humming. The low, slow buzz that gradually gathered in intensity until the sound filled her head with a steady, rhythmic chant.

He's The One, The One, The One.

It would be so easy to fall for the myth, embrace the legend that there was one right person for you and when you found that person, you should hold on with both hands and never, ever let go.

"You know what," he whispered, lowering his head so that his lips brushed against her ear.

The humming was like wildfire now, spreading throughout her body until every cell inside her vibrated with the strum.

"What?" Her chest tightened with anticipation, eager to hear what he might say. Was he going to tell her he loved her? That all this time he'd been loving her from afar? That he wanted her more than he wanted to breathe. That he'd give up everything for her. Throw away all the backup plans in the world for her.

Don't, she told herself. *Just don't.*

But try as she might, she could not quell the hope that maybe, just maybe, they could find their way through their differences and—

"Our whole trip has been just like this room," he murmured.

Huh? She blinked. He was not saying what she wanted to hear, but she gave him an endearing smile anyway. Smiling. Lightheartedness. Her defense mechanism. Sure. It's all good.

"How's that?" she asked cautiously, not sure she wanted to hear his answer.

"You took something ordinary and made it extraordinary."

Yes, yes, he covered this already. What was this new point? She saw it in his eyes. A wistful longing for things that could never be, and terror struck her.

"We made something extraordinary," she corrected.

"*We*"—he paused, pulled his head back to peer into her eyes again—"created a romantic mirage. But just like this room, tomorrow the magic will be over, and things will go back to normal."

"Normal," she repeated past the lump in her throat.

The humming was receding, taking the full body tingles with it, and where she'd once had a heart, it felt like a gaping hole. She'd been spinning romantic fantasies about a man who was still too wounded to believe in the magic of long and lasting love. She thought he'd made a lot of progress in the art class when he'd drawn his hand, but she was expecting too much of him. He was right. She couldn't fix everything with twinkle lights and tinsel.

"Aria." His voice was gravelly with emotion. "It's been so much fun living in a fantasy with you."

"You too." It was all she could force out, felt tears pressing against the back of her eyelids. He'd told her from the beginning he was broken, and she hadn't listened. She'd dared to hope. Dared to believe in the magical worlds she created. *Stupid, stupid.*

"It's been great while it lasted." He was smiling so gently, as if waking up from a sweet dream and he wanted to luxuriate in the memory of it.

"Yes." How could she argue? What if she told him she wanted more, and he didn't agree? No, the best course of action was to pretend she didn't care. She bit her bottom lip, hardened her chin, steeled her eyes. "We can't live in a romantic fantasy, can we?"

"No." Slowly he shook his head, his expression bittersweet. But he was right. None of this had been real.

"Tomorrow, we go back to our regular lives," she said with forced breeziness.

"Our trip will be just a memory."

"Yes, yes." She bobbed her head as if she agreed. "That's it."

"Should we talk about what happens when we're back in Cupid?" He canted his head, his gaze hot on her face.

"What do you mean?" she asked.

"Our families will be curious how things went. They'll ask questions."

"We tell them nothing," she said. "It's none of their business."

"We'll see each other at family gatherings."

"And we'll avoid each other the way we always have. Nothing has changed." She gave a little shrug as if it were that simple, as if she really didn't care.

"Or maybe we could tell them that during the trip we came to understand each other a little better and resolved our personality conflicts? Because we have. I understand now why you don't make backup plans."

"To what end?" she asked.

"Huh?" He looked surprised.

"Why should we do that?"

"So that we can hang out without raising eyebrows."

"For what reason?"

His eyes rounded and he looked at a loss for words. "To be around each other."

"You mean have sex?"

He lifted his shoulders. "I—"

She took a step back from him, trained her eyes on his, watching his reaction. Couples were moving around them in time to the music, but she was barely aware of them. Right here, right now, he was the center of her universe.

"Remington, I have a question for you."

"What's that?"

"Tell me the truth. Do you see any way for us to have a relationship based on anything more than great sex?"

He shifted uncomfortably, tugged at the collar of his dress shirt, and that movement was answer enough. "Honestly?"

She almost said, *no, lie to me*, but realized that being flippant was the way she protected her heart, so instead she simply nodded.

Remington gulped visibly and splayed a palm on his nape. "I can't say, Aria. Things on the road have been terrific. We had good times, and we worked through the problems we encountered. I felt like you and I were a real team. But that's within a protected, starry-eyed container. Outside of our magical little box, impacted by family influences"—he shook his head—"I have no idea if we can maintain this."

"Me either."

He looked surprised by that. What? Just because she was a romantic and loved weddings didn't mean she wasn't a realist. He was not an easy man to love. He had a brick wall built as high as his neck. He had a lot of baggage he needed to unpack from his childhood and wounds from his experiences in the military.

And while she wasn't equally emotionally encumbered, she had her own problems with staying power. As any of her former boyfriends could attest, Aria had always been the one to break up with them just when things started getting serious.

"Do you think . . ." Her voice came out in a squeak.

"Yes?" His stare anchored her to the spot.

"That you could ever fall in love with me?"

"I already love so many things about you." He reached out to brush a strand of hair behind her ear, and his touch, as always, electrified her.

Dammit.

"It's not the same thing. Do you think you can love *me*, Remington? Even when I'm flying by the seat of my pants and have absolutely no backup plan? Even when I'm impulsive and flighty and love Santa caps on armadillo statues?"

"Aria, all I can offer you is what you see standing right in front of you. I can try, but that's all I can promise."

She nodded. She suspected as much. Was he even capable of loving someone the way she ached to be loved? That forever after, complete acceptance, unconditional love kind of relationship.

"I hope you understand." To his credit he looked stricken.

"Yes, I get it because I don't know if I can fall in love with someone who can't embrace me, warts and all, one hundred percent."

"If—"

"I think it's best this way," she braved. "Before we get any more invested than we already are."

People were two-stepping around them to George Strait's "Christmas Cookies" and sending them curious glances. They were getting noticed.

"We should dance," she said, aware that they were drawing too much attention to themselves. This was Olivia and Ben's night. "Or get off the dance floor."

"I don't care who's watching."

"I do. That's one of the many things we differ on. People matter to me, Remington. I like making them happy. I like *being* happy. I don't know that you do."

"Aria, you have no idea how hard I'm trying to be a better person . . . for you."

That was it. He needed to change for him, not her. "Yes, I do know how hard you're trying. You stopped cussing in front of me. That tells me a lot about who you are, and I appreciate it. But Remy, I can't be anyone's backup plan. I can't wait around and be a second-best solution until someone better comes along. I need it all. I need someone who can be one hundred percent *in*."

"That's not what's going on here." He shook his head.

"Isn't it? You know I don't have the qualities you want in a woman. You want someone methodical and dependable. Someone who makes lists and checks them thrice. Someone who cooks meals far in advance and freezes them for future dinners. Someone who measures out ingredients instead of just flinging in whatever looks good."

"That's not true."

"Isn't it? You want the kind of girl who always has a spare tire in her trunk and puts her faith in planning instead of other people. Sure, there's sexual attraction and chemistry between us—I can't deny that. But it's just not enough for me."

He wrapped his arms around her again and moved her around the dance floor. But the magic was gone and there was no getting it back.

"Aria," he said, "I have just one question for you."

"What's that," she whispered, holding herself stiffly in his embrace. "It's a big one."

Her heart knocked. What was he going to ask? "Yes?"

"When I kiss you do you hear humming?"

Aria looked squarely into his face and told him the biggest bald-faced lie she'd ever told. She told it to protect them both.

Hitching in a breath, she said on one long exhale, "No."

CHAPTER 21

Uncouple: To release the connecting link between objects or persons.

The tip of her nose turned red when she lied, Remington realized. Mostly, Aria was painfully honest, so he hadn't noticed the telltale sign before. But her face said it all.

When he kissed her, she heard humming. Looking at her now, he knew it as surely as he knew his own name.

But she wasn't about to admit it.

Why?

She couldn't meet his gaze. Eyes gone vacant, she peered off into the distance as the music ended and the DJ took a break. Guests drifted back to the chairs.

"I have to go supervise the cutting and serving of the cake," she murmured.

He wanted to wrap his arms around her again and kiss her one more time. Kiss her until all she could hear was the legendary humming of her family's myth.

Remington was not a fanciful man. He didn't believe in fairy tales. But damned if at this very moment, he was praying it was true—that Aria was his soul mate.

The warrior in him scoffed at that. He was a realist, and fantasies had no place in his world. But the ten-year-old boy who'd lost his mother, the kid who'd spent his nights talking to his missing mom as if she could still hear him, wanted desperately to believe.

"Remington," she said.

He locked eyes with her, his palms tingling with the urge to touch her.

"Why don't you go on back to Cupid tonight? It's six o'clock now. If you leave right away, you can make it home around two A.M."

"Y-you want me gone?"

She made a face. "I think it's for the best."

"How will you get home?"

"Two of the bridesmaids are from Alpine and I can hitch a ride with them tomorrow," she said, not quite meeting his gaze.

Boggled, he stared at her. She was sending him on his way? Man, she must be spooked by what was going on between them. Really spooked.

He forced a casual smile and shrugged like he didn't care. "Don't I get a piece of wedding cake first?"

"I'll wrap up a slice to go."

Wow. Okay, message received. She no longer wanted him around.

"I was teasing," he said. "I don't want any cake. It's too damn sweet." He almost apologized for saying damn, but to hell with that. He was a grown man. He could curse if he chose.

"Okay," she said.

"But I'll stick around and help you clean up after the reception."

She shook her head. "No need. I can tap Roger and Gary to pitch in. Joel and Jana too."

"Look at you," he murmured. "You've got yourself a backup plan."

Her smile was tight. "You *have* taught me a few things, Remington Lockhart, and I am so grateful for the lessons."

Yeah, so grateful she was giving him the boot.

Well, he wasn't a clingy whiner. He got the message loud and clear. *Be gone with your bad self.*

"I do appreciate all you've done for me, but you're free to go." She waved a hand like a queen dismissing a peasant.

Olivia bopped over to them, barefoot in her wedding dress after she'd kicked off her high heels so she could fast dance. "Time for the cake," she said. "Could you get everyone's attention?"

"On it." The smile Aria gave her best friend was real, unlike the one she swung back in his direction once Olivia headed for her groom and the cake.

Everything inside Remington wanted to protest. To point out she was scared as hell about her growing feelings for him and shoving him away, but he did not. She was right. There was no reason for him to stick around. He'd served his purpose. She had plenty of other people in her life who could and would help her out.

Why prolong the inevitable? She'd decided that he wasn't the man for her and it was a smart decision. He couldn't argue with her conclusion.

Oil and water. That's how well they mixed.

"I've got to go." She gestured toward the cake.

"I know." Then before he had time to think it through, he gathered her in his arms and kissed her, not giving a good damn who was watching.

When he released her, she stumbled away from him as fast as she could without even a backward glance.

That was that, he thought. Remington went back to the Merry Cherub, gathered his things, said goodbye to the angels and the Cantrells, and hit the road home to Cupid.

He'd had enough Twilight magic to last him a lifetime.

THE NEXT MORNING, Aria and the two bridesmaids, Jyl and Paula, stuffed themselves into Jyl's Mini Cooper and headed southwest.

They had a terrific time gossiping about the wedding guests, catching up on each other's lives, and playing Christmas carpool karaoke.

Anyone on the outside looking in would see three good friends having a fabulous road trip after the wedding of their fourth friend. They'd see fresh-faced, young women, filled with joy and the spirit of Christmas.

What they might not notice, as Aria lounged in the back, wedged in between suitcases, was the sadness in her eyes and a catch in her voice when she sang the sappy Christmas tunes. The car was lively and fun, but she couldn't help comparing it to the trip up to Twilight with Remington.

"After Christmas," Jyl said, "we're hitting the road to Taos for a ski vacation, where we'll celebrate the New Year."

"Why don't you come with us," Paula invited. "Things are always more fun when you're there, Aria."

Once upon a time, she'd be all over that invitation. She wasn't much of a skier, but who cared? She didn't mind wearing cute snow clothes, sitting around the lodge, drinking hot toddies, and eyeballing the ski patrol hotties.

But now? She just wanted to go home and lick her wounds.

And see Remington?

God, no! She was staying as far away from him as she could get. Which, considering she worked on the Silver Feather, wouldn't be easy.

"Please, please, please come with us," Jyl wheedled. "We've rented a chalet on the slopes. You can stay with us for free if money is the issue. You'd only have to pay for the skiing."

"I can't." Aria shook her head. "Vivi has four weddings scheduled in January. There's too much to do."

"Wow." Paula turned around in the passenger seat to give Aria a pouty face. "You sure have changed since college. You used to be the ringleader of our shenanigans, and now you're—"

"Sedate," Jyl finished.

Aria shrugged, feeling as if she'd come home from a long journey to find everything the same while she was a different person. "Can't party forever."

"That's not what you said in college." Jyl changed lanes, zipping past a black Escalade.

Aria couldn't resist twisting in her seat to see if it was Remington. It wasn't. Her heart slid to her stomach.

"It's *him*, isn't it?" Paula asked.

"What?" Puzzled, Aria shifted to avoid the edge of the suitcase poking against her ribs. "Who?"

"The rugged good-looking dude. What's his name? Winchester?"

"Remington."

"Oh yeah, I knew it was a gun name." Paula giggled. "Either way, he's smoking hot."

"You've got it bad for him." Jyl eyed her in the rearview mirror.

"No." Aria shook her head vigorously. "Not at all. We're just friends."

"The kiss he gave you on the dance floor last night looked far from friendly to me." Jyl buzzed the Mini Cooper past a slow-moving 18-wheeler. The driver was cute. Paula rolled down the window to wave at him, letting in a blast of cold air.

The driver tooted his horn.

Jyl changed lanes to get in front of his truck.

For a few minutes Jyl and the driver played games. Slowing down. Speeding up. Exchanging honks and hot looks.

Aria resisted rolling her eyes at the highway flirtation. Had her friends always been so immature? All they seemed to care about were guys, clothes, and having a good time.

Not that there was anything wrong with that, but c'mon, you had to grow up sometime. They were all twenty-six. Not sweet young ingenues anymore.

It occurred to her then that people had been sending her the same message for the past few years. Urging her to grow up and stop being so shallow and impulsive. Embarrassed to admit she'd spent so much of her time gamboling and cavorting, she covered her head, unable to watch her friends blowing kisses at the truck driver.

"He could be a serial killer for all y'all know," Aria mumbled.

"Lighten up," Paula said. "Just because you're moping over Winchester leaving you behind doesn't mean you have to rain on our parade."

"Remington, his name is Remington."

"Okay, okay, sheesh, don't get your panties in a bunch." Paula made a face and turned back around.

"Seriously, girl"—Jyl turned her head to give Aria an exasperated look—"you *have* got it bad for Mr. Firearm."

"Stop making fun of his name." Aria snorted.

"See?" Jyl arched her eyebrows. *"B. A. D."*

"You know . . ." Paula tapped her chin with an index finger and pursed her lips in a pensive expression. "I don't ever remember you being so hung up over a guy."

She hadn't been.

"In college, you were the love 'em and leave 'em type. What was it they called you on campus?" Jyl furrowed her brow.

"Miss Hit and Run," Paula supplied.

"No, they didn't," Aria denied.

"Oh yes, they did!" Jyl and Paula said in unison.

Okay, maybe in college she hadn't been the most faithful person in the world, but she led no one on. She made it clear she was just out for a good time, and boy she'd had some wild fun.

But now? That kind of lifestyle no longer interested her.

What interests you?

The answer popped unbidden into her head.

Remington.

He's what interested her. Remington was a man of depth and substance. A man who'd seen the hard side of the world and lived to tell the tale. A complicated man with integrity and character and a bucketload of scars.

Did she really want to get weighed down by all that?

Aria sighed. If truth be known, that's exactly why she'd sent him away. The reason she hadn't encouraged him when he asked about having a relationship with her when they returned home.

He was as solid as a rock and she was flighty as a butterfly.

A butterfly couldn't change her colors after all. She was who she was, and Remington was who he was, and no matter how much she might be falling in love with him, no matter how good-looking he was or how great they were in bed together or how loudly her head hummed when he kissed her, they simply were not a good match.

"Jingle Bell Rock" came on the satellite radio, and Jyl and Paula burst into spontaneous song. Aria, never one to stay on the sidelines for long, joined in.

Pushing humor and joy into her voice to lighten the heaviness expanding inside her heart.

FOR THE DAYS leading up to Christmas, Remington avoided the big house whenever he knew Aria would be around, which really wasn't hard.

He had a lot of work to do on his little plot of land on the west side of the Silver Feather, planning his retreat center for vets with PTSD. After his experiences in Twilight, he was more committed than ever to his vision. He'd already spoken with an architect, consulted a lawyer about the business side of things, and visited the loan officer at his bank.

The trip to Twilight and the art class with Aria had helped him take positive steps in the right direction to start dealing with what had happened to him in the Middle East. Aria had changed his outlook on the world and made him more open to continuing this sort of therapy, and he was forever grateful.

He was still healing, for sure, and would be for quite some time, but he had made big strides toward acceptance of his loss and he couldn't wait to share his knowledge with others. It would take at least two years before the retreat was fully operational, but in the meantime, he'd signed up to train as a volunteer to man a hotline for vets in trouble, and he was learning the ropes.

And when Archer and Ridge had asked him to help on the ranch so the hands could have a long vacation for the holidays with their families, he'd jumped at the chance for something to do. Anything to keep from mooning over Aria.

He saw her at the annual Alzate and Lockhart Christmas Eve party at Ridge and Kaia's house, because it was unavoidable. But she'd stayed on one side of the room, and he'd staked out the other. She'd oohed and aahed over her nieces and nephews. He'd talked to his brothers about his project.

Everyone asked Kaia when she was going to have that third baby. His sister-in-law rested her hand on her extended belly and said, "When the time is right, it'll happen." The answer satisfied no one because there was way too much truth to it.

At that moment, he'd locked eyes with Aria across the room, hoping for any sign they still had a connection, but she'd quickly glanced away. Letting him know in no uncertain terms that she was sticking to her guns. What they'd shared on the road trip had been amazing, but what happened on the road, stayed on the road.

They were over.

He got it. He wasn't upset.

Not really.

Remington was just—well, for the lack of a better word—*sad*. He missed her. There. He'd admitted it, if only to himself. He missed her vivacious smile and her sweet original scent. Missed her light, enthusiastic laugh. Missed the taste of her mouth and the feel of her body beneath his palms.

Because their extended family was so big, each person only bought gifts for the children and drew names for the adults.

When Ridge, who was playing Santa, put Remington's gift in his lap and he saw Aria's name on the tag, he thought for one crazy minute that she'd got him something special.

His hopes jumped but then his gut clutched, and he thought, *I got nothing for her.* Followed immediately by another thought, *backup gift.*

During the holidays he kept two gift-wrapped presents under the seat of his SUV. One for a male, one for a female. He almost hustled out there to get the generic female gift—a bath salts set—but immediately realized how lame that would look, and Aria, with those sharp brown eyes, would see right through him.

"I drew your name."

"Oh," he replied, and realized he wasn't special to her at all.

"Open it," she urged, still sitting as far across the room from him as she could get.

Family members were watching with interested eyes, and Remington hated the spotlight.

"I'll open it later," he mumbled. "Christmas is about the kids."

Aria forced a smile but said nothing and quickly turned her attention to her sister Ember, who was holding her toddler on her lap, and she kept her distance for the rest of the day.

Later, when he got to his house, Remington unwrapped the present with great care. Inside, he found a musical snow globe of Twilight, Texas, and a note that said simply, *To remember the magic by.*

He turned the key and watched as the globe spun and played "White Christmas." A lump formed in his throat. Ah damn. The song had been his mother's favorite Christmas carol. Was it accidental? Or had she known?

Carefully, he wrapped the snow globe back in the tissue paper, put it into the box and slipped it underneath his bed. Tucking away his memories of Aria and their time together. Would he ever be able to look at it without hurting?

On Christmas Day, he declined Ridge and Kaia's offer to have dinner at their house with Vivi and Duke. He just wasn't in the mood for their lively company, and instead saddled up a horse and went to work, moving a group of cattle from one pasture to the other, and then spending the rest of the day inspecting fences. The fences were all intact, so toward sundown, the cold wind blasting across his face, Remington pulled his Stetson down low over his face and turned the horse toward home.

The sky was thick with clouds and getting dark, so he almost missed seeing it.

There, underneath a thorny mesquite, lay a little critter huddled in a reddish-brown-and-white ball.

Remington reined in his horse, swung from the saddle, and approached slowly. The poor little guy looked so wide-eyed and lonesome that Remington couldn't help thinking of how lost he himself had been after his mother's death.

"Hey, buddy," he crooned, crouching some distance away from the puppy, who looked like a red merle Australian shepherd, so as not to spook him. "What are you doing way out here?"

The puppy trembled but did not run.

Remington's heart wrenched. He didn't know why he was feeling so sentimental over a dog. He'd been to war. He'd seen horrible things. On a scale of the terrible things he'd come across, an abandoned puppy didn't even rate.

In fact, the little guy was quite lucky Remington had come along. He would not die in the cold. He ducked, walked forward.

The puppy thumped his tail, his eyes growing even wider.

Remington extended the back of his left hand so the dog could smell him.

The animal's nose twitched.

"It's okay," Remington said. "Everything will be okay."

The poor thing was so gaunt, Remington feared he might not make it. He probably had many health issues. When the vet opened tomorrow, they'd be the first in line.

Tentatively, the puppy reached out and licked Remington's hand right at the seams of where his fingers used to be. As if the dog knew he'd been hurt and was trying to salve things for him.

Stunned by the tears that sprang to his eyes, Remington viciously swiped them away. What the hell? Why was he crying over a dog? Especially a dog that was going to be A-okay now that he'd found him. Remington would absolutely make sure of that.

The puppy didn't protest when Remington picked up his quivering little body, tucked the dog against his side, and zipped up his coat tight around him. Using great care, he climbed back into the saddle and rode home, feeling the shepherd's heart beating wildly against his own.

CHAPTER 22

Hang tough: Catchphrase of encouragement and solidarity for paratroopers who endure bad weather, missed jump spots, and malfunctions.

After spending Christmas Day alone, Remington took the dog to the vet the following morning. The puppy had spent a restless night whimpering until Remington took him out of the mudroom. It seemed like a good idea to keep the untrained dog blocked in, but once he was beside Remington, the puppy calmed instantly, curled up next to him, and promptly fell asleep.

Only to wake up an hour later, licking Remington's face to let him know he needed to go outside. The process repeated itself throughout the night, until the last time, just before dawn, Remington gave up trying to sleep and went to make coffee.

He took the puppy with him as he did his chores and fed his livestock. He fed the dog a small amount of raw hamburger meat he had in the fridge, then loaded him into the SUV, and off they went to the vet.

"What am I going to call you?" Remington asked the dog as he settled him into a box and put it on the floorboard of the backseat, wanting to protect him as much as possible. He'd get a proper canine seat belt in town.

That's the moment he realized he was fully adopting the puppy.

He'd told himself during that night that the arrangement was temporary, that he'd find him a good home. He'd never had a real pet before. Sure, growing up on a ranch, there had always been lots of dogs and cats around, but he'd never claimed one as his own.

Too much trouble, he'd told himself. Animals didn't live as long as people, and he didn't want to get too attached, because eventually he'd lose the pet and it didn't seem worth the grief.

Now, looking at the dog over the back of the seat, he saw the shortsightedness of that philosophy. No one knew how long they had to live, and forsaking momentary joy to prevent long-term sorrow, well, that trait kept a guy from truly living.

"You don't know how to let love in," his first love, Maggie, had flung at him when he confronted her about her betrayal. "Until you stop being afraid of love, you'll never find it."

He'd thought it was a good thing that he hadn't fully let her into his life, or he'd have been shattered when she took off with his best friend.

But now?

It was sad really, the lengths he'd taken to avoid romantic entanglements. He'd run to the other side of the world for twelve years. Hiding out from his family, from an ordinary life, from his feelings most of all.

The veterinary clinic had just opened when Remington walked in with the puppy in his arms.

The receptionist had hopped up from her chair, making a fuss over the puppy as his sister-in-law, Kaia, waddled from the back of the clinic in a lab jacket.

"What are you doing here?" he asked.

"The regular vet has the flu, so they asked if I could fill in."

"But your third baby is due any day now."

"So? I'm not in labor now." Kaia was a tough woman, and she took motherhood in stride. She loved children and animals equally. "My obstetrician says I can work as long as I feel like it. And today I feel like it."

"What does Ridge say?"

"He says, 'whatever you want, Kaia.' There's a man who knows how to please his woman."

"Meaning?"

Kaia just shook her head at him. "Talk to your brother if you want to know the secrets to a happy marriage."

"Umm." Remington thrust the puppy at her. "Here."

"And who is this?" Kaia cooed and pulled her stethoscope from the pocket of her lab coat.

"Found him on the back forty."

"Oh dear. Lucky you found him when you did. As thin as this little guy is, he's been out there awhile. It's surprising that coyotes hadn't gotten to him. Bring him on back to the exam room." Kaia motioned.

"Do you have other patients ahead of me?"

"You get the family express pass." She smiled. "And it's early on the day after Christmas. No one else is here yet."

Clutching the puppy to his chest, Remington followed his sister-in-law to the exam room.

"Set him down," she instructed, maneuvering her expanded belly around the stainless steel exam table.

Remington settled the puppy onto the table, and the little dog peered up at him with the saddest eyes. "I'm right here, buddy. I'm not going anywhere."

"So . . ." Kaia stuck the earpieces of the stethoscope into her ears and bent over the dog. "You spent Christmas alone, out riding fences and rescuing puppies."

"No. Just the one pup."

She grinned at him. "I understand. Get the Alzates and Lockharts together en masse, and things can swiftly get overwhelming."

"Since the Middle East, loud noises . . ." He shrugged. "I'm still a work in progress."

"Aren't we all." She laughed. Then she paused before saying, "Aria didn't come to Christmas dinner either." She cut him a sideways glance as she placed the bell of the stethoscope to the puppy's chest to listen to his heartbeat.

"No?"

"She said she needed to catch up on her sleep. Apparently, I'm guessing there were a lot of sleepless nights when you guys were in Twilight?" Again, she peered up at him from a sheaf of dark hair the same color as her sister's and leveled him a knowing gaze.

His sister-in-law was fishing for info. He knew it. Aria hadn't told her a thing about what had gone down in Twilight. Remington shrugged. He didn't want to encourage Kaia's nosiness. "How's the dog?"

"Heart and lungs sound okay. Are you going to keep him?"

"He seems to have bonded with me."

"I like that idea." Kaia straightened and sent a bright smile at him. "Have you thought of a name?"

"Not yet." Remington shook his head. "How old is he?"

"He looks to be about eight weeks," she said.

"He seems much younger than that."

"It's because he's so small. He must have been the runt of the litter. And like I said, he's underweight. What did you feed him last night?"

"A little raw hamburger meat. I didn't want to overdo it, so I only gave him a big spoonful."

"I'll give you a prescription for some food to build up his health. It's pricy, but he shouldn't have to be on it for long."

"I don't mind the cost." Remington jammed his hands in his coat pockets.

"We don't know what happened to him out there, but clearly he lost his mother. It will take some time for him to heal."

Remington knew all about healing and time.

"Don't be surprised if he has some bad habits because of what he's been through. Plus, he's a puppy and, like all babies, he needs lots and lots of patience."

"Got it."

"He has some sores that look as if they're getting infected, probably from those mesquite thorns. I'll put him on an antibiotic along with giving him the shots and other medications he'll need."

"Thanks, Kaia."

"I think you've got yourself a fine companion here, Remington. Why don't you leave him with me an hour and go grab some breakfast?"

He didn't want to leave the little guy all alone, but Kaia was already shooing him out of the office. Pulling his Stetson down lower over his forehead, he sauntered outside and across the street to the diner.

Millie's Diner was a hopping place at this time of morning, the parking lot jammed with cars. When he spied Aria's car in the lot, he almost pivoted and trotted back across the road to the vet clinic.

Hell, man, you can't avoid her for the rest of your life. Make peace with the fact you're going to see her occasionally.

Yeah, okay, but did he have to make peace with it right now? His stomach was in his throat and his palms were sweating at the thought of seeing her.

Cowboy up, Lockhart. You might be a lot of things, but you're not a coward.

Tilting up his chin, he ambled into the dinner. He looked neither left nor right, just made a beeline for the barstools, in the shape of saddles, positioned at the counter. He plunked down, ordered a cup of black coffee and the sunrise special—two scrambled eggs, bacon, toast, and hash browns.

He'd just brought the coffee cup to his lips when her scent filled his nose. That sweet floral smell that would forever say "Aria" to him.

"Hey, cowboy," she said and took the saddle next to him. She motioned to the server and said, "I'll have what he's having."

Remington closed his eyes. Being in the same diner with her was one thing. Having a full-blown conversation was another.

She leaned closer and dropped her voice. "I'm sorry if I made a misstep with your Christmas gift."

He shook his head. He was so knotted up inside, he could barely speak. "You didn't."

"Didn't I? Because you sure cleared out of there pretty quickly. The minute I drew your name, I knew I should have told Kaia I wanted to draw another. But then she would want to know whose name I'd drawn, and it would turn into a thing." She flapped a hand. "I didn't want it to turn into a thing."

"It's fine. You did fine." He still couldn't look at her. Instead, he stared into his cup as if the liquid was black gold.

"Did you . . ." She paused and he could feel the heat of her gaze burning the side of his face. "Open the gift?"

He nodded.

She grabbed a napkin from the napkin holder in front of him and started pleating it with tight, precise movements. She was nervous. "Did you like it?"

Again, he nodded.

"I wanted to get you something to remind you of Twilight."

"It does."

"Good grief," she said, abandoning the napkin and shoving a hand through her hair. "Talking to you is like talking to a rock."

"This isn't the time or place, Aria."

"Time or place for what?"

"This conversation."

"And what conversation is that."

Finally, he gave her a sharp glance. "I need space from you. Is that okay?"

She looked as if he'd just slapped her. The muscle at her jaw worked and her eyes widened. She blinked hard as if trying to hold back tears.

"I don't mean to hurt you," he said. "I just can't do this."

"Do what?" she whispered.

"Pretend to be friends."

"I see," she said, then gathered up her purse and walked out the door.

Leaving Remington with two breakfasts to eat and absolutely no appetite for either.

ARIA FLED THE diner.

She would not cry. No, no, no. There was no way she was going to let that man cause her to cry, dammit. She'd known when she'd taken up with him that he was as hard as stone—at least on the surface.

Yes, he had a softer side. She'd brushed up against it in Twilight and let it trick her into thinking that underneath the gruffness, he was a comfy place to land.

But back home in Cupid, he was prickly as a cactus, and he *enjoyed* being that way. What had happened between them really was just road sex and no amount of head humming could change that.

She was just going to get over him. She'd made a mistake. They'd made a mistake. No sense compounding it by trying to be friends. He'd come across clear enough on that point.

Not knowing where else to go to salve her soul, she bopped across the road to the vet clinic to cry on Kaia's shoulder. When she got inside, she found Kaia weighing a sickly puppy.

"First patient of the day?" Aria asked, eyeing her sister's rounded belly. She wasn't about to ask her why she was working. Kaia prided herself on not letting pregnancy slow her down a bit.

"Yep."

"Whose puppy is it?"

"Remington brought him in."

At the sound of Remington's name, she felt the hole in her heart widen. Aria moved to scratch the pup behind the ears. The little dog looked up at her with the saddest eyes. Eyes that reminded her of Remington himself.

"Where'd he get him?"

"He found him while he was out riding fences on Christmas Day."

Hmm. "Remy—er—Remington didn't spend the day with you guys?"

"No." Kaia raised her eyebrows at the Remy nickname. "He was invited, just like you were."

So, she hadn't been the only one nursing her wounds alone. While she'd been watching old romantic movies on Netflix in front of the fireplace, snuggled under a blanket and eating too many Christmas cookies, Remington had done the cowboy version of self-soothing. Riding fences. In her mind's eye, she saw him loping along in the cold and finding the puppy. *Aww.*

"I'd hoped you two might have sneaked off to spend Christmas together." Kaia shook her head.

Aria grimaced. "Good gravy, why would you think that?"

"Ridge and I were thinking maybe you two had made up."

"Made up? What are you talking about? You have to have a fight with someone to make up."

"You two aren't having a disagreement?"

"No."

Kaia clicked her tongue like a mother hen calling her chicks. "You don't fool me one bit, sister."

"I'm not trying to fool you."

"Something happened between you and Remington in Twilight."

"Oh, so you have magical powers now?"

"It doesn't take magical powers to see how miserable you both are and how you avoid each other."

"We're not—" What was the point in pretending? Self-deception was not a pretty color. "Fine, something happened in Twilight."

"I knew it!" Kaia pumped her fist in the air. "Ridge owes me a hundred bucks."

"Excuse me? You and Ridge bet on us?"

"Friendly wager between husband and wife. You'll understand what I mean when you and Remington get—"

"Good Lord, Kaia! We're not getting married."

Kaia sank her hands on her hips. "You're telling me you didn't hear the humming when you kissed Remington?"

"C'mon." Aria pushed her hair back from her face with a palm. "Don't tell me you really, truly believe in Granny's silly legend."

"Don't tell me that you *don't* believe. You're the hopeless romantic in the family."

"There's romantic," she said, "and then there's loony like you and Ember and Tara when you go on about that damned humming."

Kaia gave her a cat-who-snacked-on-the-canary grin. "You heard the humming. I can see it in your eyes." She twirled in a circle with such force the hem of her lab jacket went flying up. "I knew it. How could Remington *not* be your soul mate when the rest of us locked down Lockhart men?"

Aria rolled her eyes, but her heart galloped, and she got all tingly inside. "It would be really interesting to hear what a psychologist thought about this humming and soul mate nonsense."

"You're running scared," Kaia said as she finished her pirouette. "I get it. I did the same with Ridge. He had so much baggage—"

"Look," Aria interrupted. "*If* I heard the humming, and I'm not saying I did, that doesn't mean Remington is right for me. We're just too different."

Plus, he viewed her as a backup plan. That thought stabbed her like a thorn, and she remembered why she'd pushed him away back in Twilight. Self-preservation before she got in too deep.

Face it, Alzate, you've been treading water ever since, and there's no bottom to this pond.

"You heard it, you heard it." Kaia mamboed the way she did in Zumba class, adroit for an eight-and-a-half-months pregnant woman. "The humming, the humming."

"Stop that!"

"Wait until I tell everyone."

Aria clamped a hand around her older sister's wrist, and they were kids again, Kaia bent on tattling about something Aria had done. She felt that same sense of desperation now that she'd felt back then. "You can't tell them. *Please* don't tell them."

Kaia started humming, her voice gradually growing louder and louder.

Aria let go of her sister's arm. "I'm leaving."

"You can't outrun it," Kaia called to her as Aria spun on her heels. "You can't hide."

"Watch me."

"Remington is your *destiny*."

"Bull hockey." Aria didn't have to turn around to know her sister was doing another dance move.

"Remington and Aria sitting in a tree . . ."

"I am so out of here." Aria stormed past shelves of pet food, leashes, and squeak toys and toward the front door, her throat so tight she could hardly breathe.

And she plowed right into Remington's chest.

Chapter 23

Auxiliary: Synonym for a reserve parachute, especially on a tandem harness.

Oof.

Remington put out a hand to keep Aria from stumbling on the sidewalk outside the vet clinic.

She veered away from him as if he had some highly contagious disease.

"Are you okay?" he asked.

"Terrific," she mumbled and split away from him, moving so quickly in such a blind rush he feared she would run out in front of a vehicle. Practically sprinting, she dashed across the street to her car, still parked in the diner's lot.

His pulse was racing almost as fast as her pace. He stood there in the doorway staring after her.

A lady with a Doberman on a leash came up.

"Why, thank you so much for holding the door," she said, and waltzed inside. Her dog stopped long enough to sniff Remington. "C'mon, Titan," the owner said, and guided the Dobie inside.

Remington cast one last glance over his shoulder as Aria raced her car out of the parking lot and down the street. If she didn't watch it, she was going to get a ticket. *She's not your problem. She can drive however she chooses.* Yeah? Well, that didn't stop him from worrying about her.

When he got to the desk, Kaia was already waiting on the woman with the Doberman, but she winked at him over the lady's head as she bent to fill out the medical form.

Uh-oh. What was that wink about? Had Aria said something to her sister about what had happened in Twilight?

He shook his head. He didn't think so. Aria was the one who said, *what happens on a road trip stays on the road.* And he'd agreed.

But Kaia knew her sister, and Aria had been off since they'd come home from the wedding. *And you haven't?* Had Kaia put two and two together?

"How's the puppy?" he asked once a vet tech appeared from the back to take the woman and her Doberman back to an exam room.

"Great. He's had his shots and we've run the test. He had a parasite, but the medicine I'm sending home with you will clear that right up." Kaia handed him a brown paper bag.

"Thanks."

Kaia studied his face. "Are you okay?"

He kept his expression bland. "Yes, sure, why wouldn't I be?"

Kaia hitched in her breath as if she wanted to say something but was holding herself back. He didn't dare ask her what was going on in her mind, because he feared she'd tell him. Kaia wasn't one to hold back from meddling in other people's lives if she thought she could help. She canted her head and studied him with those dark sloe eyes, so much like Aria's that he felt a pinching sensation in the center of his chest.

"The puppy?" he prodded, wary of her once-over. "Can I have him back?"

"Oh." She blinked. "Yes. Let me just go get him."

While he waited for Kaia to retrieve his dog, Remington jammed his hands into his front pockets and shifted his weight.

It occurred to him just how difficult it was going to be keeping his distance from Aria in this small town. He would run into her everywhere. Not just in Cupid, but the Silver Feather as well. She was there five days a week, Tuesday through Saturday, working for Vivi.

They hadn't really thought this through, he realized, kicking himself because he'd had no backup plan for dealing with the fallout of their road trip affair. On the surface, Aria's what-happens-on-the-road-stays-on-the-road philosophy made sense, but in reality, it wasn't sustainable.

Something *had* happened between them, and it *had not* stayed on the road.

Case in point, his bounding pulse and the way he simply could not let this go.

He should talk to her again. Clear the air. Smooth things over. But how? It felt as if things between them could never be smooth again. His fault. All of this was his fault. He messed up, and how. Like a paratrooper who'd forgotten to pack an auxiliary chute, he was free-falling and the ground was coming up fast.

Restlessly, he rubbed the spot on his left hand where his fingers had once been.

"Here he is," Kaia announced, coming back to the desk with the puppy curled in the crook of her arm.

Standing there, dread suddenly flooded Remington. What was he thinking, trying to take on a puppy? He couldn't even maintain a functioning relationship with Aria—how could he expect to take good care of a dog?

Puppies needed a lot of attention, and he just wasn't equipped to do that right now. In fact, his mind was searching for escape plans. The primary one, leave the Silver Feather. Go find some VA hospital to work for to help veterans. Forget his idea for a healing retreat. Leave all this mess behind.

"Have you thought of a name yet?" Kaia asked, scratching the puppy behind his ears.

"Auxiliary," he said.

"Excuse me?" Kaia looked confused.

"I'll call him Auggie for short."

Kaia canted her head. "Why Auxiliary?"

Because, Remington realized with a sudden bolt of insight, the dog was his backup plan. If he couldn't have Aria to love, he might as well take on an orphaned pup.

"For auxiliary chute," he mumbled.

"Um, okay." Kaia's smile was perky. "Not sure what that means, but Auggie is a cute name."

"An auxiliary chute is a paratrooper's lifeline."

"Oh," she said, her eyes widening, and in a sad, kind tone, whispered, "*oh.*"

Great. Just want he needed. His buttinsky sister-in-law feeling sorry for him.

"How much do I owe you?" he asked, taking out his wallet.

Kaia waved away his offer of money. "Family discount. It's on the house."

"No," he said firmly. "I pay my way. Always. What do I owe you, Kaia?"

"Fix things with my sister. How about that?"

That cost was way too high. Sharply, he shook his head, took out his wallet and peeled out two hundred dollars and laid the bills on the counter.

"This is much cheaper," he said, took his dog from her, and went home.

TWO DAYS LATER, Remington was in his workshop, where he'd been holed up carving on the woodworking project he'd started the day he'd returned home from taking the dog into Kaia's vet clinic.

It was challenging to keep his mind on his work, which was unusual for him. Normally, carving put him in a Zen zone, and he could work until his shoulders ached, suddenly look up and realize he'd been at it for hours. But every time he came close to his woodworking nirvana, an image of Aria would pop into his mind and he'd be back at square one, mentally battling the thing he was trying to avoid.

Abject longing.

For the woman who defied logic.

The woman who made him want to throw caution to the wind, tear up his checklist, eschew those backup plans, and just dive in headfirst. The woman who had him longing for things he never dared go after before for fear of screwing it all up.

Love.

Commitment.

A wife.

For most of his life, he'd operated on the principle that if you just planned enough, had enough auxiliary scenarios in place, had a few escape routes, you could control whatever happened to you. He'd been unable to see how that excess calculating and maneuvering had hamstrung him.

Keeping him rigid and inflexible, unable to adapt to unfolding events if he had not prepared for them in detail. And honestly, who could anticipate all eventualities?

His planning had protected him, but it also kept him sewed up. Preventing him from innovating and trying something new. His strict adherence to his method of self-protection erected barriers and kept other people at arm's length.

It had worked well for him when he was in the military. A structured environment that rewarded obedience and rule-following. But he was no longer in the military, and he recognized just how much he'd stymied his own creativity by forever insisting on a backup plan. His job had been his whole life. He'd lived and breathed combat. Knew every aspect of jumping from a plane at high altitude, but what he knew about how to navigate civilian life wouldn't fill a teacup.

"Dog, you sure took up with the wrong fellow."

Auggie sat gnawing on a chew toy at Remington's feet, and when he heard his voice his ears pricked.

"Yep, sorry to break the news to you, but unless I can change Aria's mind about me, you're stuck with a crotchety old bastard."

The sound of Ridge's King Ranch pickup truck rumbled into the driveway. Auggie lifted his head, gave a little bark, and looked at Remington for guidance. His big eyes seemed to ask, *friend or foe?*

"It's just my brother. Get used to him. He's got a tendency to stick his nose in where it's not wanted. He and his wife both."

Auggie gave a low growl that struck Remington as humorous considering such a tough sound came from such a small pup.

"Chill, my man," he murmured, and stuck out his foot and lightly touched the dog's back leg with his toe, reassuring Auggie that all was well.

The puppy turned his head, met Remington's eyes, then hopped up, the hair on his hindquarters bristling, still growling low in his throat and moving toward Ridge, who'd gotten out of his truck.

Laughing, Ridge pushed his Stetson back on his head and raised his arms in the air. "Call off your bodyguard."

Remington put down his carving knife, got to his feet, whistled low, and patted his thigh with his palm. "Heel, Auggie."

Auggie looked from Remington to Ridge and back again.

"I know you'd like to go for his throat," Remington drawled. "But come on back here, boy."

Ridge squatted in front of the dog.

Auggie backed up, barking.

"Stop monkeying with my dog," Remington said. "You're scaring him."

"You're going to have to do a lot of work with him to temper that antisocial tendency," Ridge pointed out.

"Who says he's antisocial? Maybe he just wants to be left alone."

"Isn't that the definition of antisocial?" Ridge chuckled and straightened.

"Did you come over here to criticize my dog?" Even though they both lived on the hundred-thousand-acre ranch it took over twenty minutes to drive from Ridge's side of the ranch on the east to Remington's plot of land on the west.

"Nope," Ridge said. "That's just a side benefit."

"What do you want?"

"Kaia sent me."

"She did," Remington grumbled.

"She's worried about you."

"Why?"

"You're self-isolating again."

"We all can't be extroverts." Remington picked up Auggie and held the puppy to his chest. Auggie was still eyeing Ridge like he didn't trust him.

"This is more than that. You spent Christmas riding fences."

"So?"

"We missed you." Ridge's brow knit, and he looked concerned.

"I can take care of myself." Remington drew himself up straight. He was two inches taller than Ridge's six-foot-one height, and added in a snarky tone, "Big brother."

Ridge let that pass. "This isn't healthy."

"What's not healthy? Getting a dog, or woodworking? Because the last time I checked in with my therapist, he recommended both a hobby and a pet."

"You're using them as an excuse to stay away from the family."

"What makes you say that?" Remington kept his tone mild.

Ridge pulled out his phone, switched it on, turned the screen around so Remington could see the long list of texts he'd ignored. "And that's just my messages. You've been ignoring Kaia's, Rhett's, and Ranger's messages too."

"Last time I checked, answering texts is not mandatory."

"No, but you know if you don't answer them, eventually someone will drive out here to make sure you're okay. So, the only thing I can figure is that you *wanted* me to show up, at least on a subconscious level, so here I am. What's up, baby brother?"

"How's this? I answer your texts and you go away."

"Not happening." Ridge strolled into the workshop, studied the woodworking project. "What are you working on?"

He should have been grateful for the change in topic, but he didn't want to talk about the piece either. "None of your business."

Ridge cocked his head and studied the sturdy redwood lumber. "Hey, it looks like a—"

"What'll it take?" Remington interrupted, feeling a sudden rise of panic tighten his chest.

"Hmm?" Ridge raised his head. "What's that?"

"To get you to leave me alone and keep your mouth shut about this." Remington waved at his woodworking project.

"Easy enough. Come to dinner tonight."

"Just me?"

Ridge shrugged. "You can bring the puppy. My kids could help socialize him."

"Your kids would wag him around by his hind legs."

"They would not. Kaia's taught them how to handle a puppy."

"They're four and two. I don't trust them one bit."

"Leave the pup, bring it, I don't care. Just come to dinner."

"No one else will be there? Just you and Kaia and the kids?"

"Kaia might have invited her parents."

"And that's it?"

Ridge shrugged, looked a bit sheepish.

"She invited Aria, didn't she?"

"I'm not privy to her exact guest list."

"Here's my RSVP. No."

"What is your deal?"

"I'm not fond of matchmaking."

"No one's trying to play matchmaker."

Remington shot him a look. "Seriously, bro? You're as transparent as tracing paper. Thank your wife for her efforts, but I'm a no-show."

Ridge sighed. "Kaia's gonna chew my ass for bungling this."

"Aww, poor baby. Your problem, not mine."

Ridge lifted his Stetson, scratched his head. "So, there's no way you'll save me from an ass-chewing?"

"Nope."

"You're heartless."

"And you're being shamelessly manipulative."

"What happened with you and Aria on that trip?"

"Not going there." Remington shook his head.

"Did you two—"

"I don't kiss and tell."

"So, you kissed her!"

And a lot more than that.

His secret must have shown on his face because Ridge whistled long and low and said, "Dammit, now I have to eat kale once a week for the rest of my life."

"What?"

"I bet Kaia I'd eat kale once a week if you and Aria hooked up on the trip. She swore you did. I said no way."

"A wager on me? That's low, brother."

"Please tell me you didn't sleep with Aria so I can save my taste buds."

What a conflict. Tell a lie and save his brother from kale in his diet or tell the truth and have everyone know what happened on the road.

Backup plan.

Here's where he could use a good backup plan.

"Listen," he said. "If you'll help me finish this project, I'll tell you what I'm carving and why."

A big fat grin spread across Ridge's face. "Hand me that sander, little brother, and let's make this happen."

CHAPTER 24

Undercurrent: An air current that flows below the upper or beneath the primary currents.

"Are you going to Kaia and Ridge's party?" Vivi asked.

"Huh?"

It was Thursday, December 31, New Year's Eve morning and it had been three days since Aria had seen Remington in town.

She and her boss were working to decorate the barn used for wedding receptions. Tomorrow, they had an evening wedding scheduled. Pushing the tables together to make one long table and draping them with tablecloths reminded Aria of the blue and white sheets she and Remington had used to transform the convention center in Twilight into a winter wonderland.

Her heart squeezed and she let out a heavy sigh. "I can't believe Kaia is hosting a party when she's ready to pop with that baby."

"That woman is hard-core," Vivi said. "She's the original pioneer woman."

"Yeah, she's one tough mama. Something I'll never be."

"Are you okay?" Vivi canted her head and gave Aria an assessing stare.

Aria waved a hand. "Fine. I'm fine. Don't mind me."

"You don't seem fine. In fact, you've been as moody as Remington ever since you came back from Twilight. I fear he's rubbed off on you."

Oh yeah. He'd rubbed off on her big-time.

"I'm just in a holiday funk," she said. Which was true enough. All these festivities got on her nerves.

"Hmm." Vivi gave her the side-eye. "In what way?"

"Too much cheer, I guess. Too much music, food, and company."

"But you love that stuff. It's what makes you such a good wedding planner. You live for celebrations."

Aria shrugged. "Even optimists get the blues sometimes."

"Maybe." Vivi stepped back to admire their handiwork, then moved to adjust a tablecloth that was an inch lower than the rest. "But why does this optimist have the blues?"

She wasn't getting into it with Vivi. One, it was none of her boss's business and two, she didn't want to talk about Remington. It simply hurt too much.

"You never answered my question," Vivi prodded.

"What question was that?" Ever since returning home, she'd had trouble staying on point. Briefly, she'd wondered if her dwindling attention had anything to do with the concussion she'd suffered, but in her heart of hearts, she knew it didn't.

"Are you going to Kaia and Ridge's New Year's Eve party?" Vivi repeated.

"Are you?"

"Why are you answering a question with a question?"

Aria flicked her hair over her shoulder and met her boss's inquisitive stare. "Why are you?"

"You're being evasive."

"No," she said. "I'm not going to the party."

"Why not?" Vivi asked.

"I just had dinner with Kaia and Ridge the other night." And she'd secretly hoped Remington would be there. Kaia had hinted he might be there, but he hadn't come. Which was just as well. "That's enough togetherness for one week."

"But this is New Year's Eve."

"So what?"

"You skipped out on Christmas."

"I was there on Christmas Eve."

"But you *love* New Year's Eve." Vivi moved to open the blinds to let in more light.

"Not this year."

"Why not?"

"What is this? Twenty questions?"

Why? Because Granny Blue was going to be there and inevitably, as she always did at family gatherings, she'd bring up that silly humming legend, and because Aria was the last single Alzate sister, everyone would urge her to find The One.

Well, guess what, folks? She'd found the man who made her head sing when he kissed her, and it was not all it was cracked up to be. Oh, for sure, his kisses were spectacular and the sex with Remington was out of this world, but once they were out of bed nothing about their relationship worked.

"I'm just not in the mood."

"Okay." Vivi suddenly dropped that topic, leaving Aria wondering what her boss had up her sleeve.

"Why? Are you and Duke going?"

Vivi shook her head. "We couldn't get a babysitter."

Ah, so that's what Vivi was angling for. Well, okay then. "Sure, I'll keep Reed and Rory," she said.

"I wasn't hinting around—"

"Weren't you?"

Vivi stroked her chin as if mulling that over. "Not consciously, but maybe I was. I do have this new red dress I've been dying to wear."

"Go. Have fun. Babysitting for you is a great excuse not to go to this thing."

"What . . . or should I say who . . . are you avoiding, Aria?" Vivi asked.

As if Vivi didn't know. Aria decided not to answer that. "Where are the place settings? I'll get those put out."

"Gray tub." Vivi pointed to the color-coded plastic tubs she used to store the wedding supplies, but she was always rearranging things and Aria couldn't keep up with where she put what. "And the flameless candles are in the highboy's drawer."

Aria opened the tub and started taking out the place settings for fifty guests, and as she laid the table, her mind once again returned to the memory of the last wedding she'd planned—Olivia and Ben's. Remington had been such a help.

Why couldn't she stop thinking about that man and why did her heart ache every time he popped into her head—which, let's face it, was pretty much nonstop? Even when she was asleep, she dreamed about him.

The man had burrowed under her skin and made himself at home there. Even if he didn't know it.

Even if she didn't want him there.

She thought of the people she'd met in Armadillo. Those three couples who'd been so in love—Helen and Hank, Audra and Pat, Andre and Tanya. How Pat had told her that you know when you're in love when the other person isn't around, and you miss your loved one so much it physically hurts. Which, granted, she hadn't fully understood.

But now?

Oh yeah, she got it. Ever since she'd sent Remington home from Twilight, her body had been aching for him.

Be honest, it's not just your body.

Her heart, that cranky thing, missed him too. In fact, ever since the last time they'd made love, she'd wake in the middle of the night, an impending sense of doom flooding her, her heart pounding so hard and fast she feared she might be having a heart attack.

Or a stroke.

She'd gotten up one of those times and gone to the computer, googled her symptoms, and discovered she was having a mild panic attack.

But why?

What had her so twisted in knots?

She did what she could to improve the symptoms. She'd jumped rope—her preferred form of exercise—did the deep breathing exercises that Remington had taught her from his PTSD therapist, pulled out her paints and brushes, and created art.

Heavens, had she painted! Producing painting after painting, a dozen since coming home. Using lots of blues and grays, which wasn't her usual style. Normally, she painted with vibrant yellows, oranges, and reds.

Her subject had shifted as well. Instead of brides and wedding scenes, she painted images of loneliness and isolation, a green rowboat on a blue lake with no oars to row ashore, a lost puppy curled up beneath a dead mesquite tree, a black kite crashed into a power line. It didn't take a trained psychiatrist to see from her artwork that she was sorting through some stuff.

Again, Helen's words rose in her mind, *You know when you're in love when you miss the other person so much it physically hurts.*

Even now, just looking at how pretty the table was, set for a wedding reception, her body ached for Remington.

And she worried about him too. Almost constantly. He'd shut himself up in his house on the west side of the ranch. The Lockhart who was farthest way from the rest. She'd only seen him on Christmas Eve for a couple of hours and then that disastrous little encounter in town. He'd looked as if he'd lost weight and she fretted that he wasn't eating properly.

So go to him. Tell him how you feel. What's the worst that could happen?

Um, he could tell her to get lost. That he didn't want to see her again. But she was already in so much emotional turmoil that showed up in her body as palpitations, tummy troubles, and tension headaches—how much more could his rejection hurt?

His rejection?

Ahem. She was the one who'd broken things off with him. Yes, she'd been the one to cause her own pain. Was Remington hurting as much as she was? Was he hurting because of her?

Misery stirred inside her, a murky cloud of despair.

Why did she keep pushing him away?

Fear.

It was that simple.

She'd always been the kind of person who avoided deep feelings and long-term commitment. Life was just easier when you kept things light. But something had happened in Twilight. Something magical and whimsical. The something she'd often dreamed of. The something she'd longed for but had never really expected to find.

She'd fallen for the myth, the legend, the fairy tale.

Once she held the fantasy within her grasp, she'd tossed it away like a hot potato.

She'd used the thing he treasured most against him—his backup plans—holding it up as the insurmountable barrier between them. She'd told him she wouldn't be anyone's backup plan, but in reality, he'd never treated her that way.

He'd always put her first. Bringing her a coat when she'd dashed out of the car to help that mother and her kids. Dancing with her on the deck of Joel MacGregor's paddle wheel boat. Taking her down to the fireplace at the Merry Cherub because he knew she liked spontaneity. He'd even done his best to stop cussing for her.

Why hadn't she seen all this before?

Afraid. She'd been afraid. While she loved whimsy, she never expected it to turn real, and when the fairy tale had come to life in Twilight as she'd danced in Remington's arms, she'd freaked the heck right out.

"That's it then." Vivi dusted her palms together.

"What?" Aria had been so caught up in the misery of missing Remington, she hadn't even realized she'd been operating on automatic pilot and they'd finished decorating the barn.

"We're done. We can kick back until tomorrow at noon. Go home. Grab a nap before you return to babysit my hooligans."

That wasn't happening. She'd had relentless insomnia since she'd returned from Twilight.

"Unless . . ." Vivi trailed off.

"Unless what?"

"You want to tell me what really happened in Twilight."

Aria would not tell her, had absolutely no intention of telling her.

But then Vivi came over and laid a hand on her shoulder, and all the stuff she vowed would stay on the road did not, indeed, stay there. Then tears sprang to her eyes and that was it.

Aria held nothing back. Not what had happened in Armadillo. Not the screwup she'd made by not having a backup plan when the Garzas told her their son was sick. Not the way she'd sent Remington packing. Not how he'd acted when she'd seen him at the diner.

It all came out.

She told Vivi everything she could not bring herself to tell her family. Vivi just listened. Nodded appropriately. Giving her a soft smile when Aria needed it.

"I miss him so much and it hurts so bad." Aria sniffled, hiccuped.

"I suspected." Vivi nodded, her stylish blond bob grazing her shoulders.

"How did you know?"

"You haven't been the bright light you usually are."

"I'm sorry."

"Don't apologize. I just want to see you happy."

"I don't think I'll ever be happy again. Not as long as Remington is giving me the cold shoulder."

"Sounds to me like you're falling in love."

"But Vivi I *can't* be in love with Remington."

"Why not?"

"Well, for one thing the stupid family legend and my sisters will be so smug about it."

"And you'd let that stop you from grabbing hold of love? Just so you can avoid your family's relentless teasing."

"Well, no, not really."

"What is it, *really*? Remington is a good man. You *know* that."

"He represents everything I've spent my life running from. Commitment, heavy-duty responsibility—"

"Love?" Vivi finished for her.

Miserably, Aria nodded. There it was. The irony of it all.

She, the romantic who loved planning weddings and all the hoopla surrounding romance and falling in love, was terrified of being in love herself.

That's why she'd sent Remington away. Not because he'd treated her like a backup plan, but because he'd cherished her like she was special, as if she meant something special to him.

"You're afraid of being trapped by love." Vivi said it as a statement, not a question.

Slowly, Aria nodded. "Maybe."

"You're afraid it will tie you down and close off all your options."

A hard lump formed in her throat and she tasted the salt of her unshed tears.

"It's why, when things get serious, you flutter off."

She hadn't gone to Taos with Jyl and Paula. That was progress. A year ago, she would have been shooting down the ski slopes right now.

But she didn't want to be on the Taos ski slopes. She wanted to be here. Wanted to be with Remington, but she was terrified to her core that he did not want to be with her.

"Oh," Vivi said, trying too hard to sound casual. "I almost forgot."

Aria narrowed her eyes. "Almost forgot what?"

Vivi walked to where she'd set her tote purse on the small table near the front door that they used to display the guest book during wedding receptions. She rifled through it, produced a stack of mail. "Could you take Remington his mail? He forgot to pick it up when he came by the house."

Because the four Lockhart brothers' houses were so far from the main house on the Silver Feather, the postal carrier left everyone's mail at the mansion's central location.

Vivi's eyes met Aria's. "I know it's a bit out of your way, but his mail has really been stacking up, and some of it looks important."

Her boss was giving her an excuse to go by Remington's house. She could latch on to it and take a chance, or she could say that dropping by his place was simply too far out of her way. Which, honestly, it was.

Vivi stood there, her outstretched hand filled with envelopes and catalogs.

Aria stepped back, gripped by the fear of seeing Remington again and having him turn her away. How could she blame him? From his point of view, she'd acted like an impulsive flake. "I—"

One eyebrow shot up on Vivi's forehead. "You're going to make me load up the kids and drive these over there? It's fifteen miles."

"You could send a ranch hand. Or Duke or Archer."

"The ranch hands have New Year's Eve off. Duke and Archer are helping Ridge get ready for the party—"

"His mail has been stacking up this long, it can wait another day."

"So that's a no?" Vivi looked disappointed in her and dropped her outstretched arm.

"I can't—"

"Can't or won't?"

"What's the big deal with the mail, Vivi?"

"He's got a letter in there from the VA."

A fresh fear washed over her. Was something wrong with Remington? Her throat was dry, and she swallowed hard. "W-why?"

"I suspect it's a reply to the request he made before he left for Twilight with you."

"What request is that?" Fear was a concrete wall in her chest. Was he sick?

"He's laying the groundwork for becoming part of the Wounded Warrior network when he gets his retreat up and running. Although, since he found Auggie, Duke told me Remington is thinking about training dogs to be the companions for military personnel suffering from PTSD as well. This is the information he sent away for."

"Oh, so this is good news." Relief spilled over her. Remington was okay.

"Let's hope." Vivi extended the envelopes again.

This time, Aria took them.

CHAPTER 25

Burble: The area of turbulence behind an object.

Aria drove across the plains of the ranch, the hulk of the Davis Mountains to her left, rising straight up from the flat earth, gray clouds misting around the humped mounds, giving them the foggy appearance of slumbering elephants.

They weren't *real* mountains in the parlance of the Rockies, but they were the closest Texans could claim to something taller than mere foothills. The highest of them, Mount Livermore, clocked in at a little over eight thousand feet.

No, her hometown mountain range was more whimsical than anything else. Pretending at something bigger and better and larger than life. She realized then that she was a lot like those mountains.

She glanced over at Remington's mail stacked on the passenger seat of her car. The closer she got to his house, the quicker her pulse skipped. His house was newly constructed this year. He'd had it built while he was in the hospital recovering from his wounds. Before that, his home had been a fifth wheel trailer he'd stayed in when he came home from leave.

She'd only been out here once, when he'd come home for good and the families had thrown him a combo homecoming/housewarming party. She'd never really had another reason to venture this far west on the Silver Feather.

The one-lane dirt road forked.

One branch headed north, to his older brother Ranger's Earthship home, where he and Ember and their kids stayed when they came back to visit from their home in Canada. The other road led west to Remington's place.

At the fork, she hesitated.

The north entrance would take her past Ranger's house to the highway leading to Fort Davis. From there, she could loop back east to Cupid. She didn't have to do this. She could leave Remington's mail with Ranger and Ember. They wouldn't be flying back to Canada until the day after New Year's.

She stopped the car. Pulled out her phone, texted Ember. **U home?** But the text didn't send. Blocked by the Davis Mountains, she had no service in this spot.

Just drop off the mail. It's only another mile. You don't even have to knock. Leave it on his doormat and go.

Good plan.

And then she saw it. A text that had come in while she'd been helping Vivi decorate. It was from Olivia, just back from her honeymoon.

She scrolled through the long text—anything to delay this—reading about how awesome the honeymoon in Belize had been. How wonderful it was to be married to Ben. How much she appreciated all Aria had done for her.

It was the gushy texting of a woman in love.

But then, after the long text, there was a photograph of the Sweetheart Tree in Sweetheart Park, a close-up of one of the charms on the wire frame around the tree trunk. Along with a short comment from Olivia. **Thought you should C this.**

Expecting to see some schmaltzy message from Ben to Olivia, Aria used her fingers to enlarge the picture and as she read it, all the air escaped her body, leaving her rag doll–slumped against the seat.

It was the same copper heart-shaped charm that Aria had had engraved for the tree. The charm that said, *Aria & Remington were here.*

Except the inscription had been altered. Now the charm read: *Aria & Remington fell in love here.*

Her heart hammered, slamming blood against her eardrums, tribal and primal. *Boom, boom, boom.*

Who had altered the charm?

Olivia? But why?

Could it be . . . could it be . . . *Remington?*

But when and where and why?

She desperately wished she could text Olivia and ask her if she'd been the one to etch over the initial engraving, but she had no cell service. She was on her own to sort this out.

Had Remington truly fallen in love with her? Enough so that he'd gone to the trouble of having put up a charm for everyone in Twilight to see? She had so many questions.

So, go ask him.

Driving up, she couldn't help admiring the home's sturdy neo-Craftsman architecture, so much like Remington himself. She killed the engine in his flagstone driveway and closed her eyes, imagined this place with guest cottages behind the main house for wounded war vets on their path to healing. Aria admired him for wanting to do this, loved that he cared enough about others to center his life around helping them.

Wished she could be a part of it somehow.

Maybe she could give art lessons. Art therapy was a growing field in the treatment of PTSD. Maybe she could even go back to school and become an art therapist? She had an art degree and she'd stumbled into the job as Vivi's wedding planner right out of college when she'd helped her plan Kaia and Ridge's wedding. And while she loved what she did, she couldn't help thinking it would be nice to help people who were struggling and use her love of art to do it.

After all, look what a difference it had made for Remington when he'd drawn his hand in her art class.

But where was this coming from? She'd never given art therapy a second thought before her time in Twilight with Remington. And now, out of the blue, she was thinking of a whole new career?

Maybe.

Why?

Remington. And the fact he might have put up that charm at the Sweetheart Tree.

She admired that man in so many ways. He'd been through so much. Things that would have capsized a lesser person. She couldn't even imagine what it was like to lose part of your hand. She respected the way he'd bounced back from it so quickly. He'd done everything he needed to do to deal with his trauma. He'd tackled therapy, both physical and emotional, with steadfast determination. Even better, he wanted to take what he'd learned to help others. He'd already started the process.

Glancing over at the mail in her seat, the big white envelope from the VA on top, she felt a great deal of pride in his progress.

In her eyes, he was one heck of a hero.

She loved being with him because once she got him out of his comfort zone, he liked to laugh with her. He was observant and curious and kept her on her toes. He called her on her bullshit and didn't let her wiggle off the hook. Once you got past the gruff camouflage, he was warm and understanding and patient. He was active and could be playful, and he was the most loyal man she'd ever known.

And she'd thrown it all away because she was afraid. Afraid that she could never live up to the image of herself she saw in his eyes.

Hands gripping the steering wheel, she stared at his house, took a deep breath, grabbed the mail from the seat, and got out of the car.

The cool air nipped her nose. Remington's house was in a valley deep in the shadows from the mountains, so even though it was only three o'clock, it already felt like gathering dark.

It was peaceful here, she acknowledged, quiet and beautiful in its stark isolation.

He would do good work here. She tightened her grip on his mail. He had the devotion for it.

Suddenly, all the breath left her lungs, and, with a start that shook her from the top of her head to the bottom of her fashionable boots, she knew, she knew, she knew absolutely *why* she was so dang scared. Why she'd sent him home alone from Twilight. Why she'd been avoiding him as much as possible once she'd returned.

Remington was a devoted man. He'd been devoted to his first love, Maggie, until she'd betrayed his love. Devoted to the military. Devoted to his cause of building a place for wounded warriors to heal.

Anything this man did he did with all his heart and soul. *That's* why backup plans were so important to him. He did nothing halfway, and to ensure that he could take care of those he was devoted to, he prepared.

She thought of the nights they'd spent together. How he'd been all about her pleasure before his own. Felt her cheeks burn.

He was a practical problem solver who valued having support and guidance even if it was from his own planning. He prided himself on being a dependable, committed person.

And she'd made fun of those traits.

Making fun of him. Treating the things that he held dear as if they were a joke.

Ashamed of herself, Aria ducked her head. The impulse to leave the mail on his mat and flee was back, stronger than ever.

But something stopped her.

Well, two things—the notion that he had been behind that charm and the fact she needed to apologize to him and there was no other way around it. Gathering her courage, Aria raised her fist to knock, but spied something at the corner of the house she didn't expect to see.

WHILE ARIA WAS standing on his front porch, Remington waited on the other side of the door, a bouquet of Christmas flowers clutched in his right hand, his neck sweating beneath his collar.

Knock, he thought. *Please don't just leave the mail on the mat and drive away. Just knock.*

Twenty minutes ago, Vivi had texted that Aria was on the way and he'd been standing here like a goofball ever since, his best-laid plans on the verge of collapse.

He didn't have a backup plan. No auxiliary chute. It was all or nothing. This was it. An electric thrill ran through him. Was this how Aria experienced life all the time? As one big free fall?

Wow. What a life.

She was so brave, and he loved her courage.

Holding his breath, waiting for that knock, he felt as amped up as if he was about to make a HALO jump into enemy territory at three A.M. in a hellacious sandstorm.

Knock, Zippy, knock.

He moistened his lips. He'd give her to the count of ten, and if she didn't knock, he'd open the door, anyway.

Ten.

Nine.

Eight.

For hell's—heck's sake, Aria, knock on the damn—er dang—door. Look what she'd done to him. He couldn't even cuss inside his own head anymore.

Seven.

Six.

Wait, wait, what if he opened the door and she took one look at him decked out the way he was and ran away?

It wouldn't be the first time she'd run away from him.

Why had he thought this surprise would be a good idea? Yes, it was whimsical. Yes, it would be something she would like. At least in theory . . .

Now that it was happening, Remington was flooded with doubt. It worried him. What if he'd overrepresented the attraction between them? Sure, they'd been great in bed together. Really, really great, but what if, in Aria's mind, great sex was all they'd shared?

But what about their shared history? Surely the weight of familiarity added something to the equation?

Except their past wasn't exactly friendly. As kids, they hadn't even liked each other. He'd tweaked her pigtails, and she'd shoved him on his butt.

He grinned, remembering.

And what was that saying? Familiarity breeds contempt?

Except the exact opposite had been true for him. The deeper he'd gotten to know Aria, the more he'd appreciated her. He loved the way she balanced out his pessimism with her bright optimism. How she expected the best out of people, places, and things. How funny and entertaining she was. How she encouraged him to explore and introduced him to new things. How hopeful and idealistic she was. Lively, fun-loving, curious, generous, and lighthearted, she was all the things he was not.

Big question?

Was he too stodgy for her? Too damaged? He was healing, yes, yes, yes. Already he was in such a better place personally than he'd been six months ago, and he was getting stronger every day.

Remington fisted his left hand in his pocket, or as much as he could fist it with three fingers. He'd been knocked down, but he wasn't out. In fact, he was on his way to translating his bad experiences into something good and useful that could help others, and he was damn proud of himself for that.

But if he hooked up with Aria, would his cautiousness kill her vivacious spirit? The last thing on this earth Remington wanted was to change her.

One of the flower petals broke loose from the bouquet and drifted to the floor. He stepped on it to keep Auggie from going for it. The puppy chewed on *everything*—his shoes, baseboards, the rug.

Remington smiled. He had no idea how he'd kept Auggie from eating his bow tie, but the pup seemed to know it was special.

Auggie thumped his tail and gave a little whimper.

Remington glanced down at the puppy sitting beside him. Twenty minutes was a long time to make a puppy wait.

Okay, this was it. He couldn't stand it any longer. He was just going to open—

Through the window, he saw her move to the right, as if she was going around the side of the house.

Oh, no, no, no. That would ruin everything.

Impulsively, with no forethought, Remington reached out and knocked on his side of the door.

AT THE SOUND of the knock, Aria stopped in midstep.

She thought she'd seen her four-year-old niece, Ingrid, peeping around the side of the house, but why would Ingrid be here? Her parents were getting ready for their New Year's Eve party.

Unless Uncle Remington was babysitting. But he would never leave the kids outside to play alone.

But that had to be him knocking on the inside of the door. It was the same quick, rap-tap-rappity-tap he used when they'd shared adjoining rooms at the Merry Cherub. Remembering, her face flushed.

Trembling in her shoes, she raised her hand and returned the knock. *Rap-tap-rappity-tap.*

Slowly, the door swung open.

Gulping, Aria stared, then burst out laughing at the whimsy in front of her.

There in the foyer, stood Remington wearing a navy blue suit, crisp white shirt, and a red bow tie. He clutched a bouquet of white Christmas flowers in his right hand, and sitting beside him was the most adorable Australian shepherd puppy wearing a doggy-sized version of the same outfit.

CHAPTER 26

Updraft: The ascending flow or movement of air.

"What—" She was about to ask what was going on but got no further.

"Come with me." Remington pressed the sweet-smelling flowers into her right hand and took her left in his. The joyful puppy circled around them barking.

He'd been standing in the foyer waiting on her? Why?

Hmm, he and Vivi must have been in cahoots. But what for? And why were he and the dog wearing matching suits?

It was so fun, whimsical, and unexpected, she battled disequilibrium. Especially with the puppy underfoot and Remington grinning as if he were a miner who'd struck gold in his own backyard as he dragged her through the living room.

"Where are we—"

He pulled her through the kitchen, which was laden with enough food to feed a tribe as big as the Alzates and Lockharts. Chafing dishes were lined up on the buffet. Desserts on the sideboard— cakes, pies, cookies. From the heated oven came delicious smells of an impending celebration. A Yeti cooler sat on the floor and she knew without looking it was loaded down with drinks. A beer keg rested in the farmhouse sink.

Remington was definitely having a party, but there was no one else here.

Wait a minute, just what was going on?

Still clutching the flower bouquet, Aria dug in her heels, stopped in her tracks. Remington dropped her hand, turned back.

"Who are you, and what have you done to Remy?"

He laughed, his face ringed in a smile, but she noticed his Adam's apple jumped when he gulped hard, and he ran an index finger around his collar. The man was nervous.

But so was she. Her heart beating so fast she feared he could see it pounding at the hollow of her throat.

"Do you trust me?" he asked, looking as anxious as she felt.

"Yes."

He held out his hand to her again.

"Wait," she said. "I have to know something first."

"What's that?" For a second he looked panic-stricken.

She set the bouquet on the counter to pull out her phone, found the picture in Olivia's text, held it out to him. "Are you behind this?"

He nodded.

"How?"

"I called Ryder and asked him to do it."

"When?"

"Christmas Eve. After I opened your present."

"Oh." Her eyes widened. "Why?"

He said nothing, just kept his hand outstretched, and she pocketed her phone and took his hand. She picked up the bouquet again, and he led her out the kitchen door and into his backyard oasis.

"Surprise!" their families hollered.

Startled, Aria stopped on the back steps, taking in her surroundings. Everyone she loved was standing on the patio in party clothes, outdoor gas heaters blazing a cheery warmth—her parents; Granny Blue; Archer and his wife, Casey; her sisters; his brothers; their kids playing tag. Ah-ha! She *had* seen Ingrid.

From around the side of the house, came Vivi and Duke with Rory and Reed.

What was everyone doing here? Had they switched the New Year's Eve party from Kaia and Ridge's place to Remington's?

But why?

They'd decorated the place with balloons and streamers and a massive amount of curtain twinkle lights. Then behind everyone, she finally spied it—a beautiful wedding arch. It looked handcrafted with broad sturdy legs to anchor it to the ground, thick-based and functional. This wedding arch would not collapse.

But, whimsically, the top piece was carved into the shape of a heart, and all around the heart were small intricate carvings that, as Remington led her closer to it, she could see were butterflies.

She knew without him telling her that he'd been the one to carve this beautiful arch, making it both functional and whimsical, a coming together of both their aesthetics to form the most stunning wedding arch she'd ever seen.

But what was it for?

As he led her underneath the arch and looked deeply into her eyes, *whoosh,* her heart exploded like a confetti-filled piñata whacked with a baseball bat. When she inhaled, it was as if she breathed pure shimmering magic.

Still holding her hand, Remington got down on one knee.

She was shaking all over. Leaves in a hurricane didn't shake this much. Suddenly, Kaia was there, slipping around to take the flower bouquet from her hand, and then darting out of the way again.

Stunned, Aria stared down at Remington in his suit, and that adorable puppy was sitting right beside him and looking up at her too, both with adoring eyes. Covering her mouth with her free hand, it was all she could do to hold back the tears.

Her skin turned hot, then cold, then hot again. Their audience was rustling, whispering, but she couldn't really hear them. All her attention was on the handsome man at her feet gazing up at her.

"I've got something to tell you," he murmured.

"Yes?" she whispered, barely able to hear the word over her pulse pounding in her ears.

"Aria Heloise Alzate," he said.

How did he remember her middle name? Her heart galloped, a wild filly running through the desert canyons, pumping joy throughout her body, swift and hard.

He fixed his gaze on hers, tightened his grip on her palm and gave her a sexy hope-filled grin. "Would you do me the honor of becoming my wife?"

She shook her head because she simply could not speak. Had forgotten how to speak. And her tears were falling down her face.

He looked terrified. His eyes widening and his lips parting as he whispered, "Will you . . . will you . . ."

Something occurred to her then. Something almost unbelievable, but she knew it was true. "You don't have a backup plan, do you? In case I say no."

He shook his head, looked utterly bereft, as if he'd just sawed off the limb he was perched on and realized what he'd done just a beat too late.

"I've put all my eggs in the Aria basket," he croaked. "What do you say? Will you marry me?"

She stepped closer to him.

Sweat popped out on his brow. "I know I acted like a jerk. I know I can be a bear to deal with. I know I have a lot of things to work on, but I'm one hundred percent committed to being the best man I can be for you. I love you, Aria, with all my heart and soul. And if you'll have me, I want nothing more than to be your husband."

His eyes had grown softer and his voice quieter, and darn if he wasn't holding his breath . . . waiting for her answer.

Everyone was.

Oh Lord, oh heavens, oh for crying out loud. She wanted this man more than she wanted to breathe. Tears sprang to her eyes, and he looked as if he just might be sick to his stomach.

"I'm so sorry I hurt you. I should never have—"

"Shh," she whispered. "Just shh. You didn't hurt me. I hurt you. I'm the one who sent you away. I'm the one who couldn't see love when it was standing right in front of me, I—"

He was trembling, and his eyes misted, and he said, "Is that a yes?"

She grinned and threw herself into his arms and said, "Yes, my love, yes, yes, yes."

And even before he kissed her, Aria's head was humming the song that the Blue women had heard for generations—it's him. This man is *The One, The One, The One.*

EPILOGUE

Five years later . . .

Remington surveyed the ten former military personnel sitting around the table in Aria's dedicated art room. The space was sandwiched between the meditation gardens on one side and the treatment rooms, offering massage, acupuncture, and biofeedback on the other.

The young men, all with various war wounds, were focused on drawing their model—Auggie.

The dog sat regally on the small raised stage with his head held high as if he knew he was the center of attention and loving it.

Remington's gorgeous wife, her belly rounded with their third child, stood at the front of the room demonstrating the techniques she'd taught him that wintery day at The Horny Toad Tavern in Twilight.

He was a lucky man, and he knew it. All his dreams had come true. It had taken hard work and dedication, but his retreat for wounded war veterans struggling to assimilate back into society had finally come to pass.

And he couldn't have done it without Aria's help.

She'd been there at his side the entire time. She'd gone back to school to get certified to teach art therapy and given up her job as a wedding planner to do what she told him fulfilled her more than anything ever had beyond being his wife and mother to their children.

Their oldest, Hannah, was four and such a bright little chatterbox, just like her mom. Remington freely admitted his daughter had him wrapped around her littler finger. Their son, Levi, was two. The child had a penchant for climbing on things—chairs, fences, Auggie. Aria swore the boy was going to give her a heart attack. Levi looked just like Remington when he was that age—dark-eyed and intently focused.

The baby Aria carried was another boy, who they were naming Colton. She was due to give birth in three months, on Remington's birthday as it turned out.

Aria turned, and her eyes latched onto his. A bright smile spread across her face. "Keep drawing," she instructed and rushed the length of the room to join him at the back.

"Remy," she murmured when she got close enough for him to hear.

"Hey there, Zippy." He smiled down at his beautiful wife.

"What's up?"

He took her arm and led her from the room, closing the door softly behind them. They stood on the cobblestone walkway, the Davis Mountains in front of them.

For a moment, he soaked up the sweetness of her wide eyes and flushed cheeks. He loved her more now than he had the day they'd said "I do" on this very chunk of land in their outdoor wedding Vivi had planned.

In fact, each morning that he awoke to find her in bed next to him was better than the day before, and his heart was filled with so much joy. He marveled daily that she was his wife.

"What is it?" She slanted her head and gifted him with one of her stunning grins.

"This," he said, lowering his head and pulling her against him.

Letting out a soft little purr, she stretched out her arms and went up on her tiptoes to wrap them around his neck.

Giddy with love for her, he kissed her long and hard. God, this never got old.

Smiling, she pulled back. "Let me finish this class, big man, and I'll meet you in the bedroom."

"It's a date." Chuckling, he let her go and watched her fanny sway as she walked back into the classroom.

And as Remington sauntered back to the house to strew rose petals over their bed and light scented candles, he knew that he was indeed living his very own happily-ever-after.

Keep reading for a look at

THE CHRISTMAS DARE

By Lori Wilde

Now available from Avon Books

CHAPTER 1

On a Christmas-scented Saturday morning in early December, Dallas's newly elected mayor, Filomena James, walked her only surviving daughter, Kelsey, down the pew-packed aisle of the lavishly decorated Highland Park United Methodist Church.

She slipped her arm through her daughter's, and off they went to the instrumental score of "Let Me Tell You About My Boat." Filomena had insisted on music hipper than "The Wedding March" for her child's big day.

Bucking the old guard.

That was how she won her mayoral seat. Filomena was innovative, clever, and resourceful. Never mind that Kelsey was a traditionalist. After all, Filomena was the one shelling out the big bucks for this shindig, and to quote her campaign buttons, *she* was the "rebel with a cause."

She'd insisted on the December wedding date, so as not to conflict with her mayoral bid. In mild protest, Kelsey put up a feeble fuss. Her daughter was not a fan of December in general or Christmas in particular. But as always, Filomena had prevailed.

"Lucky" for Kelsey, Mama knew best.

Everything was going as Filomena had planned. That is, until the groom hightailed it for the exit, elbows locked with his best man.

Fifteen minutes later, back in the bridal room of the church, Kelsey sat as calm as a statue, ankles crossed demurely, feet tucked underneath the bench, expression mild. Her waist-length hair twisted high in an elegant braided chignon. A bouquet of white roses and a crumpled, handwritten Dear Jane letter were lying in her lap.

Sounds of car doors slamming and hushed voices stirring gossip drifted in through the partially opened window.

The poor thing.

Do you think Kelsey suspected Clive was gay?

How does Filomena recover from this?

Exhaling deeply, Kelsey hid her smile as relief poured through her. Okay, sprinkle in a dab of sadness, a jigger of regret, and a dollop of I-do-not-want-to-face-my-mother, but other than that, Clive's abrupt adios hadn't peeled her back too far.

Hey, it wasn't the most embarrassing thing that had ever happened to her. She'd get through this.

Filomena paced. As if struck by a hundred flyswatters all slapping at once, her cheeks flushed scarlet. Black Joan Crawford eyebrows pulled into a hard V. "Do you have any idea how humiliated *I* am?" she howled.

"I'm sorry, Mother," Kelsey said by rote.

"This is your fault. If you'd slept with Clive, as I told you to, instead of sticking to that wait-until-the-wedding nonsense, *I* would not be on the hook for this nightmare."

"Yes, Mother. You're right. You're always right."

Filomena's scowl lessened. "Well, at least you admit it."

Kelsey's best friend, Tasha Williams, who'd been standing by the door, lifted the hem of her emerald green, charmeuse maid of honor dress and strode across the small room to toe off with the mayor-elect.

"Are you frigging kidding me?" Tasha's deep brown eyes narrowed and she planted her hands onto her hips, head bobbing as she spoke. "Kels got stood up, not *you*."

Yay, you. Grateful, Kelsey sent her friend a thank-you smile.

"The media will eat me for dinner over this." Through flinty eyes, Filomena's glower could wither houseplants to dust.

Uh-oh, Kelsey knew the look far too well. A clear signal to give her mother a Grand Canyon–sized berth.

"Have an inch of compassion, you witch." Tasha glared lasers at Filomena.

Proud that her bestie had not called her mother a "bitch" when she knew the word was searing the end of Tasha's tongue, Kelsey cleared her throat. Long ago, she'd learned not to throw emotional gasoline on her mother's fits of pique. Courting head-to-toe, third-degree burns was *not* her favorite pastime.

"What did you say to me?" A sharp, cutting tone curdled her mother's voice. Her icy stare could quell Katniss Everdeen.

Gulping, Tasha couldn't quite meet Filomena's eyes. "Just . . . just . . . have a heart, dammit. She's your daughter."

"Don't you lecture me, you little upstart." Filomena shoved her face in front of Tasha's nose.

In a soothing, even tone, Kelsey pressed her palms downward. "Mom, I'm fine here. Please, go do damage control. You'll find a way to turn this to your advantage. You're a master at spinning gold from straw."

"Excellent idea." With stiff-legged movements, Filomena shifted her attention off Tasha. Finger pinching the ruching at the waist of her snug-fitting mother-of-the-bride dress, she straightened herself, dusted off her shoulders, and stalked toward the door. "Clive's father owes me big-time."

Filomena's exit left Kelsey and Tasha exhaling simultaneously.

"Ah, gotta love how she turns every disaster into a political stepping stone," Tasha muttered.

"It's her superpower," Kelsey said.

"What's her kryptonite?"

Rereading Clive's scrawled letter, Kelsey didn't answer. Before Clive fled with Kevin, he'd pressed the note into the minister's hand.

Dear Kelsey,

Shabby of me to ditch you this way, but please believe me when I say I wanted to marry you. You are the kindest, most loving person I've ever met and my deep affection for you has gotten me this far. But no more cowering in the closet, praying to turn into something I'm not. You deserve better. I deserve better. I've been a coward, and you were safe. Time to stop running. Kevin and I love each other. We have for a long time. Last night after the bachelor party . . . well . . . let's just say everything changed forever. Out there somewhere is the real love of your life. Please, cash in the honeymoon tickets and spoil yourself with a trip of your own.

Best wishes,
Your friend always, Clive

Floating off the page, three words stood tall above the others, accusing her of her most glaring shortcoming.

You were safe.

Yes, she played it safe.

Without question.

Guilty as charged.

While Clive's betrayal stung, the loss and embarrassment didn't equal the pain of the truth. If she hadn't been playing it safe, going for the most accommodating, least challenging man around, she wouldn't have ended up here.

Once again, her mother was right, and this *was* her fault. To avoid a major war that she stood no chance of winning, Kelsey had kept her own wants and needs suppressed. Filomena pushed the union because Clive's father was Texas Supreme Court Justice Owen Patterson. Kelsey had meekly accepted the union.

Intelligent, witty, urbane, Clive was entertaining and erudite, and he always smelled fantastic. How easily she'd slipped into a tranquil relationship with him. When he'd told her that he was old-fashioned and wanted to wait until the wedding night before they had sex, she'd been charmed.

And it was a major red flag she'd blown right past.

"'Sweet' is code for boring," Tasha had warned when Kelsey broke the news that she and Clive weren't having sex. "Who buys a car without test driving it first?"

Now she understood why Clive avoided having sex with her. Not because she was special as he'd claimed. Nope, because he wasn't really interested. She was gullible and had taken him at his word.

What a dumbass. Wadding the letter in her fist, Kelsey tossed it into the wicker wastebasket.

"Good start." Tasha gave a gleeful grin. "Let's cash in those tickets and get this party started. You need a wild night with a hot guy. How long has it been since you've had sex?"

Well over eighteen months. Since long before she'd started dating Clive. "I don't know if I'm ready for that."

"Will you stop? You gotta get back out there. Time's a-wastin'." Tasha reached for her clutch purse, popped it open, and took out a fifth of Fireball whiskey. "I brought this for the wedding reception, but we need it *ASAP*."

"Believe me." Kelsey held up a palm. "I'm mad at myself for letting things get this far. I should have stopped the wedding, but my mother started the steamroller, and I just climbed aboard the way I always do."

"Reason enough to take a shot." Tasha chugged a mouthful of hooch, let loose with a satisfied burp, and pressed the whiskey into Kelsey's hand.

"I don't—"

"Drink," Tasha commanded.

"Good gravy, I'm not wrecked. I promise."

"But you *should* get wrecked. Get mad. Howl at the moon. Let loose." Tasha stuck her arms out at her sides as if she was an airplane. "Wing woman at your service. Never fear, Tasha is here."

Sighing, Kelsey wondered if her friend had a point. Who would judge her for getting drunk after being jilted at the altar?

With a toss of her head, she took a short swallow. The cinnamon-flavored whiskey burned and lit a warm liquid fire in the pit of her stomach.

"Take another," Tasha coached.

Opening her mouth to say no, three words flashed vivid neon in Kelsey's mind. *You were safe.*

Clive nailed it. Since her twin sister, Chelsea, drowned on Possum Kingdom Lake when they were ten, she'd been playing it safe. Honestly, even before then. "Safe" was her factory default setting. Chelsea's death only compounded her natural peacemaking tendency. No adventuresome twin around to balance her out.

With a snort, Kelsey took another drink. Longer this time, and she felt her insides unspool.

"Good girl." Tasha patted Kelsey's shoulder.

After the third shot, Kelsey felt warm and woozy and ten times better than she had half an hour ago.

"Okay, okay." With a worried expression, Tasha took the bottle away from her. "All things in moderation. I don't want to hold your hair while you puke before we ever get out of the church."

Snapping her fingers, Kelsey reached for the bottle. "Gimme, I'm done playing by the rules."

Ninja quick, Tasha hid the whiskey behind her back. "I've created a monster. I'll return it when we're in the limo."

"Bye-bye limo." Kelsey hiccupped. "Clive and Kevin took it."

"How do you know?"

"Peek at the curb."

Poking her head out the window, Tasha said, "Oh well. Uber here we come."

"Where are we going?"

"Wherever you want. In place of a honeymoon, we'll spend the next two weeks doing something wild and crazy. *Fun, fun, fun* are our buzzwords."

"Don't you have a job?"

Spinning her finger in the air helicopter-blade style, Tasha said, "I quit last week."

"Wait. What? Why?"

"Had a fight with my boss. He pinched my ass and I slapped his face, yada, yada, he wins."

"Oh Tash, I'm so sorry. Did you consult a lawyer?"

"No need. Handled it on social media." Buffing her knuckles against her shirt, Tasha grinned. "Since he owns his own business, he can't get fired, but you can bet he got a lot of angry comments and people saying they won't be using his catering company."

"Why didn't I know about this?" Kelsey asked as guilt gnawed. She'd been a shitty friend. "Why didn't you tell me?"

"Wedding prep and getting your mother elected mayor of Dallas kept you snowed. When did you have time for my drama?"

"What are friends for? I need to make it up to you."

"Then kick up your heels."

"Shouldn't you be scouting another job instead of holding my hand?"

"No worries. Already got a new one."

"When? Where?"

"You're looking at the new executive chef for La Fonda's, and I start the Monday after the New Year."

"That's awesome! I mean about the executive chef job, not getting your ass pinched. Congrats."

"Let's do this thing." With one palm raised in the air as if she was a waiter balancing a tray, Tasha pumped her hand. "Celebrate my new job and your freedom at the same time. We'll have an epic adventure."

"No doubt." She mulled over Tasha's proposition. Why not? Time to break out of her bubble.

"Where should we go? New Orleans? Eat gumbo, drink hurricanes, and get inked?" Tasha wriggled her eyebrows. "What do you think about me getting a spider tattoo on my neck?"

Wincing, Kelsey sucked in a breath through clenched teeth. "Hmm, Cajun food upsets my stomach."

"Vegas? Blow through our mad money, pick up male strippers?"

"Um, I want something more—"

"Kelsey-ish?"

Sedate was the word that had popped into her head. Sedate. Sedative. She'd been comatose too long. "Where would *you* prefer to go, Tasha? Whatever you decide, I'm good with it."

Tasha gave an exaggerated eye roll. "Girl, you got dumped on your wedding day, and I can find a party wherever I go, even in your white bread world."

She adored Tasha's spunkiness. Spunk was also the reason Filomena wasn't a big Tasha fan.

Five years earlier, Tasha and Kelsey had met when Kelsey was organizing a fundraiser during her mother's bid for a city council seat. In charge of hiring the caterers for the event at the Dallas Museum of Art, Kelsey had gone to interview Tasha's boss, Tony, the ass pincher, without knowing of course that he was the kind of person who sexually harassed his employees.

When Tasha popped a mini quiche into Kelsey's mouth, and it was the best damn thing she'd ever eaten, she'd hired the caterer on the spot, based solely on Tasha's cooking skills. After hitting it off, Kelsey stuck around to help Tasha clean up after the gala, and the rest belonged in the annals of BFF history.

"Wherever we go there must be scads of hot *straight* guys," Tasha said. "How does a dude ranch sound?"

"Good heavens, I have no idea how to ride a horse."

"Yeah, me neither."

"Wherever you want, I'll go."

"Don't make me pick. I always pick, this is for *you*. My mind is lassoed onto hot cowboys. Yum. Ropes, spurs, yeehaw."

"Let the sex stuff go, will you? I don't need to have sex."

"Oh, but you do! Great sex is exactly what you need."

"If my libido were a car on the freeway I'd putter along in the slow lane."

"Because you've never had *great* sex." Tasha chuckled. "And for eighteen months, you've been in a deep freeze. Ticktock, time to climb down from your ivory tower, Rapunzel, and reclaim your sexuality."

"I dunno . . ." Kelsey fiddled with the hem on the wedding gown that had cost as much as a new compact car. Could Filomena get a refund?

"C'mon, you gotta have hot fantasies." Tasha's voice took on a sultry quality. "What are they? A little BDM? Role playing? Booty call in scandalous places? A park bench, a pool, a carnival carousel?"

"A carousel?"

"Hey, it happens."

"Tasha, did you have sex on a carousel?"

Her friend smirked. "Maybe. Once. I'll never tell."

Lowering her eyelashes, Kelsey tossed the rose bouquet into the trash on top of Clive's crumpled letter.

You were safe.

"Quit playing coy and cough 'em up," Tasha said. "Name your fantasies. Scottish Highlander in a short kilt and no undies? Or a football player wearing those skintight pants? Fireman? Doctor? Construction worker?"

"The YMCA players . . ."

Tasha hee-hawed. "No more gay guys for you!"

"Hmm, there is *one* fantasy . . ." Kelsey mumbled.

"Just one?" Waving her hand, Tasha said, "Never mind, not judging. One is enough. What is it?"

Not what, *who*. "Forget it."

"Is he a real person?" Leaning in, Tasha's breath quickened. "A celebrity? Or . . ." Her voice dropped even lower. "Someone you've met in real life?"

Unbidden, Noah MacGregor's face popped into Kelsey's head.

In her mind's eye, Noah looked as he had the last time she'd seen him. Seventeen years old, the same age she'd been, and six-foot-five. Broad shoulders, narrow waist, lean hips. His muscular chest bare, hard abs taut. Her lipstick imprinted on his skin. Unsnapped, unzipped jeans.

Wild hair.

Wilder heart.

Rattled and rocked, her safe little world had tilted. Noah was so big, so tall, and he had a wicked glint in his eyes. An honest man, independent and sexy. One hot look from him had sent her heart scrambling.

That final night, they'd been making out on the dock at Camp Hope, a grief camp for children on Lake Twilight. That year they were both junior counselors, after having attended every summer since they were eleven as campers.

On the dock a blanket and candles and flowers. Courtesy of her romantic boyfriend.

Fever-pitch kisses.

They were ready to have sex—*finally*—when he'd jumped up, breathing hard. His angular mouth, which had tasted of peppermint and something darkly mysterious, was pressed into a wary line. Noah's thick chocolate-colored locks curling around his ears and his deep brown eyes enigmatic.

In her bikini, she'd blinked up at him, her mind a haze of teenage lust and longing. "What's wrong?"

"Did you hear something?" Noah peered into the shadows.

Propped up on her elbows, Kelsey cocked her head. Heard the croak of bullfrogs and the splash of fish breaking the surface of the water as they jumped up to catch bugs in the moonlight. "No."

Doubled fists, pricked ears, Noah remained standing, ready for a fight if one came his way. Prepared to protect her.

Her pulse sprinted.

Proud and brave and strong, he looked as if he were a hero from the cover of the romance novels that she enjoyed reading.

She'd fallen deeper in love with him at that moment. Head right over heels. Over banana splits at Rinky-Tink's ice cream parlor the week before, they had shyly said the words to each other. *I love you.* Then again when he'd carved their names in the Sweetheart Tree in Sweetheart Park near the Twilight town square. Several nights that summer they'd sneaked off for trysts after their charges were asleep.

They'd kissed and hugged and petted but hadn't yet gone past third base. Tonight was the night. She was on the pill. He brought a box of condoms. They were ready and eager. Kelsey reached for him, grabbed hold of his wrist, and tugged him to his knees. Their first time. Both eager virgins who'd dreamed of this for weeks.

Souls wide open. Hearts overflowing. Bodies eager and ready.

"Come . . ." she coaxed. "Don't worry, it's after midnight. Everyone is snug in their cabins."

Allowing her to draw him back beside her, Noah branded her with his mouth and covered her trembling body with his own.

Hot hands.

Electric touch.

Three-dimensional!

The night was sticky. Raw with heat and hunger. Calloused fingertips stroked velvet skin. The boards of the dock creaked and swayed beneath their movements as he untied her bikini top.

Footsteps.

Solid. Quick. Determined. Immediately, Kelsey recognized those footsteps.

Filomena!

From nowhere, her mother was on the dock beside them, grabbing a fistful of Kelsey's hair in her hand, and yanking her to her feet. Kelsey's bikini top flew into the lake.

Angry shouts.

Ugly accusations.

Threats.

Curses.

Regular life stuff with her mother when things didn't go Filomena's way.

Mom, dragging her to the car parked on the road. She must have driven up with the headlights off. How had her mother known they would be there? Blindsided by the realization that Filomena must have been keeping tabs by tracking her every move via her cell phone, Kelsey's fears ratcheted up into her throat.

A hard shove and Filomena stuffed Kelsey into the car's backseat and shook an angry fist at Noah, who'd followed them. Warned him to stay away. Promised litigation and other dire consequences if he dared to contact Kelsey ever again.

"Noah!" Kelsey had cried as her mother hit the door locks to prevent him from opening the door and springing her free.

Pounding on the car window, Noah demanded her mother get out and have a rational conversation with him.

Stone-faced, Filomena started the car.

"I'll come for you," Noah yelled to Kelsey. "I'll find you, and we will be together. We won't let her win."

Kelsey clung to that flimsy promise. Took it to mean something. Fervent hopes. Girlish dreams.

"Over my dead body," Filomena yelled.

"Please Noah, just go," Kelsey had said, half-afraid her mother would run over him. "We were just a summer fling."

All the fight had drained out of him then, and he'd stood in the darkness, fists clenched, face gone pale, shaking from head to toe.

Sobbing and shivering, Kelsey sat nearly naked in the backseat of her mother's Cadillac as Filomena sped all the way back to Dallas.

And Kelsey never saw Noah again.

Years later, out of curiosity, Kelsey searched for Noah and found him on social media, learning that he was a successful point guard in the NBA and married to a drop-dead gorgeous model—something she'd have already known if she had any interest in basketball. She did not friend him. It was far too late to rekindle childhood flames.

Lost hopes.

Empty dreams.

Ancient history.

Soon afterward, she'd met Clive, and that was that. But now, here she was, dumped and half-drunk, with nothing to look forward to but her mother's predictable holiday harangue. Plenty of reasons to hate the holidays. This year, she had little choice but to review her life's mistakes.

Ho, ho, ho. Merry *freaking* Christmas.